THE CRASH

When a famous and busy osteopath marries
a beautiful model-girl he may well be asking
for trouble. Clem, Charles Maddison's
efficient secretary, who had secretly loved him
for years, on the rebound marries the wrong
man. She could foresee the disaster of
Charles' marriage to the lovely Lisa but not
the air disaster which made a widow of her
and a cripple in a wheel-chair of Lisa. After
that it was a three-cornered fight — Charles,
Lisa and Clem — each battling for emotional
survival. This novel is full of the suspense and
drama, written with all Denise Robins' usual
warmth and realism.

The Crash

Denise Robins

CORONET BOOKS
Hodder Paperbacks Ltd., London

For my cousins, John and Doris Klein

Copyright © 1966 by Denise Robins
First published in Great Britain by
Hodder and Stoughton Limited 1966

Coronet edition 1970
Second edition 1975

Printed and bound in Great Britain for
Coronet Books, Hodder Paperbacks Limited,
St. Paul's House, Warwick Lane,
London, EC4P 4AH
By Cox and Wyman Limited,
London, Reading and Fakenham

ISBN 0 340 12948 4

THE CRASH

1

Some people swear they feel a presentiment before a disaster. They really seem to see into the future. But I can honestly say that when I set out in our Mini car to meet Tony at the Airport, I hadn't the slightest idea I would never meet him and that I never would see him alive again. In fact I was feeling rather cheerful. As you know, I hadn't really been getting on very well with my husband, but there is some truth in the saying that absence makes the heart grow fonder. I don't much like being alone. Tony had to go to Cairo, and in fact he booked his return for a week earlier but had to postpone it. In doing this he signed his own death warrant. Such is the grim irony of fate.

ALL this was part of the long letter Clem wrote to her closest friend who was away at the time.

It was the truth. Clem had absolutely no presentiment of evil as she drove along the Chiswick Flyover that misty November morning.

She was, in fact, looking and feeling her best. Not often did she see eye to eye with Tony—about clothes or anything else; but she knew that he liked her in this particular green wool dress and jacket which she wore with her short fur coat; that he liked her hair, which was dark, straight and glossy, dressed high with a bang across her forehead. Also he urged her to use a lot of perfume which was really against her principles. But he had brought her a large bottle of Guerlain's *Shalimar* when he last went to the Middle East. It must have been expensive—rather more than he could afford, which touched her. Clem was easily moved although under her apparent softness there lay a little core of bitterness. At times, she could be hard. She resented the way life had worked out for her. But she appreciated generosity and tried to return it. So she decided to meet Tony, wearing the clothes and the scent he liked best.

Tony Ritson, at twenty-six, was still making his way in the field of business. He worked for a British computer company. After three years of showing brains and integrity, he had just been promoted to the position of Middle East representative.

Things seemed all set for better times. Tony and Clem hoped to be able to give up the small and not very attractive flat they rented in South Kensington. In the New Year they wanted to buy a cottage in the country. Tony was prepared to commute. Clem had been brought up in the country and loved gardens. She disliked London life. She was looking forward to the move.

As she drove along the familiar route to the Airport she noticed the increasing poorness of the weather. Visibility must be almost nil. Fog was rapidly descending. The sky was dark with low-lying cloud. There was no wind to move it. It was bitterly cold. Tony would feel the sudden transition from the Egyptian sunlight, Clem thought, and was glad she had put his warm overcoat in the back of the car.

She wondered, grimacing a little, what he would bring her back this time. He never forgot some sort of *cadeau* as he called it. Unfortunately he had poor taste. Like that ghastly little ornament he had picked up for her in the Moussky after a trip to Cairo. She was far too kind to hurt his feelings by telling him that she did not like it. But his lack of taste showed itself in many directions. That was something that had piled up in her mind over the years and aggravated her.

Two years ago when they first married, he was always buying something for the flat without consulting her. A piece of furniture or ornament that would ruin Clem's décor. She had come from a beautiful home. Her own taste was excellent. It was so awkward. She didn't know how to deal with Tony. And strangely enough this failing in him had not shown itself during their engagement, or if their tastes seemed to differ, she accepted the fact.

His worst fault was that he took offence easily and on the one occasion she had openly criticised a picture he bought, he had lowered his lids and—refusing to look at her, which was his habit when he was annoyed—then asked what made her imagine that *her* taste was any better than *his*.

She might, perhaps, have tried to explain; to point out that although a person was entitled to his own taste, it should be acknowledged that everyone differs. Nowadays she realised to her cost that one had to be educated up to a knowledge of fine arts, colour, design, the difference between antiques and cheap modern furniture. But Tony didn't see things that way. In spite of the fact that he

8

loved her—and she knew he did—he could not bring himself to agree in this particular matter—or about her choice of friends. She liked to entertain artists, musicians, writers. He found them boring —they embarrassed him.

Clem knew, too late, that she should never have married Tony. But at the time she met him she was lonely and vulnerable. She had just been through a bad time. First of all, her mother to whom she was devoted, had died suddenly. Then her father, a company director and much-loved parent, was killed in a car accident. Clem had always believed he had money. But once he was dead, it seemed that his finances were more on the debit than the credit side.

Suddenly she was forced to face life alone and penniless. It was the loneliness that finally defeated her. The ghastly emptiness of living in a 'bedsit' instead of the old home, or sharing a flat with other girls who offered little but surface friendship. Finally she found her solitary state unbearable. Everything in the old home had been sold along with the estate, to settle poor Daddy's debts. She had nothing.

So Clem (christened Clementine in honour of Mrs. Winston Churchill whom Clem's mother had always thought the greatest lady in the land), turned her back on gracious living and went forth to earn her daily bread.

It was fortunate that she had taken a secretarial course when she first left Benenden, was quite a speedy typist and knew a little about book-keeping as well. At the age of twenty-two, she was qualified to earn a good salary.

She answered an advertisement in *The Times* from a well-known osteopath who wanted a personal secretary. Clem fancied this sort of job. Her grandfather had been a doctor. She had an aunt in Wales, a Miss Wright, who was a retired surgeon. Clem understood and liked a medical atmosphere.

She presented herself at the address given in *The Times*. Mr. Maddison—the osteopath, had a consulting room on the ground floor of a house in Welbeck Street. He occupied a flat there also. He interviewed Clem and she got the job.

That was how she met Charles.

There had been times in her life when she certainly wished she had never met him. Yet it should have been all right. She seemed just right for the job. He said so during their first interview.

Charles Maddison, in his early thirties, was one of the most successful manipulative surgeons of the day. He started his career as a

9

doctor after taking a degree at the Great London Hospital. But finally he decided that he didn't wish to practise medicine in the accepted way. Influenced, perhaps, by the fact that an elder brother, now dead, had been a successful osteopath, and believing fully in the ethics of osteopathy, Charles decided to transfer his allegiance to what was called 'the fringe'.

He was a brilliant young man. He had charm, looks and brains. It wasn't long before he made a name for himself in his new guise and accumulated a large practice. He was particularly good with children and old people. He cured a small 'Royal Personage' of a spinal injury, after the family doctors failed. Thus the name of Charles Maddison was made.

Clem, once installed as his secretary, plunged into a busy life. It was calculated to take her mind off her personal sorrows. She stopped grieving for her lost home and parents. She enjoyed the briskness and variety of her new job. A constant stream of patients poured into Charles Maddison's consulting room. He employed two secretaries. He could keep them both busy. Clem was his personal assistant. She dealt with most of his correspondence, and a telephone line that was red hot from nine o'clock in the morning until five. She arranged the appointments.

It was not long before she found her heart turning to Charles Maddison. He was the type women adored and men respected. But flattery never seemed to go to his head. He remained modest, charming, and sympathetic, both to patients and employees alike.

Clem, and the junior secretary, Dorothy Pugh, got on well. Dorothy was younger than Clem by two years. She was a childish type and could never become a close friend of Clem's, but nobody could help liking her. Clem found her shyness and naïvety quite endearing. Dorothy never quite knew how to deal with her attractive employer. But she adored him. In his work he seemed to work miracles. Clem and Dorothy had both seen patients walk into his room on sticks—virtually crippled—and walk out again without the sticks. They had watched him seat patients on the edge of the high couch, put his arms around them, as though clasping them to his bosom, then there would be a sharp turn, a click, a gasp from the sufferer—and a sigh of relief. The painful back seemed suddenly to be marvellously free of pain. Charles had succeeded again.

Charles once confided in Clem on one of those rare occasions when they were able to talk together.

"My patients like Dorothy. She's a nice child with her pink

10

cheeks and big bosom and that dewy, silly look that sends the older men into raptures. *You* look neither dewy nor silly, Clem, and you haven't got a big bosom. You're too thin, really. But your face is most intriguing. You have beautiful intelligent eyes. *And* a first-class mentality. Young though you are, you always seem as shrewd and quick-witted as a much older woman. You've become very necessary to me, you know. Of course—" he had added quickly with his gay smile and that funny little bow with which he sometimes punctuated his statements, "I mean that in the *nicest* way, Miss Wright. Pray don't misunderstand me!"

He laughed and Clem laughed with him.

Clem didn't misunderstand. Charles to her, always said the right, the charming things. But he never put a foot wrong. Clem knew he never would. He was far too professional to be guilty of a serious 'affair' with a woman employee.

It should, Clem knew, have been enough for her that he liked and trusted her. He left her to handle the troublesome patients, particularly those women who openly wanted sex to enter their relationship with the handsome osteopath. The way they chased him nauseated Clem. And she was proud of the good solid basic friendship that existed between Charles and herself.

But, unfortunately, she fell in love with him.

It was no mere infatuation. It was a deep, serious love very disturbing for her peace of mind. Such a thing had never happened to Clem before. There had been one boy-friend before her father's death, but he had never meant more than a dance partner, or escort for the odd party. Clem had always been rather reserved, although she tried not to let people see it. She rarely showed her feelings, neither did she let anybody know it when she was hurt.

Being in love with Charles Maddison meant that she was badly hurt. At times she felt like crawling into a corner and allowing herself to lie there, dying of starvation and neglect. She often felt appalled by the violence of her feelings for Charles Maddison.

But *he* didn't know about it.

To him Clem remained the efficient, cool, tactful secretary—the 'unflappable one' as he sometimes called her to her face.

There came an evening after she had been working for him for six months, when she was putting away some X-ray plates and reports, and about to lock up for the night—that Charles invited her to join him for a drink in his flat.

She knew that she oughtn't to accept. She believed that she should never swerve from the narrow path of complete discretion. In the present circumstances, so much more sensible not to make a personal friend of him.

But she found that she couldn't resist that invitation.

In his attractive sitting-room which was furnished much as her old home used to be, with taste and elegance, Clem found some interesting books, and one superb painting by Graham Sutherland over the fireplace.

As he poured her out a drink, Charles noticed the way she looked at the Graham Sutherland. He asked her if she liked it.

Her enthusiastic and intelligent survey had seemed to surprise him.

"Well, well! I didn't think our little Miss Wright knew so much about painting. My dear, I congratulate you on your taste. Where did you get your knowledge of art?"

That was when, for the first time, she allowed herself to tell Charles about her former life and old home, and the misfortunes that followed her father's death. Charles stopped smiling or teasing her. He showed a sympathetic interest. She saw him then not as the clever white-coated professional osteopath who employed her, but a friend—understanding and extremely kind. A man with a heart.

Without the coat that night, in casual jacket and slacks, he assumed a new personality. He looked younger. But his face, she thought, was a trifle drawn. It was an intriguing face. He had an intriguing personality to balance it. His eyes fascinated her—they were such a light innocent blue. His hair, as dark as her own, was already greying on the temples. For such a tall man, she thought, he moved with grace. She watched his hands as he poured out her sherry. She was, as usual, aware of the power that lay in those fingers which were as slim and fine as a boy's.

What was he *really* like, she wondered? He was dedicated to his work. At times she had the feeling that he was driving himself unnecessarily. He never let up. Yet she felt definitely that it was the work that mattered to him more than making money. He was not mercenary. Was he happy? What interests had he outside this flat? Was there a woman in his life? He was talked of, of course, as one of the most eligible bachelors—still so young, successful and rich. *But was he happy?* She was not, however, allowed to probe into Charles Maddison's life. He was busy questioning her about hers.

He wanted to know more about those days when she used to live in the lovely Georgian house in Sussex; about the treasures that were so sadly sold; and her subsequent battle for existence.

"You've been a plucky girl, haven't you?" he said, sitting on the arm of a chair, looking at her. He had found a box of cigarettes. They were both smoking. "Adversity is an odd thing," he went on. "It either sours a person or has the opposite effect. All that you've lost and suffered has made you mature and sympathetic. I remember being told by one friend—when I first engaged you—that you were too young for the job, but I count myself a judge of character and I haven't been proved wrong over you."

"You flatter me," said Clem.

"You're not easily flattered," he grinned at her.

"No, I don't think I am."

"What do you do with your spare time?"

"Oh, I go out with friends. One in particular—Patricia Grant—a school-friend of mine who is married to a chartered accountant and lives in Chelsea Park Gardens. I owe a lot to them both. I'm god-mother to their son and they treat me like one of the family which is nice for me."

"It doesn't sound altogether exciting." Charles smiled at her. When he smiled, she thought, there was a sparkle in those eyes which wiped the look of fatigue from his face.

"I don't seem to want a lot of excitement, really," she said. "I'm always pretty tired at the end of the day."

"Do I work you all that hard?"

"Yes," she said, and laughed.

"I expect I do," he sighed. "Have another drink?"

"No, thank you. Incidentally, *you* don't spare yourself, do you?"

"No—agreed. Thank you for all you do here, anyhow. It means a lot to me to know that one can thoroughly rely on one's secretary. You are my P.A. Dear, dimpled Dorothy doesn't really come into it. By the way—I've never asked you this before—what about the love-life?"

"Love-life?" she echoed, startled.

"Well, haven't you a boy-friend?" he asked lightly.

She looked down at the point of her cigarette.

"No, I haven't."

"You surprise me. You're an attractive girl. There ought to be dozens of men lined up, waiting and hoping."

Now her face was hot.

13

"Sorry to disappoint you but I just haven't got a boy-friend."

"I am surprised," he repeated, and again she felt flattered, but was modest enough to presume that he was just being kind. Then she felt braver and asked him a personal question.

"Have *you* got a girl-friend, Mr. Maddison?"

He stubbed his cigarette in an ashtray, folded his arms across his chest and gave her a disarming smile.

"No. I'm a born, sworn bachelor."

Suddenly Clem was frivolous.

"My father used to tell me to beware of men who labelled themselves as born, sworn bachelors, Mr. Maddison. They nearly always turn out to be nothing of the kind—so Daddy assured me."

"Perhaps Daddy was right. Perhaps quite soon a deliriously beautiful girl will come and consult me about her heavenly spine and I shall break all the rules by which we chaps work—kiss her madly and dash her off to a Register Office."

"Goodness!" Clem exclaimed rather childishly.

Charles half closed one eye and looked at Clem with the other. She smiled back—warm and happy and full of love for him, although outwardly she maintained her usual deferential attitude.

"Getting down to brass tacks," he said, "I've decided to break another golden rule this evening and ask my P.A. if she would care to dine with me."

For a moment Clem was so delighted—and excited—that she didn't answer. Then when he added that if, of course, she had another date he'd understand, she made haste to tell him that she hadn't a date and would be very pleased to dine with him.

He took her to a small, discreet restaurant in Curzon Street. There they ate Scampi Provençale and Steak-Diane, followed by an excellent Brie.

Charles was now completely relaxed. He might, she decided, have been an old friend. He didn't touch on his profession—or hers. He told her a lot about wines. He was interested in them. He chose an excellent claret for their meal. He seemed impressed when Clem aired her own knowledge of wines. Her father, like Charles, had been a *bon viveur*. Charles discussed his forthcoming holiday. He was flying to Florida to stay with a 'grateful patient' whose back he had cured.

Later they had coffee. Charles smoked a cigar and bought Clem a box of cigarettes, after which he drove her home. She had never known him in such expansive mood. He was like a boy, showing off

14

his new car, a handsome Alfa-Romeo saloon, which he liked to drive himself.

Outside the big house in Cromwell Road where Clem shared a three-roomed back flat with two other secretaries, he looked up at the rather dreary building and pursed his lips:

"This is home?" he asked.

She nodded.

"Well, well—it's really rather a shame. You're a sweet girl and a very clever one. I wish —"

"Please don't be sorry for me," she broke in hastily.

"I apologise." he said, "I certainly shouldn't feel sorry for anybody with your dignity and courage."

Her cheeks reddened.

"Thank you, and thanks awfully for the evening and the dinner which has been simply fabulous. I feel quite marvellous."

"I've enjoyed it, too, Clem. You're as good a companion as you are a P.A."

That was the first but not the last of the evenings she spent with Charles in the capacity of friend rather than secretary.

One of the girls with whom Clem shared, commented:

"Oh, oh! Watch out, Clemmie. You know what a man of thirty can be like with a pretty sec!"

"I'm not particularly pretty and he isn't at all like that," was Clem's sharp reply.

It was true. Charles never overstepped the fringe of the formality essential for their fundamental relationship. He just seemed to enjoy the little dinners they had together when he wasn't otherwise engaged.

Clem attached no particular significance to his invitations. She was quite sure that with Charles, sex didn't come into it. He had no feelings of that kind towards her. It seemed to her singularly fortunate that she had the capacity of masking her own feelings. He could not possibly guess how deeply and hopelessly she was in love with him.

There was one occasion in the car when he leaned forward and kissed her goodnight. The kiss deepened and was followed by a sudden quick, passionate embrace. She shut her eyes and felt as though time itself had stopped—as though the world spun around her and she floated in space. Then he was gone.

Clem wept into her pillow that night, fiercely reproaching herself. *It didn't mean a thing. He just felt affectionate. He kissed me as*

15

though I was his sister. Oh God! I wish I didn't love him so much.

The next day when she walked into his consulting room to take the day's letters and look at his engagement book and remind him of various meetings and consultations, she was as cool as ever. So was Charles. The dinner, the conversation, the goodnight kiss might never have taken place.

That was how things went on for the next three months.

2

IT was after Charles came back from his summer holiday—and Clem from hers (she had spent it up in Pwllheli with her aunt) that for Clem the axe fell finally and completely.

Charles had mentioned to her during that afternoon that he wanted to see her in the flat as soon as the day's work was over.

She wondered for a hopeful moment if he were going to ask her to dine with him. Perhaps tonight's engagement had suddenly fallen through; or perhaps he just wanted to talk to her.

He did want to talk. He poured out her usual sherry, then a gin and tonic for himself. He raised his glass to her.

"I'm glad this day's over. It's been too long and too sticky."

"Yes, it has," Clem agreed.

"Clem," he said, "I want you to be the first to know my news."

Startled she stared at him:

"What news?"

"I'm going to be married."

Clem managed somehow—she never quite knew how—to smile although she felt a vicious stab of pain which transfixed her. She held her breath and shut her eyes. She knew that in that split second all the happiness she had ever known during the months she had worked for and with Charles Maddison was wiped out. She had never entertained a single hope that he might think of her as a woman rather than an efficient machine, but somehow it hurt cruelly to realise beyond all doubt that he had fallen in love with someone else. She was a fool, she admonished herself. All kinds of a fool. The sooner she faced up to reality the better, and the sooner she stopped feeling emotional about Charles the better, too.

He opened a beautiful Queen Anne walnut bureau, took out a large envelope and handed Clem a colour photograph.

"How about this?" he asked.

Clem took the photograph in her hands. She looked at it. This time the pain did not spring so much from jealousy as from a very natural envy. How could Clementine Wright ever hope to attract the attention of a man like Charles Maddison when there were girls like *this one* around!

She stared at the enlargement of this fabulously beautiful girl, taken at Palm Beach. She stood with her arms high above her head, holding the sort of large white football that children like to toss to one another in the water. Her background was of blue sea and long creamy rollers. She wore a white bikini. Her long lovely limbs were brown from the sun. She had a perfect figure, Clem thought, she might be a professional model; the flawless face had a look of Rita Hayworth in her youth; with long red hair curling to her shoulders, long-lidded eyes and a wide laughing mouth.

Charles Maddison started to describe his future wife in detail.

"The colour of her hair is quite unbelievable — pure Titian — and all her own — no tinting, believe me. She has modelled clothes for most of the big boys of *haute couture*. She's a freelance now and has made quite a name for herself all over the Continent. I don't know whether you have ever heard of her, Clem? They call her *Lisa*."

"Yes," said Clem, "I have heard of Lisa, and, of course, now I realise I've often seen her photo in *Vogue*."

"Her real name is Elisabeth Fannington. As a matter of fact, her father was one of the big military chiefs of the last war. General Sir Miles Fannington, D.S.O. and the rest. He died about three years ago. Her mother is an American, now married again and living in Florida. You know I've just come back from there."

"Yes," said Clem without taking her gaze from the face of the girl in the photograph, "I remember."

Lisa was almost frighteningly lovely — but what really worried Clem was her reaction to the announcement of Charles's engagement. Apart from her own feelings she was afraid for him. Was it not madness for a hardworking man in his profession to marry a model-girl like Lisa? Would she ever settle down to being his wife, living here in London; having to give way to his busy life and share his difficulties? To Clem this seemed problematical. Yet she could understand why Charles had fallen in love with Lisa. Physical beauty was of great importance to any man. And anyhow for all she knew, Lisa might prove as intelligent as she was beautiful.

Charles seemed to have no doubts that Lisa was right for him. He raved on — rather like a love-sick schoolboy, Clem thought, with some dismay — then despised herself for being jealous. Filthily so, she thought with a bitterness she could not restrain.

She handed the photograph back to Charles.

"Congratulations," she said, "Miss Fannington looks quite gorgeous."

"She is," he said.

He seemed pleased to have someone to whom he could open his heart. He told Clem that he had met Lisa at a party in Florida. They had fallen in love at first sight. He was a lucky chap. He could never have believed that such a glorious creature would fall for him.

"Heavens, why not!" muttered Clem, but he didn't seem to hear her.

Lisa was in Florida at this moment, telling her mother about the forthcoming engagement. Charles admitted that he wasn't a great admirer of his future mother-in-law. She was what he called a typical American socialite, married for the second time to a man younger than herself. Walter Cain had money, and so far the pair seemed happy enough. Lisa's mother was like a lot of American women—money-conscious, health-conscious, and unhappy unless she could rush round the world and organise everything and everybody. However, Charles said that he got on quite well with her. She liked his profession. She had told him that if he cared to leave London and work over in America, she could get him any number of wealthy patients. He would make his fortune rapidly.

Clem's sore heart plunged a trifle lower.

"Is that what you'll do, then?"

"No," he said, "I couldn't abide the American way of life. Besides I'm quite happy in my own capital, thank you very much."

She was relieved—but silent.

He had more to say about Lisa. In spite of her love of fashion and her genius for wearing clothes, she wasn't a frivolous type. She had a serious side. What had really astonished him—apart from that devastating beauty—was that she had inherited from her English soldier-father quite a sincere affection for country-life. The General had taught her to fish when she was in her teens. She could cast quite a pretty fly, said Charles proudly. When her mother was busy with her social activities, Lisa used to accompany the General on his holidays to Ireland for the salmon-fishing. This had been a point of contact between Charles and Lisa when they first met.

"Modelling clothes and dry-fly fishing don't seem to go together, do they?" Charles asked Clem, grinning.

"No," she said.

"In fact," he went on, "when Lisa and I are married, I propose to keep my flat on here for us to live in during the week, and perhaps

19

take the first floor in addition. Then buy a small house in Berkshire on the river, where we can get some trout-fishing. You know, Clem, I can't believe my luck—finding a girl as glamorous as Lisa who really would enjoy sitting beside me on a green bank, waiting for the trout to rise. What a prospect!"

Clem nodded. As far as she was concerned, the prospect was one of funereal gloom. That this girl had so much more than mere physical beauty to give Charles meant, of course, that he would be for ever bound to her. For him she, Clem, must be glad. For herself, it was bitter and hard to swallow.

But she had no reason to feel bitter. He had *never* given her, his secretary, the slightest reason to suppose that he was interested in her in *that* way. She thought:

I'm round the bend. I think the best thing I can do is to find another job at once.

But she didn't.

She hadn't the strength of mind to tear herself away from this man who had become the centre of her universe; upon whose every word she hung. To serve him was her privilege and her pride. To leave him would mean unbearable pain.

She only knew that it was more than possible that never again would she be asked to dine with him alone in Curzon Street. Never more be on those old friendly terms—and certainly never feel the friendly touch of his lips upon hers. He wouldn't kiss her good-night any more. Lisa—the beautiful Lisa—would become a high impregnable wall between them.

Clem had built up an image of herself as permanently necessary to Charles. Now it no longer existed. Her love for him had always been one-sided and rootless. She should have realised that one day he would fall in love—and not with *her*.

She heard his voice.

"I must say I'm immensely happy, Clem."

Her lips writhed into a fixed smile.

"I'm sure you are. And now"—she even managed to laugh—"what about that 'born, sworn bachelor'? Daddy was right, wasn't he?"

Charles echoed the laugh, picked up Lisa's photograph and looked at it.

"Daddy was right," he echoed, "Lisa did not beware."

God! thought Clem. *The way he looks at her face. I wish I could die.*

20

But she didn't die. Two months later, she went calmly with Dorothy Pugh to the Maddison-Fannington wedding at St. Paul's, Knightsbridge.

Amongst the hundreds of guests—a large number of them Charles's patients—were Lisa's American friends who flew over from the States for the occasion.

Clem knelt in a crowded pew and prayed for Charles's happiness. She was utterly miserable.

She watched the bride and groom come down the aisle. He was smiling. She was radiant. Clem went to the reception, listened to the speeches, drank all the toasts, and ate wedding cake, feeling that it choked her. With the other guests she saw the happy couple off on the honeymoon (they were flying to Bermuda).

For weeks Clem looked stonily at dozens of photographs which appeared in every paper or fashionable magazine. She made light and flippant replies when plump, cheerful Dorothy remarked that 'our Mr. Maddison looks years younger'. And she agreed that no bride could have looked more entrancing than Lisa as she came down the aisle on her husband's arm. Almost as tall as he—a Russian diadem crowned that lovely red head; folds of tulle drifted about her like a mist; the classic white satin dress, specially designed for her by Hartnell, for whom she used to model, showed every curve of her exquisite figure. And all the time, Clem nursed her private misery and was well aware that it was both tragic and stupid of her.

She kept remembering the reception. When it was her turn to shake hands with the happy pair, she did so, smiling brightly, murmuring a few conventional words of congratulation. Charles Maddison's fine blue eyes looked at her kindly. He turned to his bride and said:

"Clem is my right hand—the perfect secretary, as I've told you many times, darling."

Lisa condescended to smile with friendliness at Clem who at once felt several sizes too short and too small.

"Charles says you're marvellous."

She had a low, husky, attractive voice.

The praise should have pleased Clem, but it didn't. She gazed up into Lisa's brilliant eyes with their heavy black lashes; eyes so attractively set in a face as finely moulded as Dietrich's *and hated her*.

After the wedding, Clem grew used to the presence of the glamorous Mrs. Charles Maddison in the Welbeck Street flat. She even offered her personal services to Lisa and Charles when they bought a small period house near the River Kennet just outside Hungerford. One could get used to anything. Soon she was able to work with Charles Maddison once more without feeling the knife turn in her heart. Although, she had to admit she could hardly bear the sight of that big framed photograph of Lisa which now stood on Charles's desk. The flowers beside it, Lisa fixed for him these days. It used to be Clem's privilege.

She tried hard to be glad that Charles seemed so happy—and, so far, Clem even if she had wished to do so, couldn't really find anything to say against Mrs. Maddison. Lisa appeared to have settled down to being the wife of a famous manipulative surgeon and was playing the part well. For the time being, anyhow, she showed no inclination to return to her old exciting life. She neither gave nor attended parties which did not include her husband.

The day came inevitably when Clem could not go on. She decided that she did not want to continue working for Charles. It was as though the whole soul had gone out of her job. Lisa had ruined things. Clem knew it was wrong of her to feel this way. She tried to control it but found it impossible.

It was at this psychological moment that she met Anthony Ritson —Tony.

He was the antithesis of Charles. On the short side, fair, hazel-eyed with a rather chubby boy's face. Like herself, Tony was an orphan and lonely. He was also a hard worker. He neither drank a lot or had much to do with girls. He was a good, middle-class fellow. He did not move in the Maddison social strata.

His education had been paid for by an uncle who was now dead. Tony had won a scholarship for Bradfield. His was a good all-round intelligence. If he excelled in anything particular, it was maths. After leaving school, he trained in a big firm of computers. He was ambitious and had reached his present job by sheer hard work. When he first met Clem, he was, in fact, subconsciously looking for a wife. He had begun to feel that he needed a woman's company and a proper home. Clem was certainly not looking for a husband. But Tony got her on the rebound.

She was still suffering from what she supposed was her 'ridiculous infatuation' for Charles. She turned to Tony for comfort. She needed him and his ardent admiration to restore her self-confidence.

He was nice and not ungenerous. He took her out to dinner and

22

the theatre. He had a small comfortable car and drove her into the country on the fine Sundays and gave her lunch by the sea or the river. He told her that he thought her wonderful and that he was in love with her. Gradually she regained her *amour propre* and the spirit she had lost so badly towards the end of her job with Charles.

Then she spent a night with Tony. She had never slept with any man before. He, of course, had had his 'moments', and owned to one or two minor affairs. But Clem was his first real love.

He proved an eager and a passionate lover. Clem was so utterly dejected at that time, she found it easy to turn to him. So she decided that the best thing she could do was to marry Tony and settle down. She wanted a home, and she must put Charles Maddison out of her life and heart for good and all.

It was about a year after Charles's marriage to Lisa that Clem went to the altar with Anthony Ritson. She sent the Maddisons an invitation to the wedding. Lisa wrote a gracious note saying how sorry Charles was in particular, that they couldn't make it; but they were going to be away.

Charles sent his former secretary a handsome present—the most beautiful of them all in her opinion; a lovely little oil by a contemporary French artist which she knew was good and would increase in value as time went on. It was chosen with Charles's impeccable taste (so well remembered).

The first really bitter dispute Clem ever had with Tony was over that painting. He shrugged his shoulders and declared that he 'didn't see anything in it', and thought Mr. Maddison might have given her something 'more useful'. That infuriated Clem. She forgave Tony at the time, but their heated argument on art was the first of many, in the days to come. It was also the first of many over Charles Maddison whom Tony never really liked. He had only met him once but described him to Clem as a 'smooth type'. This, Clem had resented. She openly defended her former employer. Mr. Maddison, she declared, did an immense amount of good in his profession, was a man of integral character and most generous. It was all part of the 'bedside manner' if a doctor was 'smooth'.

For the first six months, Clem's marriage was not unsuccessful, but finally she was forced to face up to the rather crude fact that they 'got on in bed' but nowhere else. And for the first time she had to realise that she possessed a very definite physical side, and needed to love and to have a lover. She enjoyed a home of her own. Being family-minded, she also wanted a baby. She hoped she would have

23

one immediately, but didn't. At the end of her second year with Tony there was still no pregnancy, which disappointed her, although Tony did not seem to care. He thought it better for them not to start a family until he had consolidated his financial position.

They made many friends and went out or entertained in their own home. Clem became quite a capable cook. She almost forgot that she had ever been a secretary. But she never forgot Charles.

The time came when she could come across a photograph of Charles and the famous beauty he had married, without it hurting — but deep down, his memory haunted her and it was a disturbing ghost. She was pleased for his sake, however, when she met her former colleague, Dorothy, who was still with Charles Maddison, and heard that his marriage seemed an enormous success. Only one piece of news was disquieting. Dorothy described Charles as looking 'terribly ill'. She was sure, she told Clem, that the social whirl of the life he now led with his wife, combined with strenuous work, was far too much for him.

But even that worry didn't cut too deeply into Clem's newly-acquired content. She had set herself out to be a good wife to Tony and she was busy doing it. Her life was fully occupied and not altogether dull. The only thing that troubled her was the way she and Tony argued. The constant disputes over minor things had inevitably led to major differences of opinion. The time came when she faced the fact that she was no longer in love with her husband and that in fact he annoyed her. But she tried to console herself with the cynical thought that that was what happened in most marriages and that she — like a thousand other wives — had to make the best of it.

Then came the November day when Charles Maddison came back into Clem's life and thoughts in a sudden, quite horrifying fashion.

3

THE fog had thickened by the time Clem reached London Airport.

She parked the car, grimaced at the sky and blew her nose, smelling the acrid, damp odour of the gathering mists. The cold was piercing. It wasn't a very nice day for Tony to fly. She even began to wonder whether his plane—it was a Comet—would be allowed to land. Perhaps they would divert it. Visibility here was so poor.

She was mildly pleased that Tony was coming home. She was still fond of him in a way, and had made up her mind to put an end to all this silly bickering.

She felt a conscience about their marriage—she had done Tony a wrong by marrying him. He was really so amiable and anxious to please, but he irritated her so madly at times. The irritation had even begun to creep into their intimacy. She no longer wanted him to make love to her. The memory of how she used to feel about Charles Maddison came creeping back. A rather crippling memory —a harmful one because it separated her completely in her mind from Tony. She could imagine how horrified Charles would be if he knew. But of course so far as he was concerned, his one-time secretary, little Miss Wright, had never meant anything much and had gone out of his life for ever.

Clem began to imagine that she was fundamentally a one-man woman. The man she had married couldn't, whatever he did, have really replaced Charles in her mind and heart.

She was thinking of him as she drove to the Airport. Her old passion for him was returning in all kinds of silly unexpected little ways. For instance the other night Tony ordered a poor wine, arguing that it was darned good, and she knew that it wasn't. But she dare not say: 'Charles told me that such and such a vintage was best. Charles knew . . .' And one warm evening in the summer, when Tony insisted on sitting around the flat with his shirt off, his hair tousled and chin unshaven, Clem would remember how immaculate Charles used to look even on the hottest day. *Too smooth*, Tony would call it. He was surprised and aggrieved when she begged him to go and take a bath and freshen up. In the end he usually did as she asked, but she felt that she oughtn't to nag. She wished he was more fastidious. He called her 'Little Mrs. Particular'. That irritated her, too. In the early days, when he had satisfied the urge of her young, yearning body, she had let her own passionate response blind her to his shortcomings. They had shared some good moments. At times he had tried to show more sensibility—to get closer to her.

Sometimes now he was depressed by her attitude to him.

"I don't believe you love me any more. I don't ever really feel I possess you, even while we're making love."

Once she had felt able to assure him that he was wrong, but during these last few months, things had changed—for no specific reason. She had lied in order to soothe him. But she was sure he was right. She never *would* give herself absolutely to Tony. With Charles it would have been so different.

With Charles! Oh, God!

She supposed she might have felt better if she could have poured all her heart's hunger into love for a child. Her marriage was surely doomed if she didn't soon conceive. She decided to go to a gynaecologist and find out if there was anything wrong with her inside. Of course, it might be Tony's fault. They would have to see about that, too, if Tony would take a test.

She was thinking about Charles on this foggy morning at London Airport. Rather shamefaced she turned her mind to her husband and his return. She knew exactly what would happen tonight. It was always the same after Tony had been away from her. He would be in a good mood—especially if he had been successful with his business. After giving her his present, he would take her in his arms, kiss her on the mouth and ask:

"What are *you* going to give *me* as a welcome, darling?"

They would have lunch—his favourite—to celebrate the homecoming, then there would be—the bed. Well, perhaps one day one of these big reunions might end in a pregnancy for her. That was all Clem could hope for. She also told herself that she ought to be grateful to the gods for bringing Tony into her life. He was really a devoted husband. She had no right to complain. She might have been very lonely like some of her unmarried girl-friends.

As she began to walk through a maze of vehicles in the car park, suddenly she caught sight of a long, low, beautiful Alfa-Romeo. Surely it was Charles Maddison's—or one exactly like it?

The sight of the car—so well known to her—gave Clem such a pang that she stopped and blinked at it through the fog. Poignant memories sprang to life. Then she saw Charles getting out of the car.

Her heart leaped. She ran towards him.

"Mr. Maddison . . . Charles! . . ."

He swung round. They hadn't met for nearly two years. He looked exactly the same; his dark head with the greying wings, he never used a hat; he wore a thick tweed coat with collar turned up and a dark-blue striped silk scarf. Charles always liked scarves. He drew off one of his leather driving gloves and grinned at her like a delighted boy.

"Blow me down, if it isn't my little Miss Wright. No—of course not, Mrs. er—Oh lord! . . . don't tell me I've forgotten your married name!"

"Ritson."

"That's it, Mrs. Ritson . . ." His hand shot out. "How are you, Clem?"

"I'm fine."

"You look it. No, you don't. I think you're a bit on the thin side— yes—I swear you've grown smaller."

He smiled down at her. She looked up into those blue curiously light eyes and felt the old deep thrill of pleasure.

"I haven't shrunk as far as I know," she laughed.

"I expect it's because I've got so used to being with my tall wife. She's a *very* tall girl, you know."

"Yes, I know. How is she?"

"As beautiful as ever."

"I'm sure she is," said Clem politely.

"I should think rather more so than usual at this moment because she's been down in Cannes, and Italy. They've had a fair share of sunshine. Lisa adores the sun. She gets tanned quickly. They've had marvellous weather. She says, I made her go. She was a bit off colour. She flew over to Nice with friends. This foggy *bloody* weather in London doesn't suit my Lisa."

"It doesn't suit any of us," said Clem dryly.

"I wished I could have gone with her. But I couldn't get away. I think I'm a bit busier even than when you were working for me."

"Then that's too busy. You worked quite hard enough as it was."

"It's been hell lately. I've had such a hopeless secretary, Dorothy is still with me, but, as you know, she has few brains, poor pet. I've actually had two good P.A.s since you left. But they both got married, like yourself. My present one is indifferent and I fear I shall have to let her go. As you will remember, Clem, I never had a

27

good memory and hers is worse, so between us we get into a lot of trouble."

"I'm so sorry," said Clem.

He gave her a regretful look.

"You were exceptional. I never had to remind you of a thing."

She thought:

Keep your head, Clementine. Don't be too easily flattered and don't go on looking up into those damnably attractive blue eyes of his or you'll be sunk.

She explained that she was meeting her husband. Charles said that he had come to meet the same aircraft. It touched down at Rome on its way from the Middle East. Lisa had spent the last two days in Rome with some Italian friends. She was booked back on this flight.

Charles, in a friendly way, tucked an arm through Clem's and walked with her towards the building marked '*Arrivals*'.

"This really is fun—the pair of us meeting our better halves. And it's so very nice to see you, little Clem."

"It's nice to see you, Charles."

"What have you been doing?"

She told him vaguely about her life with Tony, and how he had just gone over to Cairo to represent the computer company he worked for.

"Computers," said Charles, nodding. "All those punch cards and electronic brains. Fascinating! He must be a clever chap."

"Yes, he is."

"Things been going well for you?"

"Very," she brightly, "and I'm sure I don't need to ask about *you*. Whenever I open a Glossy, I see a picture of you and your beautiful wife together at some smart function or other."

He stopped and glanced at the sky.

"I don't like this fog. When I phoned from Welbeck Street just before I set out, they told me they thought the Comet might be delayed, but I hope not diverted."

"It doesn't look at all good to me," said Clem.

Once inside the building, Charles went across to the Information Bureau. He returned to Clem, shaking his head and looking slightly put out.

"We've had it. They have diverted our aircraft to Gatwick where there appears to be no fog at all. It is not usual, Gatwick told me, but necessary. Isn't it the end?"

"The end," echoed Clem, "I hate driving in fog. I've a good mind to go back and let Tony find his own way home. Gatwick is quite a long way from here."

"It appears the Comet was hung up with engine trouble in Rome and won't be landing for another hour or two. How about leaving your car here and letting me drive you to Gatwick in the Alfa? There is plenty of room in the back for your husband on the return journey, and I can drop you off at your place. Where do you live?"

"South Kensington," she said.

"Well, that's fine. We'll come in over the Albert Bridge. I can take you and your husband to South Ken. then carry on to Welbeck Street."

"But what about my little Mini?" she began.

"Oh, your husband could fetch that when the fog lifts, couldn't he?"

So like Charles, thought Clem. There never seemed a bar to things he wanted to do. But she could just imagine Tony's grumbles if he had to go to London Airport tonight or tomorrow to pick up his car.

She was also not sure he would like being met by her ex-employer, 'that smooth chap', whom he didn't care for.

However, the temptation to accept Charles's invitation was too strong. It would be wonderful to drive to Gatwick in the Alfa-Romeo. Clem surrendered. A moment later she was sitting beside Charles snuggling under the cashmere rug which he had presumably brought for his wife. Charles drove slowly and carefully through the fog.

It was like the old days. It wasn't the first time she had been out in the Alfa. On several occasions when the weather was particularly bad, he used to take her home in his car rather than allow her to wait for a bus.

He began to talk about his wife. Silently Clem listened. It seemed almost to her as though the personality of the beautiful model-girl who all these years had seemed rather unreal—crystallised now into a real person.

It was fairly obvious that Charles was still deeply in love with his wife. Yet Clem found it hard to believe that she really suited him. How could a famous, busy medical man be wholly satisfied with a glamour-girl for a wife. Besides, Lisa herself was a personality in her own sphere. She had her own life to lead. He talked of their social life, and her popularity and successes. Wherever he took her, he said she was the loveliest girl in the room. With her fabulous face

29

and the clothes made for her by the leading couturiers of Paris, Rome or London—she put every other woman in the shade. He was enormously proud of her. His flat—once so quiet (the home of the 'born, sworn bachelor'—(a sidelong, laughing look at Clem), was quite changed. It had become the background for Lisa Maddison's parties. Her dinners were famous. She and Charles entertained the well-known people in Charles's own profession as well as her friends and associates. She liked music—gay dance stuff, rather than the classics. Musicians and composers wandered in and out of her *salon*. A few artists and writers were thrown in. But most of her friends were in *haute couture* or the photographic world.

Clem must come to one of their parties, Charles said. Lisa was a magnificent hostess. She knew a lot about food. She usually imported a first-class French cook for the dinner parties. They only had one Italian maid resident in the flat. The same old 'daily' who had been there in Clem's time, still cleaned the consulting and waiting rooms, but Clem wouldn't know the place, Charles continued. He rented the first-floor flat now as well as his own. Lisa had converted the two front rooms upstairs into one. It made a thirty-four foot long room with four tall windows overlooking Welbeck Street. Ideal for entertaining. The décor Lisa chose was a little extreme for Charles's taste; he really liked a quieter elegance, but he was growing used to her flamboyance and it was all very effective—gay with much gilding, crystal, and brilliant materials.

Clem took in all she heard, reflecting that Charles didn't seem to be able to stop talking about his wife. She had become his life. He hardly mentioned his work. In the old days he used to talk of little else even when he was 'on duty'. What a change! Clem didn't know that she altogether cared for the metamorphosis, but if Lisa made him happy—what did it matter? Before they reached Gatwick, he hinted that he was hoping in a year or two's time to take a partner and slacken off work and get abroad more often with his wife. She was really happier on the French or Italian Riviera than in England. She adored the sun.

"And what about the fishing?" Clem asked a trifle dryly.

Charles laughed.

"Oh, the fishing! Well, as a matter of fact, there hasn't been much of that lately."

"Didn't you go to Ireland this year for the salmon?"

"No. We had our ten days booked, but my mother-in-law in Florida phoned us in the middle of the night—she always forgets what time it is in London—and begged us to fly over there instead. Lisa wanted to go so I found myself in Palm Beach. The salmon-fishing went west."

He spoke lightly. Clem could hardly believe her ears. Lisa must be more than an enchantress in order to cast such a spell upon Charles Maddison that he had given up his salmon-fishing. She also wondered just how much 'Lisa the Magnificent' *really* enjoyed fishing, anyhow.

Clem began to feel just a trifle uncomfortable about Lisa.

They had crawled out of London. Suddenly, by some freak of nature, they came into bright sunshine. The countryside was clear. Gatwick Airport was in sight.

As Charles speeded up, he turned and glanced at his companion.

"I say, Clem, I've been talking far too much about myself and Lisa. What about you and your life?"

"Oh, everything's fine, thanks," she said lightly and without looking at him.

"Husband doing well?"

"Very. He's just had a good promotion."

"No family yet?"

Clem continued to stare ahead at the tall control tower of the Airport.

"Afraid not. Wish I could say 'yes'. I'd like an infant."

"Oh, well, my dear, there's plenty of time," said Charles cheerfully. "Same applies to us. Lisa wants to spread her wings a bit before settling down to being a mother."

Clem thought:

I wonder if dear Lisa will ever want to spoil that luscious figure. I can't imagine her wanting to lose the upward tilt of those wonderful breasts.

Then she felt mean and malicious—without real justification. What did it matter to her, anyhow—any of it? But somehow the very sound of Lisa's name disturbed Clem. She couldn't of course, deny that she still loved Charles. And up there in the sky she would soon be seeing the big jet airliner that was carrying Tony home.

She thought of Tony—and tonight. Suddenly she felt cold and a little sick.

As they pulled up at the Airport, Charles said:

"I'll drop you at the main door, Clem, and join you when I've parked the car."

She nodded, and walked through one of the glass doors towards the 'Arrivals'.

Charles found a place for the Alfa and locked the doors.

He was as excited as a schoolboy, waiting to see his Lisa again. Two whole weeks without her had made him realise to the full how madly he still loved her. He had never ceased to be grateful for his luck in having won this dazzling creature. If he had had to submerge some of his own ideas and wishes in order to please her, he didn't resent it. The only thing that troubled him at times was that their hectic social life had begun to undermine his health. Often he felt desperately tired at the end of a day's manipulative work which required all his physical strength and mental concentration. He would like to have spent a more relaxed time in the evening, but Lisa wasn't very fond of staying at home. Her own energy seemed inexhaustible. She had only to put her arms around his neck, shake back that long rich red hair, and nuzzle his cheek with her lips to make him forget everything except that he adored her and must let her have her own way.

"You're a witch. You put a spell on me," he had told her the night before she went away.

She had smiled.

"I may be a witch, but I'm not a *bitch*—am I?" she had laughed and spread out her fine slender hands with the long newly-varnished nails for him to admire. She was trying a new colour. Did he like it? He kissed the hands. She lapped up flattery and he flattered her generously. He did not find it difficult. There was so much to admire.

Certainly he never thought of his wife as a *bitch*. She was far too nice to people. Everybody liked her. And, of course, the men milled around. Old flames, new flames—one couldn't expect a girl like Lisa not to have admirers.

Charles was naturally jealous. What man wouldn't be—with Lisa for a wife? But the three years he had spent with her—glorious, fatiguing, exhilarating, slightly stupefying years—had taught him that he needn't doubt her fidelity as a wife. He was sure that she was faithful to him. She was always generous and responsive in his arms. Their passion had lost none of its fervour. At least that was how it used to be. But he had to admit that there hadn't been much love-making lately. Her superb health seemed to flag. She grew quieter—even apathetic. She cancelled many of her social engagements. She was also losing too much weight. She was accustomed to rigid dieting—she did not intend her vital statistics to rise above the level that had made her figure famous. But she was a bit too thin now even for her own liking.

Charles called in a physician from the Great London Hospital—a former colleague and friend—to give her a check-up. The result was —nothing radically wrong. Just tension, was the consultant's verdict—too many late nights, too much excitement, too little rest.

Charles decided not to worry. He packed his Lisa off to Cannes. Today when he was about to get her back (her absence had seemed interminable—at times intolerable) he felt immensely happy.

It was going to be wonderful to see her again.

He planned a long weekend at Lockbridge House, their Hungerford home. He would stand firm and insist upon no parties—no guests. He'd just have her to himself.

Charles stopped thinking about his wife and turned his thoughts to the girl he had driven to the Airport. Dear little Clem! How very nice it was seeing her again. It revived the pleasant memories of old days when she had worked so hard both for and with him. He was glad she seemed fit and happy. There was something very soothing about Clem. He remembered how pleasant it used to be to share a friendly meal and talk with her, outside the sphere of work.

She was looking more attractive these days, he thought. Marriage had matured her. Her eyes were beautiful and she had fine bones. He understood her rather reserved, cool personality. He always admired that side of Clem. There were many qualities in her that he had found admirable and missed after she left him. He wondered if he could persuade her to come back to help him during the next few weeks. It was going to be quite hellish while his present P.A. was in hospital. The girl had to have a minor operation and was expecting to be sent for any day. Dorothy was never any use except as a typist. It was always Clem who used so well to deal with the difficult moments; the awkward patients. *Could* he persuade her to work for him again, temporarily? Would her husband mind? Charles was a bit vague about Tony Ritson. What was he like? Rather uninteresting so far as Charles could remember. He had been a bit surprised at Clem's choice when she introduced her future husband. However, one could never judge what went on in a woman's mind—what sort of fellow attracted them.

Charles lit a cigar. Lately he had taken to smoking them rather than cigarettes. Lisa liked the odour of cigars. She liked everything expensive, and why not, he thought, feeling warm and tolerant.

While she had been away, he had had time to go into matters with his accountant and had been a little disturbed to find that in spite of the money he was making, they were living well above his means. He kept having to sell shares. Darling Lisa was nothing if not extravagant. But whenever he tried to talk to her about money, she would give him one of her ravishing smiles and say:

"Oh, darling, please don't. I do *hate* discussing money. It worries me."

That made him laugh at the time. Darling Lisa didn't perhaps realise that *he* was more than a little worried about his finances. However, he saw no real reason to be distressed. His income was ever-increasing, and he didn't want to cut down Lisa's fun. His practice gave no cause for anxiety. His fame was spreading and lately there had been talk about him flying out to India—with Lisa—at the expense of a Maharajah whose son needed a really good osteopath's attention. Charles had asked for an enormous fee—and been promised it. It might be amusing—a few days in Delhi in the palace of a millionaire. Lisa would adore it. All those gorgeous saris and silks and jewels of India would look well on that lissom, famous figure.

Charles stopped being bothered about money as he put his cigar between his teeth and walked into the Airport this morning. His one desire was to see and hold his Lisa in his arms again.

4

CLEM first realised that something was very wrong when she walked up to the desk marked '*Enquiries*'. She found a crowd milling around—a variety of people looking excited and upset. Clem fingered a piece of paper with the flight number of the jet which should have landed at London Airport. Pushing her way through to the counter, she asked a receptionist when the Rome aircraft was expected at Gatwick.

The girl whispered to a male official behind her. Then she came round to Clem. She seemed nervous. Her hands, holding a lot of papers, trembled obviously.

"You have a relative on this flight?" she asked.

"Yes, my husband. Mr. Ritson—initial 'A'."

The girl gave her an awkward glance, went away and whispered to two other men in uniform. Now Clem heard a sound which chilled her blood. A penetrating noise rising above the nasal sound of flight numbers being called out over the tannoy. The sad harsh wail of sirens, from ambulances, or fire-engines. Clem looked anxiously around. She noticed a group of people on her right with a Gatwick official. One woman was sobbing. The whole atmosphere suddenly seemed frightening—sinister.

"Is anything wrong?" Clem asked the girl to whom she had just given Tony's name.

"I'm afraid I have bad news for you, Mrs. Ritson —" the girl began awkwardly.

Clem stood still. She gave a nervous cough and felt the blood drain from her face.

"There has been an accident, hasn't there?" she asked.

"Yes. Would you like to come into one of the waiting rooms —" the girl went on.

"Is my husband —" Clem stammered and broke off. The sweat-beads broke out on her forehead.

"Come into the enquiry office, please."

"Has the plane crashed?" Clem persisted harshly.

"Yes, Mrs. Ritson."

"When? Where?"

"It—it was landing here," the girl said, her own face pale—her eyes scared. "We don't know yet how the accident happened." She added the word helplessly and looked to the man beside her for support. He came forward and took Clem's arm.

"Mrs.—er—Ritson, do let us take you to a quiet place —" he began.

She pulled away from him.

"I want to know what's happened to my husband. Please tell me now. I'm quite all right, I assure you."

He coughed and said:

"The Jet from Cairo was diverted, as you know, because of fog. I'm afraid it's a piece of frightful irony. She might just as well have been talked down *there*. She came over Gatwick about twenty minutes ago, touched down, and crashed. There are two dead and one injured. They were all flung out of the aircraft; one man has been identified as your husband, Mr. Anthony Ritson. We were trying to get in touch with you at your home, Mrs. Ritson, but there was no answer when we phoned you. I suppose you were already waiting at London Airport."

"Yes," she said.

She stood like a frozen figure. It was all such a shock that she could hardly take it in. She tried to compose herself and figure it all out. There had been a crash-landing here. No fog—it happened in sunlight, right here, at Gatwick Airport where everything should have been all right. Where the jet had come for safe landing. And Tony was dead. *Tony was dead.*

"Oh, God," she whispered.

"Come with us—you must have a brandy—something —" began an official.

"No, thank you," said Clem, "I'm all right. Where—is my husband?"

"The ambulance has just brought him in. I expect they will want you to—to identify the—the body."

"Yes, of course," said Clem.

She prided herself on being a strong, controlled person, but she felt so sick that she wondered whether in a moment she would not have to accept that brandy. Those words—*the body*—stunned her. Tony, Tony, her husband had become a *body*.

She would never see him alive again. There would be no special lunch—no reunion. Tony had been taken from her with the most

36

appalling suddenness. But it was not so much of her own loss she was thinking. It was of his. He had been still so young, so full of life, and well on the way to success. To die like this in a crash landing was a terrible tragedy. Poor, poor Tony!

Suddenly her bemused mind turned to that other important passenger—the one Charles was meeting. Clem pressed her hands against her cheeks. She said:

"There's a Mrs. Charles Maddison on the same flight. Her husband and I actually drove here together. Is Mrs. Maddison—*is she*—" Clem could not get out the rest of the question. She stood trembling, staring at the official who had told her about Tony. He looked down at his papers.

"Mrs. Charles Maddison—yes, she was injured. She is being taken to hospital—on her way now actually. She's still alive, don't worry. Three-quarters of the passengers weren't hurt at all—only bruised and shocked. It was the few sitting in front who were thrown out. Our air hostess among them. She's dead. Such bloody awful bad luck . . ."

The man could say no more. He turned and walked away.

Then Clem saw Charles walking quickly across the hall towards her. She could see at once that he knew. He looked awful. He came up to her.

"Clem—isn't this ghastly—oh, my God, why did this have to happen? Why the hell did they ever divert the Jet?"

"We don't know the real cause of the accident yet, sir," said the girl in uniform. She spoke a trifle stiffly.

"There are only two dead and my husband is one of them," said Clem in a strange cold voice.

"Christ!" said Charles under his breath. "My poor, poor Clem. Lisa has a fractured hip and a broken arm and superficial cuts. They've rushed her off to hospital in Redhill for a blood-transfusion. I didn't know about your husband, Clem. I came to tell you I am just off to the hospital. I must be with Lisa."

He let his cigar fall on to the floor and stamped on it.

She took his arm, dissolving suddenly into tears.

"Let me come with you. I can't face being left here alone."

"We'd like you to identify your husband first if you would, Mrs. Ritson," began the girl, awkwardly.

"Yes, of course. I'd forgotten," said Clem and shut her eyes.

Charles held tightly on to her hand.

"I'll stay with you, Clem. Then we'll go to Redhill together. Yes, of course, you want someone with you. Lisa is in no danger, so they've assured me—but she's unconscious and lost a lot of blood. It's all ghastly, but she's lucky to be alive."

The two of them exchanged a look of grief and horror. Charles was recovering from the initial shock. He was lucky, he thought, his wife was neither dying nor dead like poor Tony.

Charles had not seen his wife. She had been taken off to Redhill just before he and Clem arrived at Gatwick.

"I'll come with you to the mortuary, then we'll drive to the hospital together," he repeated, taking Clem's hand. "That is, unless you'd prefer to go straight home."

"No, oh no," she said, the tears blinding her eyes. "There might be something I can do for *you*. I—I don't want to go home and be alone. Let me stay with you, please."

He pressed her hand—his own fingers shaking. He hated to see her stricken face.

Later, they drove to Redhill. A very different couple from the laughing, talkative pair who had driven down the road in the Alfa-Romeo to meet the diverted aircraft.

They sat in shocked silence; only after driving for about five miles did they begin to discuss the details of the crash.

Charles kept saying:

"I'm so terribly sorry for you, poor Clem. So deeply sorry."

"I'm sorry about Lisa. It's terrible for you. You must be so worried," was Clem's reply. She felt numb—quite stupid. None of this seemed real.

She could not forget the moment when, with Charles holding her arm tightly, she had looked down on Tony's dead body. It was macabre and seemed to her like a bad dream. There he lay, still in his dark blue overcoat, with the red and yellow silk scarf she had given him among other birthday presents, a few months ago. His face was hidden in bandages—like his head. They told her that he must have fallen on that poor face. One of his hands was covered. The other, wearing his signet ring, had made identification easy for her.

They gave her his Airways bag which, miraculously, had been flung out with him and was still closed. They had found his passport and ticket inside. The rest of his luggage was intact they told her, and would be sent to her.

Mrs. Charles Maddison's Airways bag had also been handed to her husband. The square red leather case in which she always carried her jewellery and make-up had burst. But they had picked up everything they could find; the jewels, some papers, a few scattered letters and a wallet. They put them all in another bag. Clem took charge of it. It was in her hands now.

Charles looked so haggard that it made Clem's heart ache. How happy he had been an hour ago! Full of anticipation—right on top of the world. Now he began to talk about Lisa's injuries rather quickly and incoherently, swinging from hope to fear and back again.

"One never knows what will happen . . . these preliminary examinations are so cursory. I wish I had been the one to deal with her first, poor darling. She must have been so terrified. But no, she was not conscious, of course. I can't bear to think of her having been flung out of the aircraft like that. They were so near to landing safely. It seems such hideously bad luck. Of course, the pilot may have been at fault or it was just a mechanical failure—some defect in the undercarriage probably. Only the enquiry will show. I saw some of the other passengers being taken off—in a state of shock—looking pretty awful. Someone told me about it just as I was going to join you. I heard those damn fire-engines and ambulances and it made my blood run cold."

"Mine, too," said Clem.

"Lisa's fractured hip is what worries me," he went on. "I hope to God it's not too serious. Then there's the broken arm. She'll be in considerable pain when she comes-to, poor darling. I must take her to the Great London, to my friend, Trevor-Johns, as soon as possible. He's one of the best orthopaedic surgeons in the country. We don't always see eye to eye so far as my work is concerned, but we're great friends and he knows I respect his surgery. After all, he and I qualified at the Great London together."

Clem let Charles talk. He seemed to be in the excitable, disturbed state that needed an outlet. He kept trying to curb himself, and swing the conversation from Lisa to Tony and back again.

'You must be in a hideous state, my poor Clem. Did they give you a drink?"

"They offered it."

He gave her a quick look. Her face was white and pinched. Her eyes looked sunken.

"God, I'm sorry about Tony," Charles muttered, clearing his throat.

"I don't suppose he knew a thing. They say he wouldn't have suffered. His head was injured."

39

"That's a mercy."

Clem shut her eyes and shuddered.

"Isn't it grim? Tony was so young and strong. He had wonderful health. He was so fond of sport!"

"A bloody business," said Charles.

"I'm afraid I can't really take it in yet. I can't believe it," she began. Then the tears began to roll down her cheeks and she wept. "Yes, I can. When I saw him lying there . . . he was so still. I realised then that he wouldn't move any more. Death is so terrible, Charles. Specially sudden and violent death. No wonder in the Prayer Book we ask to be delivered from it."

Charles passed his tongue over his dry lips.

"I don't suppose it matters much if death is painless and quick. One has to be realistic. Better Tony should have died this way than like a young osteopath colleague of mine — same age — had cancer — a pretty grim, long drawn-out ending."

Clem buried her face in her hands. She was angry with herself for her sudden loss of control.

"Don't take any notice of me," she whispered.

He felt full of pity for her. His imagination was vivid. He couldn't have borne to have looked at Lisa's dead body as she had just looked at Tony's. At least, his wife was alive and as a man of medicine, he knew what miracles they could perform these days. She would get well in time. But Clem had lost her husband. She must at this moment be inconsolable.

Clem was glad when they reached the hospital in Redhill. It had been an unbearable drive from Gatwick. She hated the thought of Tony's death. Equally she hated herself because she could not feel as profoundly grieved as she knew she *ought* to feel. As no doubt Charles imagined she was feeling. But then, Charles didn't know about the breach that had recently widened between Tony and herself. And of course he didn't know about her feelings for him — her first great love.

Later on, Clem sat in one of the Ward-Sister's rooms where a sympathetic nurse listened to the story of the crash and brought her tea and a sedative. Charles had been taken straight to his wife. When he came back to Clem, she looked at him anxiously. He was obviously under a great strain. His eyes were rimmed with red. Sister eyed him as she handed him a cup of strong tea. Everybody knew the famous Mr. Maddison. How attractive he was, she thought. He must be terribly shocked. That poor beautiful girl—she was pretty badly hurt from what Sister had heard in Casualty.

Charles sat down, sipped his tea and lit a cigar, sighing deeply.

"How is Lisa?" Clem asked him.

"Still unconscious. They haven't a private room vacant. She's in the Casualty Ward. I'll contact Trevor-Johns as soon as I can. She must be moved to the Private Wing at the Great London."

"Do they know any more about her injuries?"

Charles stared blindly into space. He knew too much . . . They hadn't been able to hoodwink *him* with all the set meant-to-be-kind phrases.

'It's too early to tell until we've seen the X-rays . . .'

'It may not be as bad as one thinks at first . . .'

'Concussed, of course.'

'There are a lot of nasty cuts . . . superficial, we hope. Don't worry too much.'

But Charles was worried out of his wits. It was ghastly seeing his wife lying motionless there in the hospital bed, with that deceptive sun-tan that made her face look so brown against the white capelline bandage across her brow and over her head. The beautiful face was miraculously untouched, but he had shuddered to imagine the bruises, the broken bones, the agony she must go through when she was no longer under full sedation. It was the thought of her hip injuries, or possibly her spine that drove him frantic with anxiety for her.

"What are you going to do now?" he heard Clem's tired voice. The question brought back the remembrance of her own tragedy—so much worse than his.

"What about you, Clem?" he began.

"I'm all right," she broke in and repeated, "What are you going to do now?"

"I must go home and see about having Lisa moved to the Great London. There's nothing more I can do at the moment. They'll ring me the moment she's conscious."

"Maybe you'd drive me home, then," said Clem in that same weary voice.

"What about . . . what are they arranging at the Airport for—for—?" he stammered and stopped, feeling awkward.

She said:

"About Tony's funeral. Yes, they're going to contact me."

"Must you be alone tonight?"

"I shall phone my aunt in Pwllheli. She's a retired doctor. She'll be very helpful. I know she'll come straight down to me. Tony has no relations in the South. His cousins are all in Lincolnshire where Tony came from."

"If I can be of any help, Clem, you must let me know," said Charles.

They drove back to London in silence.

When they were outside her block of flats, a hideous feeling of misery suddenly threatened to destroy Clem's self-control again. Charles would be leaving her now. Probably he would go out of her life again; just as he had gone before.

"This isn't the time to discuss it, but let me know if you'd like a temporary job to take your mind off your miseries, Clem. I could do with my old secretary and —" he stopped, spreading out a hand.

"Oh, Charles!" she said with a lump in her throat. "It would be a help. As soon as I've settled my affairs, I'll phone you. I assure you I'd love to work for you again."

He drove away.

She went slowly up to the flat and let herself in. It seemed very quiet and deserted; yet the sitting-room looked attractive—with the flowers she had arranged for Tony's home-coming. A bottle of white wine stood on the table which she had already laid with gay yellow linen mats and Danish cutlery. In the small kitchen, a peach-baked ham was waiting, and Tony's favourite Stilton cheese. She had even ground the coffee. It was all ready—the lunch they should have eaten together. Now it was long past five o'clock in the afternoon.

Taking off her coat, she walked into the bedroom and sat down on the edge of the double bed which she had shared—sometimes gladly, more often than not reluctantly—with her husband.

A pipe that Tony had left behind in an ashtray on the table at his side of the bed was still there. She could see his thick Jaeger dressing-gown hanging on the door in the adjoining bathroom. She stared at it. She felt dizzy and ill as though she had been hit over the head.

It was all over—the life they had led together. The sense of loss—the finality of his death inevitably turned her thoughts to the earlier days when she used to imagine she had found real happiness.

Now she felt guilty because she knew that her initial love for Charles had never died—love that she should have given completely to Tony.

42

Suddenly she realised that she was still clutching the zip-bag that was full of the scattered contents of Lisa's case. She thought, dully:

I must take it back to Charles.

It would be a great comfort to be able to work for Charles again. She knew that he would need her; he used always to rely on her. There would be a lot of publicity for him to face now. The reporters and photographers would buzz around like hornets. Charles wouldn't want to be bothered with them or things like Lisa's jewellery and private letters. She would go through the bag and try to sort things out and give the valuables to Charles to put in his safe.

She put the bag down and picked up the telephone receiver to call Wales.

Just before they got to town, Charles had said:

"Sure you aren't going to be alone, Clem?"

She had given him a noncommittal answer. Aunt Anne couldn't get down tonight. It was a seven hours' journey. But knowing her aunt, Clem was quite sure she would take the night express and arrive at the flat for breakfast tomorrow.

Clem didn't really want anybody with her tonight. She wasn't the type to enjoy sobbing on somebody's shoulder. Her reserve had, at times, been of value to her and at other times, made life more diffi-cult. Tonight she wanted to creep into a corner alone, to nurse her wounds. It was particularly sad that her great friend, Patricia Grant, was away. The whole Grant family were down in Devonshire with Guy's parents. Timothy had had very bad measles and needed a complete change so the whole family had taken this week off.

She would be quite alone tonight; and she did not care.

The flat was still full of Tony. She couldn't think of much else. As time passed, she tried to grasp the fact that she had just left his dead body lying there at the airport; that he would never come back to the flat; that she would have to live her life in future without him. It seemed impossible to believe that anybody could be wiped so suddenly and completely out of existence. Whether you were deeply in love with your husband or not, he was still your husband, and once dear and close to you. Clem had been fond of Tony. She had tried hard to make a go of things, despite their incompatibility. She felt a genuine grief for his passing.

She made herself a cup of coffee. She found the tears would keep trickling down her cheeks. A sickening sense of loss began to creep into her consciousness.

One thing Clem had always despised was hypocrisy. She refused

43

now to be a hypocrite over the death of her husband. Cynically, she reflected, that once a man died one was apt to put a halo over his head; to remember all the nice things and none of the unpleasant ones.

She found herself thinking of their early days when she and Tony had enjoyed the fervour of their clamouring, passionate union. She recalled the moments when she used to feel physically so close to him that she could deceive herself into believing that he was right for her. She remembered his amiable, jocular side, his bright eyes, that rather endearing 'puppy-like' devotion he used to give her.

She tried to forget the fact that he had been really rather stupid about their emotional life; never had a clue as to how *she* felt or what she needed. Poor dear Tony! She refused to dwell on the way they had begun to argue—to disagree; or on the thought of how often he had bored her. She must admit that she had probably bored him, too, because she had rarely really enjoyed the 'pub-crawling' which he liked; or drinking with his friends, or, for instance, getting frozen whilst watching a Soccer match.

She tried only to remember his best points now. And the fact that this might not be the end of a perfect marriage—but of a young, useful life. Besides she must face the fact that she was a widow. A widow—how odd that sounded!

Clem began to laugh hysterically, her face pressed against her pillow. Then she dissolved into tears.

The story of the aircraft disaster at Gatwick was in the evening papers. The Press sent reporters to Clem to get her particular story. Soon the telephone started to ring. Tony's London director called her from his private house. One or two of his immediate colleagues at the office and some of their more intimate friends, telephoned. She had to bear an interminable succession of futile, well-meant conversations; the usual expressions of formal sympathy.

'We're all so shocked . . .'

'He was such a splendid worker . . .'

'Oh, poor darling Tony! Ghastly for him and for you. Poor darling Clem! . . .'

That night, she crawled into bed, exhausted. She tried to shut her mind to the fact that this was only the beginning of misery and loneliness. Awful to think that the other side of the big double bed would never again be filled by Tony's warm, friendly figure.

Later when she had fallen into a state of semi-coma, haunted by a vivid picture of the crash, and Tony being hurled to his death, she was woken up by a telephone call.

It was Charles.

She raised herself on an elbow. A degree of warmth and comfort crept over her as she heard that much-loved voice:

"Am I too late? I had to call you. I've been thinking of you so much, poor Clem. Are you all right, my dear? Is somebody staying with you? I do hope so."

"Nobody, but I'm all right. I'd rather be alone. I could have had a friend along if I'd wanted. Lots of them offered to come, but I'd really rather be by myself."

"I think I understand. I just wanted to make sure you were all right."

"Good of you, Charles. What about Lisa?"

"Nothing very concrete. I've just got back from the hospital. I've been there most of the evening. Trevor-Johns is unfortunately not available—out of England—but I managed to phone him in Paris. He's flying home first thing tomorrow morning and he'll see that she's taken to the Great London."

"Meanwhile what does Redhill think of her?"

"They're a bit cagey—even with a professional like myself. I don't like the fact that I haven't been able to speak to her. She's still unconscious. But her general condition seems satisfactory—heart, blood, and so on—amazing really, considering what happened. She has a strong constitution. No internal injuries, but a lot of external bruising, poor darling. Fortunately, she was in good health when it all happened which will help."

"Does her mother know about it?"

"Yes, I phoned her."

"Is she coming over?"

"Yes. Poor Jackie—you know, don't you—Jacqueline is Lisa's mother—she was in a hell of a state, naturally, but she won't fly. She never has liked flying. Maybe she's wise in the face of what's happened and now, of course, she'll never be converted. But she's got a passage on the 'Queen Elizabeth' and should be over in a few days."

"I hope she'll be helpful to you, Charles."

"That I very much doubt," came his reply with a dry laugh. "Dear Jackie is not a restful or helpful character. She's very generous and she'll be filled with the desire to help, but she'll try and talk down everything I want to do for Lisa. She's got a 'thing' about American doctors and surgeons and how much better they are than ours, etc., and I very much fear that husband of hers will be coming with her to complicate matters. She never leaves him behind."

"What is her name now?"

"Mrs. Walter Cain. She calls him Wally. He's rather a smooth 'precious' type. Has a lot of money and owns a flourishing firm of interior decorators in New York."

Charles talked on about the man his mother-in-law had married as though he wanted to talk to Clem about anybody—anything. Clem realised that he was tense—suffering from reaction. "Wally Cain," he went on, "is the health-conscious type. He produces a slipped disc as soon as he sees me. I don't know how my Mama-in-law stands him, but she needs a slave and he's just that."

"Well, I suppose nothing matters to you so long as Lisa continues to improve," said Clem and closed her eyes. They felt sore and inflamed.

"There will be a public enquiry but they seem to have a bit more information now about the crash," went on Charles. "It was the undercarriage—touched down on one wing, then went on fire. Thank God they soon got *that* under control. They were coming down, you know, at one hundred and twenty miles an hour. One can imagine why some of the windows were shattered, but only three people were thrown out. They say the safety belts—Lisa's and Tony's—were not fastened. And the air hostess was standing up, presumably. Well, there you are!"

"Yes, there you are," said Clem, shivering.

"I must go. Glad to be in touch with you again, dear Clem. Goodnight. I'll call you in the morning."

He didn't call. She took it for granted that he was far too occupied getting Lisa transferred to Great London.

It was she who called him the day after that to make sure Lisa was all right.

He seemed happier about things in general. Lisa had recovered consciousness and recognised him.

"She seems anxious about a case she was holding when they crashed. It was apparently lost," he said.

"No," said Clem. "Some of her things were found near her, picked up and put into another bag which they handed to me. I forgot to give it to you, Charles. I'll bring it round."

"Any time. I don't think she needs it really. It was her make-up and jewel case. Now I remember. Poor darling, she certainly won't be wanting jewellery or cosmetics just yet. They're keeping her under sedation most of the time. Bring the case around to Welbeck Street when you have a moment, Clem. And incidentally—this may not be the time to broach the subject—but you will remember that I told you my present secretary is due for a slight operation soon?"

"Yes."

"When she goes, if you'd like some work to take your mind off —" he stopped, awkwardly. She filled in the gap.

"Take my mind off my own troubles—yes. It's exactly what I need. Can I come, Charles?"

"You certainly can. You'd be a godsend."

"Tony's being buried the day after tomorrow. My aunt, Dr. Wright, has arrived and is staying with me. I told you she was a retired doctor, didn't I? But I'll come to you when you want me."

"You're sure you can manage it?"

"Yes," said Clem. "Oh, *yes*."

Charles said goodbye.

Clem walked into the sitting-room where Dr. Wright was busily writing a few business letters for her niece.

"Who was that, dear? I wish they would leave you alone. People are so thoughtless phoning all the time."

"Actually I made the call. It was to Mr. Maddison—the osteopath I used to work for."

"Oh, yes. The one who's wife was on the same plane as your poor Tony."

"Yes, she's going to be all right, it seems. Anyhow, he is in a flat spin at the moment and after next week he wants me to help him out. His secretary has to go into hospital."

Dr. Wright looked over her horn-rims at her niece. She thought that Clem looked very pinched and pale—and exhausted. But no wonder! This must have been a terrible experience for her. Dr. Wright was devoted to Clem. She admired the girl very much. She had always been such a courageous little thing, tackling the problems of life as they came along. But Dr. Wright was no fool—not to be misled by outward appearances. She had never personally cared much for the man Clem married nor did she think that in recent months Clem had found her marriage wholly acceptable. But Tony's sudden ghastly death must have shaken her to the core—of that the doctor was sure. And it worried her to think that poor little Clem would soon be quite alone.

"I don't think it's a bad idea for you to do a bit of work, but wouldn't you like to come up to Pwllheli and live with me for the next few months, anyhow?"

"Thank you, darling Aunt Anne, but I couldn't afford to and I'm not having you keep me," said Clem. "I must earn my own living."

But she looked with affection at the doctor. She and Aunt Anne were alike; both small and dark-haired with camellia-pale skin and fine-cut lips. Of course, Aunt Anne was now quite grey, and lined for her sixty years. But they had similar characters; that was why they understood each other so well. Aunt Anne didn't argue when Clem protested that she wished to remain alone and be quite independent.

"Well, dear, just as you say, but you know my home is yours if and when you need it. I suppose you will have to work, because this letter we are just answering from Tony's solicitors isn't too reassuring, is it?"

"Not very," said Clem with a faint smile.

One rarely knew all the facts—even about the man you were married to, she thought. She had imagined that Tony was pretty sound, but now it seemed he had been somewhat vague and neglectful over money matters. There were too many outstanding bills and a life insurance of only two thousand pounds which, when invested, would barely bring her one hundred a year. True, she could get out of this flat, but she would need most of the contents even in a smaller, cheaper one. There would be compensation from the airline company. Tony's lawyer, Mr. Spaxton, had been in touch with her and informed her that the amount paid would be decided after the enquiry and depend on how much Tony was worth—what his future prospects would have been. Mr. Spaxton didn't think it would amount to much more than a couple of thousand pounds, if that. Anyhow it would be three or four months before anything was settled.

Clem would not be sufficiently well off to remain idle. She must find a job. She wanted one. She could not have borne to remain idle and to start by standing in for Charles's secretary would be more than she dared hope for.

She sat down opposite Aunt Anne. They still had to sift through the contents of Tony's deed-box.

5

DR. WRIGHT left her niece the week following Tony's funeral. She would have stayed longer, but there were several important reasons why she must get back to Wales. Although she left Clem with reluctance, the girl assured her that there was no need for her to worry. Dr. Wright returned home rather more than usually full of admiration for her. After the first terrible shock, she had behaved with such admirable calm and fortitude. The cremation took place at Golders Green. It was a grim day for Clem and she shed bitter tears in the little chapel—tears for *him* so much more than for herself. Then with her characteristic calm, her philosophical acceptance of fate, she set to work to settle up Tony's estate, and reorientate her own life.

Dr. Wright could well understand why the famous Mr. Maddison needed his old P.A. Clem, for her age, was so competent. It was also at the back of Dr. Wright's mind that as her niece was still so young, she might one day meet somebody else; even remarry; Clem (feeling secretly as she did about Charles Maddison) had told her aunt she was quite sure this would never be.

'I shall never marry again.'

But Dr. Wright had looked into her niece's eyes—those long-lashed velvety brown eyes which were unusually sad, and shook her head. It wasn't the time to say so, but she didn't for a moment think Clementine would remain alone. Behind that quiet exterior there lay a warm passionate nature—of that Dr. Wright was positive. She knew her Clem.

Once Aunt Anne had gone, Clem realised to the full how empty life was in the flat without Tony. She must move. Besides, it was bigger and more expensive than she could now afford. She placed the flat in the hands of a local agent and started to look for one with two rooms, kitchen and bath. She would, of course, also have to find a permanent job. She was sure Charles would recommend her to a fellow practitioner, as she was so familiar with his type of work.

He *might*, of course, ask her to go back to him altogether. Hadn't he mentioned that he meant to give the present girl notice? Clem was stirred by a small secret hope that this might happen, but there was no certainty.

Clem suddenly remembered that she had never returned Lisa's case. How awful! She had forgotten to take it round to Charles. She was a person who rarely forgot things, but might be excused after such a harrowing and busy week. She had been in daily touch with Charles. They had talked together every night on the telephone about Lisa. The most serious of her injuries was to the lower spine, but until they got her on to the operating table today, Charles was not able to give Clem any details. Trevor-Johns had the case under control now. Lisa had already had one operation on her hip and the broken arm had been set. But she was still concussed. Charles said he had not yet had one coherent conversation with her. She would just open her eyes, smile at him and mutter, then sleep again. He would hold her hand and look at her, Charles told Clem rather pathetically, thankful that she had been spared to him, but horrified that his beautiful radiant wife had been reduced to such a state.

Anyhow, she didn't seem to need the make-up case or the jewels so Clem hoped her omission did not matter.

There had been nothing in the papers about poor Tony after the first mention that he was among the dead, but both the daily and Sunday papers publicised Lisa—the beautiful, famous model-girl. Her photographs and the bulletins about her condition were 'news'.

Clem began to look forward to working with Charles again. It would be wonderful; a great comfort.

She opened Lisa's bag and began to tidy up the bottles and pots—some of which were cracked and only fit to throw away. Then she found a pile of letters. Clem was not normally a person who read other people's letters, but the words on the top one were startling enough to fascinate and hold her attention:

She felt stunned as she went on reading the first paragraph:

> You've got to tell Charles. You belonged to me last night as you've never done to him. I love you madly. I can give you all the things he can never give. You know that. If you don't telephone by the end of this week and tell me that you'll leave him for me, I shall fly over and fetch you. Lisa, OH MY LISA . . .

Bewildered, Clem sat there taking in the full significance of those words: 'You belonged to me last night as you've never done to him.'

Bewilderment gave place to indignation. This was *horrible*. To be the wife of a man like Charles Maddison—adored and spoiled and to be unfaithful to him . . . it was *horrible*.

Long afterwards, Clem's conscience pricked her. She felt guilty and ashamed of having read somebody else's private correspondence. But strong, resolute character though she was, this temptation was too much even for Clem. She loved Charles. He was obviously being made a fool of and betrayed. It was more than she could stand. She must find out more.

Now she began to read more of the letters. One had been sent from Cannes to the villa where Lisa had stayed in Rome.

The writer was named Max. It seemed that he owned a yacht which was at this moment in harbour there. It was called '*Lisavetta*'.

It wasn't difficult for Clem to gather most of the story. 'Max' seemed to be a literary sort of man. He had poured his feelings out on paper. There were six, big, transparent pages of foreign notepaper, closely written on in a small, at times, almost indecipherable hand.

The rest of the letters were from a hotel in Rome—short, passionate—filled with exotic reminders of the hours he and Lisa had spent together. The first in the packet explained most things to a dazed and fascinated Clem.

Lisa—you have only just left Nice Airport. I stood for five or ten minutes looking up at the sky after the Caravelle vanished from my sight. I knew before that I loved you, but as I stared at that empty sky, I realised that my love for you was different from the idle passion I have felt for other women in my life.

There have been others. I'd be stupid to pretend otherwise. I've been married and that marriage ended. Since then I have had a great many love affairs. Each one has left me with the wretched, morbid sensation that they meant little and that by enjoying them, I had debased any grain of nobility that there was in my character. I don't pretend that I am ever really a noble person, but I have a contempt for petty men. I am the grandson of a millionaire. I have inherited his wealth. Nothing has ever been denied me. I can buy what I want but nothing ever satisfies me for long. That is the hell reserved for most men who have inherited wealth. They haven't even experienced the thrill of making it. You have everything and nothing. I had

51

begun to feel hopeless of ever finding real happiness. Then I met you.

When I first caught sight of you at that party in Venice, you remember the one given by Prince Varioni, I knew my life was about to change.

You wore classic Greek draperies and among all the other fancy-dresses—fussy and flamboyant—you triumphed. It was perfect. So were you as a Vestal Virgin. You were more than exquisite. Yes, it was as though there was a fire burning through all the whiteness. Your fantastic red hair floated over your naked shoulders, like a flame. When I looked more closely at you, and you lifted those long silken lids, I saw your strange green eyes and I was convinced that passion was there, there, too, in the curve of your moist pink mouth. You seemed to me voluptuously beautiful, yet coldly pure. An intriguing combination.

After we had danced together, we went down to the bridge and stood looking into the canal watching the moonlight dip into those mysterious waters and I felt like a man under a spell. It is a spell that has never lifted.

The fact that you are married to this English doctor doesn't particularly alarm me. I have seen many marriages break up and I admit that I have helped to break up one or two, then walked out on the girl because I couldn't face the rest of my life with her. I am not proud of it, but it's true. With you it's different. If you decide to break with Charles Maddison and come to me, I'll never leave you. I am bound to you for life.

When you left Venice and went back to London, our separation only confirmed my absolute belief in my love for you. Do you remember our first kiss? Oh, Lisa—if ever there was to be a last kiss, I would not want to go on living.

You told me the other day that you thought it might destroy Maddison if you left him, but I'm afraid I can't help that, or even be sorry for him. He had his chance and lost it.

This is the strongest passion of my life. Lisa, dearest, I mean to grasp you and hold you for ever—no matter at what cost to anybody else.

LATER

Seeing you again in Cannes has only confirmed all that I have just said. Those two marvellous unforgettable nights that

52

we spent on my yacht proved not only that you are the most fascinating and glorious woman I have ever loved, but that you love me, too. You told me that you accepted the admiration of other men—and you've had plenty—without being moved, but that with me things were different. You need me as much as I need you. You have convinced me that the fact that I am a millionaire is of no importance and that if I lost every penny, you would still want to come with me. The only doubt in your mind seems to be whether you should hurt your husband. Yet you admit that he bores you and that as a lover he means nothing; that at the time you married him you thought yourself in love, but found it a mistake once you and I met each other. On the face of this, you cannot go on living with him. You must come to me.

My lovely, adorable Lisa. What absolute heaven it was on the yacht! I bought her because she had long, classic, beautiful lines—I knew you would admire her and grace her. And you know why I called her 'Lisavetta'—in honour of you, my adored darling.

I find a new excitement in the thought that my bank-balance will allow me to buy you anything in the world you want. When you leave Maddison and join me, we'll go round the world together. I'll marry you the moment Charles sets you free.

You shall have not only one beautiful home, but many—in London—Paris—Rome—New York. Last night I wrote to my grandfather in Hamburg. As I've told you our family fortune comes from the shipbuilding company we own there. They have made a remarkable recovery since the Second World War. I don't often see my old grandfather, but I am fond of him. I wrote to him about you and sent him a snapshot of you. He thinks it marvellous. He was quite a lover, in his own day. It's a curious thing that the Von Kernhardts have always admired English women. Both my grandmother and my mother were English. You've told me so often that you find little of the German in me. Well, after all, I was educated at Eton and Oxford and I have my mother's tall thin English figure and grey eyes, and only my blond hair (which I hate) to remind me that I am on one side, a Prussian. But at least I have the Von Kernhardt's fortune to lay at your feet, and as you don't care for Germany, I am glad that I became an

53

American citizen. I think you will prefer the name Kern, which I took when I first made a home there. You will be Mrs. Max Kern—and you'll find as I do, that an American passport and dollars, rather than marks, make life easier and less awkward. There is still so much anti-Nazi feeling left in the world.

Lisa, belovèd one, this is the longest letter I have ever written to anybody in my life. But now you are away from me, I want to pour my heart out to you.

I used to love poetry when I was a boy at University reading English. I remember two lines of Lord Tennyson:

> 'A daughter of the gods, divinely tall
> and most divinely fair.'

That describes you. YOU are my divine Lisa. You are my soul. Please I implore you, tell Charles how we feel about each other. Tell him as soon as you get back to England.

Clem was trembling when she finished this long, lucid, extraordinary letter. She felt as though she had smashed a mirror, walked through and found herself in another world. A world she hadn't really wanted to enter, and in which she had no place. Such a revelation of fierce passion and desire fascinated but terrified her. More especially as it was directed at Charles's wife.

Little had been left to Clem's imagination. Max Kern's long letter was verbose, poetic and really rather un-English. But his meaning was plain.

He was the wealthy owner of a famous shipbuilding concern in Hamburg. He had become an American citizen. And he was madly and desperately in love with Lisa. They were lovers. And from what Max said, Lisa was as deeply involved as her millionaire. Whether she was truly in love this time, or whether it was just the lure of money—Clem could not judge. But the salient fact was that Lisa must have given Max Kern reason to believe that she intended to ask Charles for a divorce.

Clem could hardly believe it. Her indignation and resentment grew with every minute that passed. She, herself, loved Charles so much that she couldn't understand another girl being married to him and so much as looking at anyone else. It seemed incredible. Yet the words were there. Lisa had told Max that Charles, and her marriage, *bored her*. That she never should have married him in the first place.

Clem lit a cigarette. Her fingers shook so that she could hardly hold the match. Feeling sick to the pit of her stomach, she opened one or two more of Max's letters, shorter notes, written from the Hassler Hotel in Rome. He had followed Lisa, unable to keep away. He had seen as much of her as he could while she was staying with her friends.

Whatever Clem thought about the rights or wrongs of it, she had to admit that Max Kern was a most persistent lover. He wasn't going to let Lisa slip through his fingers. He wrote to her every night; every day. One letter began:—

Lisa, Lisa, you are driving me quite mad. Last night was the most marvellous we have ever spent together . . .

What followed was intimate enough to make Clem's cheeks burn. Hastily she folded the note then put all the letters back in their envelopes.

She got up and began to walk to and fro in a state of agitation.

For Lisa to have kept those letters—God knew they were incriminating enough to make any divorce possible—could only suggest that she did indeed mean to leave her husband. She would never have brought them over like this in her bag, had she not made the decision.

In her semi-comatose condition at the hospital, Lisa had no doubt remembered the existence of those burning, damning letters and been anxious about them. Very soon she would ask about them.

What *should* she do, Clem asked herself. She felt that she couldn't bear the prospect of Charles being brought face to face with the proof of Lisa's infidelity. It would kill everything in him. He was utterly in love with his wife. He believed in her. She had deceived him and got away with it. The dates on those notes showed Clem this hot love affair must have been going on for several months. She remembered now that Charles had told her that he had taken Lisa over to Venice for the VARIONI masked ball which was held annually and always a sensation.

Clem shut her eyes. Oh God, poor Charles, poor darling Charles! In her own small way, she knew what torture unrequited love could be. To have had Lisa then lose her in this way would be *murderous* for him.

Clem looked further ahead. She began to wonder what difference this terrible accident would make both to Lisa and her lover. Would she delay the confession to her husband until she was on her feet? (Always supposing that she *could* stand on those lovely feet again. Who was to know the full extent of her injuries until Trevor-Johns gave the final verdict?) Or would she reorientate her whole life and decide to stay with Charles?

What would have happened if I had given this bag to Charles that night—if he had read the letters, Clem suddenly felt sick again as she asked herself this question.

Her lapse of memory was a stroke of luck. Was it up to her now to make sure that Charles never did read those letters? At any rate, she must tell Lisa about the letters as soon as she was conscious, and ask her what she meant to do about Charles.

Never had Clem been more uncertain as to which step she should take. It was not her business she well knew but, unfortunately, her lapse of honour in reading those incriminating letters had made it so. She must now try to save Charles. She cared what happened to Lisa only insofar as it affected *him*.

It would seem that the crux of the situation was what Max Kern would do. It just might happen that he would not have heard about this accident. Suddenly, feverishly, Clem sifted through Lisa's letters again and pulled out the one which was obviously the last he had written from the Hassler Hotel:

I have been awake all night thinking of you. I find it unbearable that you should be flying back to your husband tomorrow morning and that immediately you have gone I must fly to Kennedy Airport alone. You have become my life. I can only bear the present because you promised to join me as soon as I get back from New York. I'm committed to attend some business there or I would have come with you to London and stayed there until you were ready to break all the ties and join me. Don't let him touch you tomorrow night or ever again. Remember you have sworn that, Lisa . . .

Shivering violently, Clem folded this note and shoved it back into its envelope. The sickness which she felt was of disgust for Lisa and of terror for Charles who loved her so much.

Oh God, how could she? *How could she?*

How debased, and two-faced, she must have been all this time, going straight from her lover to her husband—capable of playing the part so well that Charles had never guessed. And no doubt because of her unholy vow to Max, she had refused to give herself to him on the grounds of fatigue or ill-health, or by telling some lie which would keep them apart.

In all my life, Clem thought, *I have never hated or despised anybody more.*

But now the name 'New York' leapt at her from the page she had been reading—this mad love-letter written by Max Kern. It looked as though he would have already been in the air, flying to Kennedy International Airport, when Lisa reached England. He was unlikely to have heard about the accident. It was not a great world-shaking catastrophe. The great majority of the passengers had escaped death or even injury. Fire had been immediately brought under control. The report in all probability would occupy only a small paragraph in the American papers. More especially as it was not a Trans-atlantic flight. There had been no Americans aboard.

So, Clem went on thinking, there was a very good chance that the accident to Lisa hadn't yet been brought to Max's notice. *So far,* Charles was safe.

Suddenly, Clem's way seemed clear. She must protect Charles. To do this she would have to keep all her wits about her. Acting as his secretary again would make things easier. She would be in control of the post. She used always to sift the personal and private letters in the morning before Charles appeared. True that had been altered once Mrs. Charles Maddison took up residence, but now that Lisa was no longer at Welbeck Street, they would doubtless revert to the old habits.

Anyhow, should there be a letter or a telephone message from America for Lisa, it wouldn't strike Charles as being untoward since her mother lived there.

Clem was frantic with anxiety to see Lisa as soon as she was permitted to do so. No matter what story she told —what excuse she trumped up—she must find out what Lisa intended to do.

The difficulty was largely solved by the unsuspecting Charles himself. He telephoned Clem early that next morning.

"Hello—I'm at the Great London. Lisa is recovering at last. She has asked to see you."

"To see *me*!" echoed Clem, feeling rather stupid. She had only just woken up.

"Yes. I've been with her most of the night. She didn't want me to go. She's in a pretty miserable state of nerves. I don't understand why but she keeps asking for her jewel case. She says that it's because she is afraid the ring I gave her for our engagement—her

57

emerald—may have been stolen. Anyhow, when I told her you were looking after the case she asked if you would go at once to the hospital and hand it over to her personally. I offered to collect it but she wants you. It's a bit odd but people in her shocked state often are. I feel it is best for us to humour her, poor love."

Now Clem understood. With some cynicism her lips twisted. It wasn't the emerald Lisa was worried about!

Charles added in a tired voice:

"I'm all in at the moment, Clem dear. I'm going back to have a bath and get half an hour's sleep before I start seeing patients. I've had to cancel several appointments. I've also heard from Dorothy that Miss Garner—my P.A.—isn't turning up. She tried to contact me but couldn't get an answer on the phone so she got hold of Dorothy last night, Dorothy told me. There seems to be a hoodoo over us all. Miss Garner is in hospital herself—with an appendix."

"That settles that," said Clem promptly, "I'll get round to Welbeck Street as soon as I can."

"Bless you, I knew you would. Take a taxi on me to the Great London and back. My poor Lisa seems so concerned about her damned jewels—as if I would mind how many emeralds she lost, so long as *she's* all right."

As Clem put down the receiver, she drew a deep, bitter sigh. It seemed so awful to *know* why Lisa was concerned.

In a way, thought Clem, *it's as well I pandered to my lower instincts and read those damned letters*.

Why had Lisa asked for *her*.

Possibly to try and make an ally of her, although she must be too ill at the moment to be able to deal with any of her affairs very sensibly.

When Clem reached the Great London, she was at once taken to Mrs. Maddison's private room. The Sister had her orders.

The Maddisons were great friends of Mr. Trevor-Johns. That name spelt magic in the great hospital.

Clem seated herself beside Lisa's bed. The contempt, the disgust she had felt for this girl dissolved into pity as she looked at the white bandages. How changed she was. Her arm in a splint; her figure immobile; her face almost unrecognisable without make-up; the pale lips were pitiful; the eyes staring up at Clem, were bright with fear. Clem had never seen such a tell-tale expression.

Lisa whispered:

"My—things—they say the case burst—what has happened to—the contents?"

Clem unzipped the bag. She pulled out the bundle of letters.

"These are what you are looking for, aren't they, Mrs. Maddison?"

Now a look of unholy joy and relief crossed that tortured face. Lisa's free hand gripped the packet of letters.

"Yes — thank you."

She seemed so weak that she could only speak in that husky whisper. Then she looked up.

"Has . . . my husband . . . seen these?"

"No. He gave me the bag at the Airport and I hung on to it. We were both in such a state that your case was forgotten."

Again the relief. Then the whisper:

"Thank you. I . . . Charles tells me . . . you are going to work for him again."

"For the time being, yes."

"Listen. There may be a telephone call and a cable or some letter from America for me. Please let me have them. Don't give them to him. I — don't quite know how to explain but —"

"Mrs. Maddison," Clem broke in coldly, "please don't upset yourself. You can be quite frank with me. I know everything."

Lisa's face flushed scarlet. She gasped and stared incredulously at the girl who had once been Charles's trusted secretary.

"What do you mean?"

"I think it's better," said Clem, "that I tell you straight away that I read your letters. I had absolutely no right. It was a shocking thing for me to do. I'm not really that sort of person, but I happened to catch sight of one paragraph in one of the notes that had no envelope. It disturbed me to such an extent that I just had to go on reading. You may hate me, Mrs. Maddison, but I feel now it was for the best. You see — I am very devoted to — Charles. He loves you so much; I'd hate him to learn the truth. Besides — since your accident you may have changed your mind. You may not want him ever to know. I assure you I want to do what I can for both of you. I'll help all I can. You may think me untrustworthy, but I'm not. You have my word that Charles will never know about Mr. Kern if you don't want him to and I can handle any phone calls or cables that come for you. Just brief me."

After this long speech, Clem stopped, feeling highly embarrassed but at the same time thankful to have it all off her chest. Her conscience had been troubling her.

Lisa didn't speak for several minutes. She seemed stupefied. Clem could see her struggling with her emotions. Once again she pitied Charles's wife. It must be terrible to have had your life planned—to have been so full of self-confidence—so crazily in love (even if with the wrong man) then to find oneself helpless and on the edge of an emotional disaster that might be even worse than the calamity which had overtaken her at Gatwick.

Then Lisa gave a great gasping sob.

"How dared you? How *dared* you read my letters?"

"I've admitted it was wrong of me. But look at this calmly, Mrs. Maddison. Isn't it better I should know everything and be able to help you? Or do you want your husband to find out that you are on the verge of leaving him?"

Lisa's face contorted. She moved her head from side to side, as though in physical pain.

"No, he mustn't know. Not now."

"Then I *can* help."

"Why should you?" Lisa began to cry like a child. "Why don't you give me away?"

"I've told you. I don't want him to be hurt. He's a wonderful man and he worships you. It would kill him."

"Why wasn't I killed in the crash?"

"It isn't much good thinking like that."

"You must be in love with my husband!" broke out Lisa, suddenly, viciously.

Clem set her teeth.

"I don't think that comes into it. But I don't want him to be hurt, and I'd like to help you while you are so helpless."

"Ought I to thank you?"

"This isn't the time for thanks. Or for us to crack at each other. Tell me what you want me to do. Possibly I can intercept the mail, but I can't prevent Mr. Kern from coming over here. What if he turns up?"

"He mustn't," said Lisa feverishly. "I couldn't face all the upheaval and publicity now. I feel too ill. Besides I may never walk again. They don't know yet. My spine is fractured. I may have 'had it'. They can't fool me."

Once more Clem was full of pity. She said in a more gentle voice:

"You're in good hands. Everything will be all right. Let's just face the immediate trouble. What do you suggest?"

"You must send a cable to Max at once."

In business-like fashion, Clem pulled a pad and pencil from the large bag she always carried.

"Where is he, Mrs. Maddison?"

"In New York. He wouldn't have heard about the crash yet—I'm sure. There has been no letter, no phone call for me, has there?"

"Not if Charles hasn't said anything to you that I don't know. But I'm going round now to see to his correspondence. I'll make discreet enquiries."

"There *may* be a letter. Keep it for me."

"Yes."

"And please," said Lisa, with the tears running down her cheeks, "take these . . .' she handed Max's love-letters back to Clem. "Burn them. I daren't keep them now."

Clem put the letters into her bag. She felt extraordinarily calm and unemotional, she could only hope that what she was doing might save Charles from complete and utter disillusionment.

"Please dictate your cable," she said, "and give me the address. I swear by all that I hold holy that I will respect your confidence and do all I can to keep the facts away from Charles."

Lisa, still weeping, snuffling, gasping like a child—her spirit broken by the awful shock to her whole system, nodded. She whispered the message:

DO NOT CONTACT ME STOP WILL WRITE STOP CIRCUMSTANCES
HAVE CHANGED STOP IT IS IMPOSSIBLE FOR ME TO LEAVE
CHARLES JUST NOW STOP I BEG YOU NOT TO TRY AND GET IN
TOUCH WITH ME UNTIL I GIVE YOU THE WORD LISA

Clem, taking this down in shorthand, flinched at those two words 'just now'. Her heart was heavy. Did this mean that Lisa was only marking time? When eventually did she mean to deliver the *coup de grâce* to poor Charles?

6

It was a Christmas that Clem was never to forget. For a month before Christmas Day she had been living, literally, in a whirl. The days had been hectic and the nights hateful. She could not get accustomed to living alone again, nor to the memory of Tony's sudden death, which haunted her.

A dozen times a day she needed Tony to lean on, but learned that she must fend for herself and ask for no outside support. Fortunately, because Clem had never been the clinging or helpless type, she was able to stand up to the rigorous change better than some women. A great deal of her grief and shock gradually disappeared. Her practical side asserted itself.

She spent Christmas week with her friends, Pat and Guy Grant. She tried to forget Tony's death and the tragedy of the Maddisons. She concentrated on her small godson, but she remained haunted by the disaster. She and Pat had always been great friends. They could talk things over; but she could not tell even Pat the truth about Lisa. Clem had to listen in silence when Pat said 'how terrible it was for poor Mrs. Maddison'. Pat did at least know what the position had been between Clem and Tony so there was no need for hypocrisy.

"You'll miss him, but you'll get back to normal soon and it's a good thing you are able to work for Charles Maddison again," Pat said before Clem left the house.

Yes, Clem knew it was a good thing, but she was so deeply involved in Lisa's duplicity, things were far from easy for her. Trying to keep Charles from learning the unfortunate truth about his wife was no mean task. It became of paramount importance in Clem's life.

It was strange, she often reflected, how in a queer way a person can become attached to the person who is causing all the trouble. Looking after Lisa meant caring for an invalid, a cripple. A job necessitating many unpleasant tasks, nevertheless essential, and heaven alone knew she found it singularly unpleasant to have to be the buffer between Charles and Max Kern — with a miserable weeping Lisa in between.

Clem found that the whole personality of Lisa, the once-Magnificent, had changed. She was no longer the much to be envied model-girl who had married Charles. She was a wreck. The wreck Clem was trying to salvage—for Charles. She did more now for Lisa than for anyone. She began to feel, somewhat cynically, that fate must have saved her from bearing a child to Tony in order that she could 'mother' Lisa. And even though this strange child was often abhorrent to Clem she could still find it in her heart to try her best to make things easy for Lisa as well as her husband.

Lisa seemed to go to pieces during the weeks that followed the crash. Because Clem, and Clem only, knew the truth, she clung to her in a despairing fashion.

"Don't go away—don't leave Charles or me—stay and look after our interests, for God's sake," she kept saying with the tears pouring down that beautiful, ravaged face.

How could Clem do anything but say 'yes'. Charles for the moment still had his illusions. Lisa was bitterly unhappy because Max seemed to have deserted her. Once he had been madly in love with her, but with this new Lisa, the helpless invalid, he seemed to be proving less devoted.

The three weeks preceding Christmas had been chaotic and difficult for everybody. Lisa's mother and her young husband arrived from Florida. As soon as Clem saw Mrs. Wally Cain, she found fresh grounds to pity Charles. He had the worst type of mother-in-law. A spoiled, domineering woman, who at the age of forty-five was made-up and dressed to look half her age and behaved like a pampered doll. But under the 'doll' exterior, she was as hard as flint. She must have led General Fannington a dance, Clem decided. But he had apparently been a strong man who had some control over his wife in his lifetime.

Wally Cain had none. He was effeminate; a 'yes' man. He trailed after Jackie and seemed a little afraid of her. She had complete control of him. Even Clem had to admit that Lisa's mother was still a beauty. The same red hair that had been bequeathed to Lisa, and those green, magnificent eyes. But she was more *petite* than her daughter, and had an over-abundant vitality. She tired everybody out.

Jackie Cain's genius lay in colour and design. She had proved a great help to Wally in his particular field of interior decorating. The pair had become very popular and successful in Florida.

One thing Clem soon learned was that Mrs. Wally Cain wanted

her own way in most things and when she didn't get it, could be extremely unpleasant. Even Lisa seemed to dread seeing too much of 'Mummy'.

The Cains stayed at Claridges, bombarded Charles when he was busy, or exhausted him after his day's work.

Jackie made herself a menace at the Great London where doctors and nurses dreaded her visits. She disapproved of everything that was being done for Lisa. She ended up by quarrelling with Charles who bluntly told his mother-in-law that she didn't know what she was talking about and that he wished her to leave his wife's treatment to him. Jackie rushed to the hospital complaining bitterly of her treatment, and begged Lisa to go out to Florida to her as soon as she was able to travel. But, for once, Lisa was on her husband's side. She couldn't bear any more of her mother's scenes.

"Oh, for heaven's sake, you go home, Mummy, and take Wally with you," she exclaimed.

Whereupon the Wally Cains packed up and left England.

Charles, trying to keep a sense of humour, had described to Clem his final parting with his mother-in-law.

"She practically accused me of being the cause of all Lisa's spinal trouble, making no mention of the accident," he said grimly. "What a woman! And that ghastly husband of hers, tripping around my house, telling me how 'divine' all my furniture is. Thank goodness Lisa doesn't resemble her mother. Physically, perhaps, in a way, but in character I reckon Lisa is more like her father."

Clem had often thought over those words; wondering whether Lisa wasn't in fact just as pampered and exhausting as her mother.

But Charles's eyes were not yet opened.

Came the day when Clem, back in harness at Welbeck Street, had to cope with Max Kern. The long-awaited telephone call came from Philadelphia. Dorothy Pugh took it, but handed the telephone to the senior secretary.

"From the States—asking for Mrs. Maddison."

Clem was prepared for this. She sent Dorothy out on a mission which took her to a stationers to buy blotting paper (not really needed) but which got her out of the house. Then, satisfied that Charles was busy with a patient, Clem answered the call.

It was Max Kern.

Clem told him quietly, but pulling no punches, all that had happened to Lisa.

At first Max seemed genuinely shocked—even distraught.

64

"I can't believe it. I must fly over at once."

"Haven't you had her cable, Mr. Kern?"

"No. Where was it sent?"

"To your apartment in New York."

"I haven't been there. Ever since I got back to America from Cannes, I've been here in Philadelphia on urgent business that kept me. When I phoned my secretary in New York I told her to hold up any mail or messages. I never anticipated such a cable from Lisa. What did it say?"

Clem repeated the message. Max then demanded every detail of Lisa's crash. Clem told him everything, but made it clear that Lisa did not wish him to come over to her. She could not go away with him now, as she had hoped to do.

"You know about us, then?"

"Yes, I know. I'm in Mrs. Maddison's confidence. She's very sick, Mr. Kern. The best thing you can do for her is to leave her alone and let her get over this terrible shock."

"But I *must* write. I *must* send flowers. What hospital is she in?"

"She doesn't wish you to know. She thinks it best that there should be complete silence between you—for the moment, anyhow. You understand? In the circumstances, there must be no outward break between her and her husband."

It took Max Kern some time to accept this, but in the end he did so.

There followed other telephone calls from New York and finally one from Cannes. Max, by that time, had flown back to Europe to make arrangements about his yacht. He was planning to spend Christmas in Nassau.

Trevor-Johns held out only small hope that Lisa would make a complete recovery but at least he could assure Charles that his wife might not be permanently disabled. Her paralysis could be cured in time. But for many more months she must lie in plaster, then have to sit in a wheel-chair. A long-drawn-out period of treatment might, he hoped, put her on her feet again. But he was more hopeful than convinced.

It fell to Clem to deliver this grim news to Max. He had just telephoned from Cannes for the latest bulletin.

He expressed horror and grief. But after questioning Clem repeatedly, and receiving always the same answer, that it might be a year before Lisa would walk again and then only if things went well, Max admitted that there seemed no future for them now.

"It's too terrible, but I suppose I must accept the blow. Our hopes are at an end, for the time being anyhow."

Clem's lips curled. So this was the great lover! Max wasn't really interested in a girl who couldn't walk. When she thought of Charles whose devotion to Lisa never wavered and who spent every possible hour at her bedside, rushing madly between Welbeck Street and the Great London—wearing himself out in the effort to comfort her; to make the long hours less tedious, Clem thought it ironic. Ironic and sad that Lisa should ever have contemplated leaving this man for the other.

"Of course, I must eventually see her," Max said with emotion, "I'll come to London very soon and we'll talk things over."

"I doubt if that would be wise, Mr. Kern."

"Naturally, I won't give anything away, but I *must* see her."

"For what reason? Just to upset her?"

"Don't be so destructive. I am sure Lisa wants me to come; and I want her to know how I feel."

"I'll tell her, Mr. Kern."

"I think you overstep the mark," Max's voice suddenly sounded angry. The spoiled millionaire took the place of the heartbroken lover. "Please do not dictate to me. I shall do what I think best and when I am in London, I intend to see Mrs. Maddison."

"As you wish," said Clem coldly. "Possibly when she is able to do so, Lisa will write to you, herself, and you will, I am sure, abide by her decisions."

Max rang off.

Clem repeated this conversation to Lisa. She had taken down every word that Max had said, so that she should deliver the messages faithfully.

When she saw Lisa's face crumple up and the tears spring to the beautiful heavily-fringed eyes, she could almost weep with her. Poor unhappy Lisa—once so confident that every man in the world was her slave; so sure that she had only to call the tune and Max would dance to it. Now she must learn that all men are different and that Max was the type who could not take this kind of blow on the chin. He was not going to put himself out for her for the present, anyhow.

Lisa burst into tears.

"Listen," said Clem, "surely you won't be too upset if Max goes out of your life. You've already told me you don't want to leave Charles now."

Lisa chewed at her lower lip, tasting the salt of her own tears of self-pity.

"No, I don't—while I'm so helpless. But give Max time. If I keep writing to him, I know he'll come back to me and show more concern."

"He showed plenty on the phone, but men are not like women, you know. If they see that it's best to end something, they cut away ruthlessly and quickly. It's the women who want to hang on and play the game to the bitter end. And you must realise, Lisa, that as things are with you today the end is inevitable."

Lisa sighed deeply. With bitterness and chagrin, she remembered the mad unrestrained hours in Max's arms, both in France and Italy. She remembered the power of her beauty, the triumph of her passion for Max and the glamorous prospect she had once entertained of a future as Mrs. Max Kern. It was appallingly difficult for her to settle down to being a cripple—a girl who would eventually crawl around on crutches.

Lisa began to cry.

"I don't know how you can be so cool and practical, Clem. You aren't human. You've no real feelings. I don't understand you."

Clem, who was sitting beside the hospital bed, made notes that didn't mean anything, on her stenographer's pad. No feelings! *Dear God!* She thought of Charles as he had been when she saw him alone for a few moments after the last patient left. He had lost half a stone since Lisa's accident. His eyes were sunken—bright with the pain of his anxiety and concern. All for Lisa; none for himself. Clem had felt heartbroken for him.

"How can I help Lisa? How can I make her feel that life will still be worth living?" he had asked Clem, wearily. "If she wants, I'll even give up my job and live on the money I've saved, so that I can look after her completely."

Lisa stopped crying. She glanced forlornly at Clem. Sometimes she hated Charles's trusted secretary, yet she herself had to trust Clem. There was something so strong and composed about her; in a queer way it irritated Lisa. She knew for instance that Clem had been widowed in that crash. She must be going through a hard time yet she never complained. Lisa was sure Clem was more than ordinarily interested in Charles. She brooded over this fact

67

spitefully. Clem really loved Charles—she was not grieving for that husband who had died. Lisa was not jealous. She no longer cared about Charles but it was a case of 'dog in the manger'. She didn't want Clem to get him.

As the days drifted on, Lisa lost interest in Clem and thought of nothing but Max and of trying to get him back. She felt scant gratitude or loyalty towards her husband. She decided to do everything possible to revive Max's interest in her. She knew this was infamous after all that Charles had done for her. She kept excusing herself. She wasn't as strong or brave as Clem. Everything that used to make life exciting and worth living had been taken from her. She couldn't stand up to it.

"I've decided to send for Max."

She flung this statement at Clem one afternoon towards the end of January.

"But you can't," said Clem, shocked.

"I can and I will. It doesn't mean I have no feelings just because I'm semi-paralysed."

"I agree. But a divorce *now* would—would be hopeless," exclaimed Clem, her face hot and worried. "Besides, you can't expect Mr. Kern to —"

"I don't expect anything," broke in Lisa. "The question of divorce doesn't come into it; I just want to be with Max. He can do more for me in every way than Charles. He has much more money and more leisure. He would fly me down to Cannes. I could lie on his yacht and we'd cruise round the Mediterranean. I could go round the world with him if he wanted that. I could have everything I wanted. He would like that. I know Max. It was only the idea of divorce and marriage that got him down when you last spoke to him. Now I can tell him I just want to be with him and find a cure. And I'm still attractive. My face hasn't changed. I still look beautiful, don't I? *Don't I?*"

Clem stared. Yes, Lisa was still beautiful. Her sun-tan had vanished. Her skin was like milk; the long red hair, regularly coiffured, curled, satin-smooth down on to her shoulders; she looked pathetically fragile. Her filmy white negligée with the white swansdown collar added to her glamour. Difficult to realise that those long lovely legs were immobile and that it would mean long months of therapy, of specialised treatment to get the strength back into the wasting muscles.

The crash had been a ghastly tragedy for Lisa. Clem admitted it;

68

but how could she feel *really* sympathetic when, with every breath Lisa drew, she made it obvious that she no longer cared a damn for Charles's feelings.

"Charles gets on my nerves," Lisa kept saying. "Always telling me not to mind, and that *he*'ll look after me. I don't *want* him to."

"That's not true. That's only how you feel at the moment," Clem tried to protest. "You'll forget Max if you'll only make an effort."

"I shall not and I'm going to write and tell him so." Clem's eyes suddenly flashed with anger.

"Lisa, please don't. Please don't start things up again. It will all settle down if you'll only leave it alone. You, yourself, said in the beginning that you thought it best."

"I know, but I've had time to think things over," said Lisa sulkily, "and I can't stand just being wheeled around in our country home by Charles, and made to do exercises and then begin to crawl like a crab with mechanical aid. My God! Just imagine my life down there without my friends—or parties; any real fun. If I were with Max he could arrange any amount of fun for me. He could afford to. And once he realises how I still feel, I know he'll want to take me away. I should think even Charles will understand if I go."

Clem kept silence. She was too shocked to reply. It seemed monstrous that Lisa should be so utterly egotistical, so lacking in gratitude. Apart from forsaking Charles how could she beg a man like Max Kern to take over the task of her rehabilitation? And it was all monstrously ungrateful to Charles. Of course, Clem didn't for a moment think Max would 'play' even if Lisa wrote to him. *But, supposing he did?* Supposing he still wanted her and flew over and Charles found out. The fat would be in the fire indeed.

Nothing she could say that afternoon would alter Lisa's decision to contact Max again. Clem left her in a state of deep depression.

The depression and uncertainty continued right through the week that followed, and so into February. Lisa did, in fact, start communicating with Max again. She wrote feverish letters to him and to Clem's dismay, he began to reply with all the old fervour. He seemed agreeable to the idea of waiting a month or two until Lisa was stronger—then coming to England to discuss the future with her.

"He still loves me. He still wants to be with me and he'll do all he can to help me. I knew he would!" Lisa told Clem triumphantly one cold February evening. She had just been reading a long letter from Max.

"I think it's *awful* of you!" Clem protested, feeling this to be a feeble, childish comment.

"You must think as you like. But I knew that you were wrong and that Max wouldn't walk out on me once he knew how *I* felt, and if I didn't insist on divorce or remarriage. When he told you that things were at an end, it was because *you* made him believe that *I* wanted to tie him down—to a cripple—I'm sure."

"Well, I thought you did want to marry him," said Clem.

"Well, now you know differently," Lisa spoke to her with sudden insolence.

She was growing more used to her physical disability. She continually held parties in her private room—received dozens of visitors, all of whom sympathised, petted and spoiled her.

The great surgeon, Trevor-Johns himself, was symbolically at her feet. To the nurses she was a very glamorous figure. It was only Clem who looked at her with knowledge—with cold accusing eyes. Lisa hated her for this fact but dared not make an enemy of her. For the moment, Clem was an excellent intermediary. It did not suit Lisa—or Max—for Charles to be told the truth yet. It was Trevor-Johns' opinion that it would be a good six months more before the invalid would be fit to travel.

Clem said suddenly:

"Charles will collapse if you drive him too hard. He's absolutely exhausted."

"Poor dear Charles! You must look after him then," said Lisa, sarcastically. "I rely on you. I really rely on you for everything," she added with one of her sudden dazzling smiles and put out a long lovely hand and touched Clem on the shoulder.

Clem moved away as though the fingers burnt her. She couldn't bear any physical contact with this girl.

"You will go on helping me, won't you, Clem?" Lisa asked.

"I won't help you to leave Charles even if Max Kern tries to take you, but I'll do all I can to *save* Charles—and make *you* see sense in time!" said Clem furiously.

Lisa pushed the rich waves of hair back from her forehead. She picked up a mirror and looked at herself. She was not only beginning to feel better, but to look it, she thought. Thank God her glorious head and shoulders had been left untouched. The broken arm was fast healing. Oh damn, damn, *damn* the fractured hip! But she was far less depressed than she had been at first. She was particularly cheered by a paragraph in Max's last letter:

> I realise that a divorce and a remarriage might be difficult under the circumstances, but my beautiful darling, if you need me—and you seem to—I shall not desert you. I shall take care of you. The moment you can leave the hospital and come to me, I'll have a plane especially prepared for you. You shall be flown where you wish to go. I'll engage a special nurse and I'll take you all over Europe to see every specialist in the world in the hope that we might find a cure.

That was what gave her confidence. In time, Max and his dollars would put her right on the map again.

This morning Lisa eyed Charles's secretary through her lashes, covertly, trying to pick holes in her. She wondered if it were possible that Charles found her attractive as well as useful. No, not Charles! He wouldn't look at anybody but his wife. But how did Clementine Ritson strike *other* men?

Lisa knew enough about the way a girl should look to be able to size Clem up fairly. Somewhat to her astonishment, she had to admit that Clem won, on many points. Men *would* look at her twice. She was small but neatly made. She had a slim waist and boyish hips. She looked good in that short, tight jersey skirt with the black polo-necked sweater which showed her small pointed breasts. Her hair was always well-groomed, dark as an Italian's. Lisa remembered Charles telling her that Clem's family were of Sussex origin. But the darkness of Clem's hair and the pallor of her skin had been inherited from her Welsh mother.

She is good looking, and damnably efficient, Lisa thought, and she thought, too, with bitterest envy; *she can run around and dance and do all the things I may never be able to do again, even if I learn to stagger around on crutches.*

What she resented most was her present total dependence on Clem.

At the Great London they had decided to send Lisa down to Stoke Mandeville. This hospital dealt with cases like hers. She might have to stay in Stoke Mandeville for a few months before going back to her own home. She must, therefore, write to Max, tell him about it and warn him not to fly over to London and do anything rash until she had been finally discharged from hospital.

"Is there anything else I can do for you?" Clem asked coldly, after

71

the long silence, during which she had tried to smother her resentment against Lisa.

"Yes—just be patient with me," Lisa said in her sweetest voice and gave Clem such a melting look from her fabulous green eyes that the girl felt uncomfortable. She put her biro into her purse and stood up.

"You won't do anything drastic about Max yet—will you?" she asked Lisa almost pleadingly.

"No, I can't until I've finished at Stoke Mandeville anyhow. They're taking me down by helicopter tomorrow. Did I tell you?"

"No."

"Well, that ought to please you," said Lisa. "It will mean Charles will have to stay in Town, and he won't be able to visit me every day so he won't get so tired. You can't bear Charles to be tired, can you?"

"No, I can't," said Clem quietly, determined not to be riled.

She left the Great London feeling in poor humour. Everything was very difficult. Lisa was such a tricky customer. And Charles was in deadly peril. How right Lisa was! She *couldn't* bear him to be so tired. She would fight for him now as hard as she could, and for as long as she could.

Certainly she was rather glad to hear that Lisa was being taken to Stoke Mandeville.

She drove herself home. She still had the old car. Charles had refused to let her sell it.

"I'll license and run it for you," he had said. "There is so much running around Town for you to do for me nowadays. It can become the secretarial waggon."

He had refused to let her argue about it.

It had been rather a memorable week. The unsatisfactory Miss Garner, whom Clem had never seen, did not return to Welbeck Street after her operation. Charles had asked Clem to fill the post again as a permanence. She had agreed to do so with gratitude.

The very force of that gratitude which she concealed from Charles made her feel curiously disloyal to Tony's memory.

She was not deeply religious—although she had been brought up in a home where both parents were regular church-goers. Sometimes she went to church and reproached herself because she did no more about her religion. Often she wondered what, indeed, happened to those who died. Where had Tony gone—and the nice father to whom she had been so devoted? Both these men had died sudden and violent deaths—still in the prime of life. Where were they now?

Clem seldom allowed herself to brood on the problem of life after death. It was all beyond her. She, herself, was still alive, still very young. She had, she hoped, long years ahead. The pace today was almost unbearably fast. It seemed to her that people were once more in the grip of the law of the primeval forest. *Survival of the fittest.* Truly, only the very strong, physically and mentally, could survive the rat-race of the twentieth century.

It was strange, Clem thought, how far away Tony had gone. He seemed to be close to her for a day or two after his death. Now the distance between them was like the span between heaven and earth. But, of course, things had changed so much. Her whole life had altered.

She had got rid of the flat; that hadn't been difficult and it so happened that the young couple who took it over had a two-roomed flat of their own on a long lease, so they just made the necessary exchange. The landlord had put up the rent of the two rooms, but it was no more than Clem could afford, for with what Tony had left her, and her salary from Charles, she could not count herself impoverished.

Her new home was in a modern block just off Marylebone High Street; nearer Welbeck Street which was better for Clem. Just a short walk.

Sometimes when she got home at the end of a day's work, she would look around and think how completely different it was from the old days. Tony's things had been put away. The new décor she, and she alone, had chosen. The books and pictures were all hers. The colour scheme was as she had wanted it—dark green with white paint. Her bedroom was pale grey, with dusty rose and green chintzes.

Nothing was left of Tony but the one photograph on her desk. Sometimes she would look at it with sadness and a dim sense of loss, but even that was gradually fading. She felt that she owed him something that she could never repay now that he was gone. This disturbed her at moments. She would look at his pleasant, cheerful face and think:

I know it's wrong of me, but I don't miss you as much as I should. If you can see and hear—forgive me, Tony. I gave you as much love as I could and thank you for being kind and good to me.

73

But we didn't really get on. I won't forget you. But I loved Charles first, you know that. I've always loved him. I hope, wherever you are, you understand, poor dear Tony!

The night before Lisa left the Great London, Charles asked Clem to stay and talk to him when work ended.

One of her greatest joys was the knowledge that he seemed to need her company these days. Since the Gatwick crash, he had cancelled practically all the old social activities. When he was not working he was with his wife. Tonight he was not going to Great London. They were keeping Lisa especially quiet; under sedation, before making the journey by ambulance and helicopter from London to Stoke Mandeville. Hence, Charles had this quiet hour to spare and, as he told Clem, he liked to relax which he could always do in her company.

He started by giving her a sherry, poured himself out a whisky, then began to discuss a case that was on his mind.

"That woman, Mrs. What's-her-name from Singapore —"

"Mrs. Cornelius," put in Clem.

"That's right. What a memory you've got! Mrs. Cornelius seems to have had quite a bit of reaction since those neuromuscular treatments we're given her spine. Her husband is delighted."

Clem gave a faint smile.

"I like the 'we'. You mean the treatment that *you've* given her!"

"If you want to be so precise," he smiled in his friendly way.

"It's been an interesting case," said Clem.

"Mainly because the medicoes are puzzled and think she might be suffering from a tumour of the brain and I had other ideas."

"I'm glad Mrs. Cornelius came to you."

"Well, I hoped it was going to be no more than spinal adjustment," said Charles, looked at his drink thoughtfully and drank it down.

Clem felt warm and almost happy. It didn't matter at all that outside it was one of the coldest nights of February, and snowing hard.

It was wonderful to be able to talk like this to Charles; to know that he trusted her and came to her with most of his worries.

Inevitably, the conversation turned to Lisa.

"I shall be glad to get her to Stoke," Charles said. "They're absolutely marvellous there with these cases."

Clem eyed him thoughtfully.

"How difficult it must be for you, an osteopath, to consign her to orthodox medical treatment."

"Oh, I don't know. I trust Trevor-Johns which is why I left her so long at the Great London. And anyhow, osteopathy must involve certain treatments which differ from the old precepts. *And*, as you have heard me say or write so often, the spinal column is the main concern in my profession. But I can't treat my own wife."

"Poor Lisa!" Clem said under her breath.

Charles got up and began to walk restlessly to and fro.

"The great thing to do will be to get her back to Hungerford soon."

Clem felt uneasy, remembering what Lisa had said about this. She ventured:

"Don't you think it might be a little boring for her — tucked away in the country?"

Charles stopped and looked down at Clem with some surprise.

"Boring?" he repeated, "but she loves Lockbridge House. The spring is coming — she'll have the garden. We'll find her a nurse with special knowledge of these spinal cases. We'll all wheel her around and cheer her on when they first get her on her feet again" — his face suddenly broke into a boyish smile — "she might even like me to wheel her to the river-bank. I could cast a line for her and she could catch the trout."

Clem nodded, but her heart sank lower. She wished to God she didn't know so much about Lisa. It thoroughly upset her, listening to Charles. He was so trusting. So *stupid* about his wife, Clem thought in sudden helpless anger. As if she would take an interest in fly-fishing when she was only waiting to recover.

"I'm always talking about Lisa or myself," said Charles suddenly, "when do we talk about *you*? You've been through a pretty hellish time since the crash, my poor Clem."

She stared at the ground. She didn't want to look too long or too deeply into Charles Maddison's clear blue eyes. She hunched her shoulder and muttered:

"Oh, don't talk about me, please. I'm fine."

"You'd say that even if you weren't. I've got to know you pretty well these last few months. I thought I knew you in the old days before you left me to get married. By God, you're brave and you've proved a Rock of Gibraltar for us all. Lisa agreed when we discussed you the other day. She said how much you helped her."

75

"Good," said Clem. She snapped the word so that Charles was momentarily puzzled. Clem was not usually so remote and unfriendly. He often told himself that he had grown very attached to this girl. He admired her tremendously. She was so much more to him than an ordinary personal secretary nowadays. She was a great friend. But, of course, she was reserved—always had been. How much, he wondered, had the loss of that chap, Tony, really meant to her? Obviously she had been shocked and upset. But Charles wouldn't have said that his death had broken her heart. What *did* she feel behind that calm, stoic façade?

"Have another drink," he said and held out the sherry bottle.

She shook her head.

"No. I must be getting on. You'll be travelling with Lisa to Stoke. I'll hold the fort here. You're all clear. I particularly left tomorrow morning quite free for you."

"Thanks, my efficient one."

"You'll be back by two-thirty, won't you?"

"What have I got at two-thirty?"

"That old misery, Lord Beckenham."

"Ah, yes," said Charles reflectively. "Do you remember, Clem, he thought he was dying, poor chap, when he woke up and found he couldn't move that right arm. Mind you—these frozen shoulders are very scaring to elderly patients. What am I giving him? Just a general treatment?"

"Yes. Then you've got that pet patient of yours, old Miss Pinkney."

"Delightful old girl. Never a grouse or a grumble and she has a lot of pain. Those old girls are as brave as they're tough. Has she been keeping to her diet, do you know?"

"She says so and she assured me that she was what she called 'feeling invigorated'. She thinks you're God."

Charles's light-hearted mood vanished.

"I wish I were. *How* I wish I were God just for a moment. Then I could cure my Lisa—not just watch her totter a few steps with help—but dance again—ski—move as she used to do."

Clem shut her eyes but opened them immediately and tightened her mouth.

"Try not to fret, Charles, she's not as bad as we all thought at first."

"No, thank the stars, at least she and I have each other. That helps."

Again Clem shut her eyes.

"Yes." She had to force the word.

"*You* must be finding it pretty lonely, Clem. I wish you weren't living by yourself," he said gently and put out a hand and touched her shoulder.

She moved away. Her whole body felt tense. She thought if he spoke to her like that, looked at her with pity, *pitied her* because of Tony, she would scream.

"Goodnight, Charles," she said abruptly. "See you tomorrow."

After she had gone, Charles walked up to his room, contemplating a hot bath and a quiet meal at home.

He was fortunate, he decided, that he had a first-rate couple now to run the place. Carmella, the Italian girl, had found herself a Neapolitan husband named Luigi. Luigi cooked divinely. Carmella was a delightful if temperamental maid. But even with the mistress of the house away, things ran smoothly. With most of his friends complaining about the hopeless domestic situation, Charles counted himself fortunate. Of course, he knew there would soon be a child and Carmella would be temporarily missing, but he and Lisa had talked things over and decided that they wouldn't let Carmella or Luigi go even if it meant housing the child. The couple seemed devoted and just as pleased to go down to Lockbridge House to work, as stay here in Welbeck Street.

He was lucky in a hundred ways, thought Charles as he stretched luxuriously in the hot bath, shut his eyes and contemplated life. But his heart bled for Lisa. Poor helpless sweet. Thank God, he could prove his love for her by giving her everything he'd got to give. One of his best friends had dared suggest that life must be pretty difficult for him with a crippled wife. Charles, in response, had expressed his indignation. He didn't want pity. He considered it a privilege to be able to look after Lisa for the rest of her life. His main concern was that *she* should be happy.

His thoughts turned to Clem. What a hell of a nice girl she was! She didn't want pity, either. Yet *she* had lost everything. He thought her extraordinarily courageous, and he was deeply grateful for her loyalty. She seemed to mind, in a personal way, what happened to him; that could not be denied. Charles—sensitive to the feelings of others—could not be altogether blind to the fact that Clem was personally attached to him. But the word 'sex' did not enter his mind. The feeling between Clem and himself, was, in his estimation, purely friendly. Thank the stars it *was* so. It could be pretty awkward with a girl like that if sex entered the relationship.

Once Charles had employed a very attractive woman secretary and had had to get rid of her quickly because she made things so awkward for him. Some men had affairs with their secretaries. Charles was not that type and in his position it would be both difficult and dangerous. Little Clem's utter reliability and emotional detachment were exactly what he needed.

But what, he asked himself rather uneasily tonight, was wrong with Clem. She had seemed tense and miserable. She never discussed her troubles. He wondered if there *was* another man in her life now. He had soon guessed that Tony Ritson was not right for her. Why had she married him? What story lay behind the masklike face that Clem showed the world?

Charles suddenly remembered another disturbing point about Clem.

Lisa, in a bad mood, had recently discussed her with Charles and with a disparagement that surprised him.

"Oh, I know your wonderful P.A. is a marvel and you couldn't replace her, and this and that, but I think you ought to be a *little* careful, Charles. I don't altogether trust our Clementine. I don't of course mean over work or money, but *men*. These quiet types can be dynamite."

"I don't know what on earth you mean," Charles replied.

"Oh, never mind, *I* couldn't care less," Lisa had added with a shrug. "I shouldn't have said anything."

With so many worries about her health, and several troublesome cases on his mind, Charles forgot the conversation. But the memory returned this evening. It perplexed him. Women were odd about each other. He was sure Lisa's implications were without foundation. Anyhow, what did it matter to him what Clem did outside her work? It wasn't his business. She could have a dozen men in her life and sleep around with impunity, for all he minded. Still he couldn't imagine Clem as sexually 'dynamite'. She wasn't like that. Lisa was barking up the wrong tree.

Anyhow, he couldn't do without his dear secretary and he saw no reason why he should.

He dozed off in the bath; woke up with a jerk to find the water tepid, and stepped out, swearing. He was always warning people against 'dropping off' in the bath. Now that *was* dangerous.

He ate his meal, then made a phone call to a friend in his

78

profession whom he wanted to talk to about a patient. Later he drove over to Hampstead to see this man for an hour. Afterwards Charles intended to have an early night.

Tomorrow, Lisa would be leaving London.

He thought no more about Clem. He concentrated wholly on the thought of his wife.

7

ONE cool wet morning in June, Clem sat in the train on her way to Hungerford.

She found it a good deal quicker going the sixty miles by rail rather than by car, these days.

She had left her employer in town.

Charles had been in bed with a chill and temperature all this week. His doctor had confirmed Clem's suspicions that Charles was exhausting himself, rushing between his work and his invalid wife. He insisted upon driving the Alfa-Romeo down to Stoke Mandeville in order to sit with her, either early or late—whenever he could best get away.

Now he had agreed as soon as possible to cancel his appointments and take a week's rest. He had to be sensible and admit that he couldn't do his job thoroughly—couldn't do justice to his patients in his present debilitated condition.

Clem had had plenty to do, what with the cancellations, placating disappointed patients, and writing letters. She, herself, was pretty tired because Dorothy Pugh had been off for three days with flu and Clem had to cope with the work of two secretaries. This had meant that when Clem got home at the end of the day she was so tired, she just cooked herself a quick meal then went to bed.

Tomorrow would mark an important event in Lisa's life. The girl who had been so badly injured was to leave Stoke Mandeville and be taken by ambulance to her country home.

The lower limbs were out of the plaster. The spinal cord had not been broken, but the bone was badly bruised. With pressure on the cord, some paralysis, was, for the moment, inevitable. But as Charles had joyfully told Clem after Lisa's last examination, he was hoping that the blood clots round the spinal cord would gradually be absorbed. And the treatment at Stoke had definitely got her back on to her feet.

There would be many hours in bed or her chair, and slow but certain increase of activity. Once she was home, what with her osteopath husband and a trained attendant, she could continue the hydrotherapy, and even sport, to help the muscles. In the end, with the aid of calipers and crutches, she would be able to walk perhaps twenty or thirty yards. This was, of course, a tremendous improvement. The trouble was that she still lacked sensation and, although she felt no pain, she suffered from continual discomfort which made her nervous and irritable. She had no patience and the progress was in her opinion lamentably slow.

It took all that Charles could give to lift her out of the fits of depression into which she fell so quickly and easily.

Clem had been sent down to Hungerford today to make sure that all the arrangements for Lisa's return were in order. Carmella was already there—Luigi had stayed behind with Charles and would drive down with him tomorrow. They had been lucky enough to find a very nice woman in the village, a Mrs. Fairhead, who was usually going to help Carmella in the mornings, and return to do the evening meal.

Then, of course, there was the central figure of the nurse who was going to live with Lisa and attend her, indefinitely.

This was where Charles Maddison with his big reputation both in his own profession and out of it, had been lucky and found an excellent woman. Janet Laurie had worked for three years in an orthopaedic hospital. She knew her stuff. Then she married and left the profession. But like Clem, she had lost her husband, suddenly, in an accident, and she had returned to her old job. When Charles, who had met her on one or two occasions 'put on the charm' and begged her to take this private nursing job with his wife—she accepted. Clem made all the arrangements.

She had met Sister Laurie and liked her. In her thirties, Janet was a tall, strong, intelligent woman who came originally from the Hebrides. She had the soft, soothing, gentle voice of her race, but spoke without much accent. She had lived a long time away from the Islands. She was neither beautiful nor smart. She was too big-boned and had rather fuzzy hair that had gone prematurely grey. She looked ten years older than she really was. She had a sunny temper and possessed various attributes essential in her profession—she was strong-willed, self-confident and tactful. She would be able to handle a patient who was fractious and hard to please, like Lisa, with the necessary diplomacy. She also had an immense respect and admiration for Mr. Maddison. When he had said:

"Do everything you can to make my wife happy," Janet Laurie had answered:

"That's a promise, Mr. Maddison."

Clem was at least sure that she and Lisa's nurse would not clash. They had liked each other at first meeting. For Charles's sake, when Sister Laurie asked Clem what sort of a patient Mrs. Maddison was likely to be, Clem had tried to let Lisa down lightly.

"Oh, of course, she's difficult at the moment—nothing pleases her, but one can understand it. It must be a terrible hardship for her—all this treatment and helplessness. Think of what she used to get out of life—a gorgeous model-girl like that. And she's still so lovely."

Sister Laurie agreed.

Clem went on making notes in the train.

Carmella was not much of a cook, but could make an omelette for Clem tonight. Charles expected to arrive with Luigi before ten to-morrow morning. Sister Laurie was coming at the same time. The ambulance from Stoke would bring Lisa home at midday.

Clem thought of all the things that she would have to order and buy in Hungerford later this afternoon; Lisa did not seem able to eat rich food with any enjoyment, and had grown very fussy about her diet. For her, there must be a grilled sole, and fruit. Charles had ordered champagne. On the luggage rack above Clem's head lay a huge bunch of glorious yellow roses to be arranged in Lisa's bedroom. From Charles, of course. With some bitterness, Clem thought about the whole set-up. It was very unsatisfactory from her point of view—and most of all from Charles's, although *he* didn't know it.

Clem faced a new crisis in her personal life that also occupied her thoughts during the journey to Hungerford.

Since Tony's death—now seven months ago—Clem had concentrated on her job. She hadn't even found time to go up to Wales to visit Aunt Anne.

Clem invited few people to the flat these days except Pat and Guy Grant, her closest friends. She nearly always had Sunday supper with them. She loved the Grants' attractive Chelsea home. They made Clem feel one of the family. Pat was not artistic, but very domesticated; interested in cooking and at this time taking Cordon Bleu classes; otherwise she was fully engaged with her small son.

Guy was a warm-hearted schoolboy type of man with a keen sense of humour; sound at his job. He was a partner in a London firm of accountants. His hobby was photography. His latest purchase was a stereoscopic '3-D' camera. He spent his time photographing family and friends. They were all made to look in the little box at the delicious coloured slides that were more like living tableaux than photographs. '3-D' fascinated everybody. One shot Guy had recently taken was of Clem sitting in the garden, her dark, luxuriant hair unpinned and falling about her face. She had been sunbathing. It was a warm May weekend. When Clem eventually saw this picture, she almost received a shock. This was not Charles Maddison's sedate, tight-lipped, personal assistant. This was the Clem she used to be—bright-eyed, vivacious, quite attractive—she had to admit it—smiling gaily into the camera.

"I wish you looked like that more often," Pat sighed.

Guy Grant added:

"You're quite a doll with your hair down, honey, as they say in little old New York. My old girl had better look out."

Clem laughed back.

"Oh, no! Pat's a good cook. The woman who can tempt the brute with marvellous dishes is the one who can count on keeping her man."

Nevertheless Clem felt flattered, and nostalgic about her extreme youth—the happy days before sorrow had touched her, leaving its indelible mark. She did not often look like 'a doll' these days. She knew it. She was quite frightened by the way her hopeless love for Charles, combined with the shock of Tony's death, had changed her.

Charles had become an *idée fixe* with Clem. It was having an almost paralytic effect upon her life. As Pat remarked one day when the two girls talked together:

"It isn't right for you to be so much in love with a man you can never hope to marry, or even live with. You're only in your early twenties—it's making you far too serious and introspective."

But Clem's answer was firm:

"I don't care what it makes me. I love Charles. Now—I've told you, Pat, although I expect you've guessed it ages ago—I love him. I'll never stop loving him and I don't want to."

"But you get nothing out of it but your work!"

"I get the knowledge that I'm useful to him. And"—Clem turned from her friend—"more use than I can ever tell you about. That's enough for me."

Pat did not altogether understand but she was warmly sympathetic. She had met Charles. She admitted that he was most

83

attractive. She understood why Clem's passion for him had lasted so long and even blotted out the brief consolation of her marriage.

Pat and Guy had both realised long ago that Tony did not make Clem altogether happy. He was a nice boy but too crude—too materialistic for the sensitive, reserved, deeply affectionate Clem. But Pat wished her friend need not waste her affection on a married man.

With feminine guile and out of her love for Clem, Pat now set to work to try and find a new interest for her.

She held an intimate little party one evening. The dinner was cooked by herself. She invited a man named Hammond Portal to meet Clem and make the fourth.

Pat 'wrote Clem up' to Hammond before the two ever met. She convinced him that the young, widowed Mrs. Ritson was as intelligent as she was good-looking.

The cunning Pat played a similar game with Clem. To her, Pat described Hammond as being an exceptional person. He was a good ten years older than Guy, but he had known Guy's father. Hammond's elder brother had served in the Navy under Admiral Grant, during the last war; he had often been to their house and later, Hammond and Guy had become friends.

Hammond was a confirmed bachelor. There *had* been a girl in his life, but the affair ended tragically. She had contracted polio and died. He hadn't seemed able to replace her.

He was a Lloyds Underwriter, comfortably off, and lived in a bachelor flat just off St. James's Street. Lately, he had bought a small house on the river at Hurley. He liked the river. He used to row when he was at Oxford. He intended shortly to buy a boat.

Pat told Clem.

"I know you two will like each other. Guy was only saying the other day, you should have met before, only we didn't ask Ham when Tony was alive as he wasn't really Tony's sort."

That was exactly what Clem discovered.

Hammond was impressive at first meeting; a huge man with a head of thick fair auburn hair and very large blue eyes with slightly drooping lids. He was extraordinarily handsome in the classic style of Ancient Rome. The Grants had christened him 'The Emperor'. It was plain for Clem to understand why. She immediately thought that given a toga and a laurel wreath, Hammond could pose for any Caesar.

He seemed genial and good-tempered, but had a sharp, witty tongue which could at times be malicious. The amusing wit behind his criticisms of others, however, excused the malice. He had an extremely kind side and—so Pat told Clem—a generous one. He helped those friends who were less monied than himself. His hobby lay in collecting paintings of worth and travelling all over Europe. He frequently bought rare pictures and sold them at a profit. On the night he first met Clem, he told her the exciting news that he had just found a small oil painting by a Dutch Master, hidden away under a load of rubbish in a shabby little shop in Ireland. He had sold it at Sotheby's for four figures.

"Are you interested in pictures?" he had asked Clem.

With truth she had been able to answer 'yes'. She had always loved beautiful paintings and before the decline in her family's fortunes, her parents had taken her to see most of the famous galleries in Paris, Rome and Holland. She particularly remembered the glorious one in the National Park outside Amsterdam. Before long, Clem found herself enthusiastically discussing classic art—Van Gogh, Matisse and the modern painters, as opposed to Van Dyke, Vermeer and the Rembrandt.

Dinner finished, Hammond lifted his glass and drank a toast to Clem.

"To that rare creature, a girl who is really interested in painting—and intelligent about it."

Clem felt quite pleased, and blushed a little. In fact she spent a very pleasant evening in Hammond Portal's company, and when he asked if he might take her to a private view of some French pictures at Tooth's Gallery, she accepted; then refused:

"Oh, how stupid of me—I can't. I shall be working."

"Could you get the morning off?"

She explained that her job was with an osteopath named Charles Maddison and that he was far too busy to give her even an hour's grace.

Hammond then gave his booming laugh and said:

"Good gracious me! I know Maddison. I went to him when I slipped a disc about a year ago. Damned clever fellow."

"You must have become his patient after I left—I used to be his secretary before I married."

"Well, well," said Hammond, then, removing his mind from the subject of painting remembered what his hostess had told him about this girl. Her husband had been killed in an air crash at Gatwick a month before Christmas. Yes, he remembered reading about that, too. Suddenly he said:

"Wasn't Charles Maddison's wife seriously injured —?" he began, then stopped, embarrassed, not wishing to upset Clem.

She answered quietly.

"Yes. Poor Mrs. Maddison's spine was injured. She still can't walk."

"Oh, lord, she was a great beauty, too—a model, wasn't she?"

"Yes," said Clem, and was glad that Pat caught her eye. They walked out of the dining-room together leaving the two men to their cigars.

"He's rather a poppet, don't you think?" Pat asked Clem.

"Very unusual and amusing, and what is better—highly cultured," Clem said. "I find his conversation fascinating."

Later, before she went home in Hammond Portal's rather old-fashioned sedate Daimler with which he refused to part, Pat whispered to Clem.

"You've made a conquest, sweetie. The Emperor thinks you're marvellous. He always falls for the little dark girls because he's so big and fair himself. But your brain attracts him."

For the second time that evening, Clem blushed.

It became obvious that Hammond Portal liked her. When they said goodnight, he kissed her right hand in a gallant, Continental fashion and asked her if she would dine with him next week.

"Do you know Rules?" he asked.

When she told him that she didn't, he explained that it was in Covent Garden, much used by writers, painters and the Press, and was full of old engravings which he found delicious.

"I'd like to introduce you to Rules," he said. "They have good food and wine as well as a truly old-world atmosphere. As you may have gathered, I'm right out of my time and disinterested in space or indeed any of the modern discoveries. I should really have been born in the nineteenth century."

"I think that's rather nice," Clem smiled.

"I think *you're* very nice," he said, "you're quite an old-world type yourself—you haven't a modern face, you know. You don't hide it behind a lot of untidy hair that makes girls look like poodles these days. I think Manet would have enjoyed painting you. You have that heart-shaped face and the delicate lips he admired, and with your smooth, dark hair, you should be wearing an Edwardian dress, and a little black velvet ribbon around your throat."

She found that charming and laughed. She didn't laugh often

86

these days and she was glad to be able to do so. She shook hands with Hammond Portal feeling that she had made a new friend.

She dined with him at Rules, a week later.

She had seldom eaten a more perfectly chosen meal, although, loyal to her memories of those little dinner *à deux* with Charles, she didn't think Hammond Portal any more of a connoisseur of food and wine than Charles. And much as she enjoyed listening to Hammond talk, she went home that evening feeling as sad and lonely as ever.

Pat plugged the fact that Hammond was more interested in her than he had been in any girl for years. Clem knew that the Grants both wanted her to be interested—to find a boy-friend who might eventually replace Tony. But she could not even begin to think of Hammond in *that* way.

The fact that he was fifteen years older than herself didn't matter. She quite liked older men and she continued to find Hammond's company stimulating. But her loyalties were far too firmly implanted in her love for Charles. Constantly, the image of Hammond's square handsome face and leonine head faded easily from her sight. She could only see Charles—thin, haggard, exhausted. She could only suffer for him and dread the edge of the axe that Lisa had turned towards him. She was fast reaching a point when she felt that she would willingly die rather than allow Charles to discover the truth.

But she must not be either stupid or inhibited about him—she was aware of that, too. She must accept the fact that life goes on—that other men were bound to come into her life and Hammond Portal was the first to try and establish any kind of personal relationship with her since Tony's death.

She began to dine with Hammond regularly.

One Sunday, he drove her, and the Grants, to Hurley where they spent a fascinating day helping Hammond sort out the things which he had sent down, soon after taking over his new establishment.

Clem found Hurley an adorable village, still unspoiled. Clock Cottage—Hammond's weekend hideout, was quite a find. He had, of course, paid a tidy sum for it. Properties in that part of the world were not cheap, and Clock Cottage was on the river's edge, with a small velvety green lawn stretching down to the water, and a garden gay with flowers.

The house was of Georgian design, small, white-painted, with green shutters. Hammond had knocked the two downstairs rooms into one and built bookcases on either side the fireplace. He had brought from Town one or two of his favourite paintings—those he considered most suitable for the country. The curtains had been made by a specialist. He had inherited a great deal of beautiful Queen Anne furniture. Clem and the Grants proved adept helpers, and it wasn't long before Persian rugs were laid on the polished floors, and the furniture in place. Clem was given the task of unpacking Hammond's books and placing them on the shelves.

Outside in the little garden, an old man whose services Hammond had already procured (he managed these things with a combination of charm and hard cash) was already at work. There were two beds of the beautiful 'Super Star' roses in full bloom. The June day was fine and warm and Clem felt quite light-hearted and happy. It was lovely, this little house, and the river perfect at this time of year.

They all lunched at the Old Bell, in the village, where the food was superlative. While they were at the long bar, drinking their aperitifs, Hammond suddenly said to Clem:

"I go abroad a great deal—I practically abandon Lloyds these days. I don't seem to make any more money when I'm there than when I'm not. Anyhow I've quite decided to spend all my capital, before it's taken from me. What I'm driving at, Clem, is that I shall not be using Clock Cottage much until the autumn. I'd like to give you the key and feel that you would go down there and rest whenever you wanted. I am sure you work too hard."

"It's frightfully good of you," said Clem, gratefully. It was a handsome offer and she found herself accepting it.

"You could always bring a friend," Hammond added.

Guy Grant who had overheard this last remark, intervened with an impish grin.

"A *boy*-friend, eh? Are you leading our little Clementine into sin, my dear Ham? A lovely, lonely cottage on the river—*and* the key. But how tempting!"

"I don't in the least object to sin," said Hammond in his rather clear, high-pitched voice, "providing it is committed with grace and artistry. It is the appallingly vulgar way which the human race sins these days which I deplore."

"Really, Emperor!" protested Pat, giggling.

Clem looked at him with a faintly ironic smile.

"I don't think you need worry about me using Clock Cottage for sinning. It's much more likely that I'll come down quite by myself and sleep twenty-three hours out of the twenty-four. I shall be completely relaxed. I adore the sound of running water and of laughter, as people drift by in their boats. In fact, I find Clock Cottage very romantic."

"And I find *you* most intriguing," Ham said in a voice that only she could hear.

That was when an inner little voice warned Clem that she must go carefully. If Hammond were really intrigued by her—she mustn't accept too many favours. It wouldn't be fair. Pat had already said that he was falling in love. She didn't want that. He could be a wonderful friend and God alone knew one needed friends—but she could not think of Hammond in other terms. She did not want to become too involved. Charles was still far too much in the foreground of her thoughts and emotions.

Her thoughts strayed now from Hammond back to Charles and Lisa.

During the long months that Lisa had been at Stoke Mandeville she had been in constant touch by post and telephone with Max. He had flown over to see her twice on days when Charles was always fully occupied and not expected at the hospital.

Lisa seemed to take a sadistic delight in torturing Clem by her descriptions of Max's visits.

In order not to attract too much attention so that the news of Max's visits got back to Charles, she asked him not to shower her with extravagant gifts. He had contented himself by bringing her flowers, candies from a particularly expensive shop in Fifth Avenue which he knew she liked, and tall flagons of her favourite perfume. The nurses looked upon him as 'the special boy-friend'. Lisa was so beautiful—they were not surprised she had a string of admirers.

"When Max is alone with me," Lisa told Clem with a satisfied gleam in her eyes, "he seems as much in love as ever. He can't stop telling me how heavenly I still look and how little he minds that I am temporarily paralysed. He would consider it a privilege, he said, to carry me around in his arms, find every gadget money could provide to make me more comfortable, and take me all over the world with him. It makes him feel that at last, his money could be used to good purpose. He's carrying a torch about me. Looking after me would become his main objective in life. Already he has found out about some marvellous doctor in Geneva. He cured someone who was semi-paralysed and on crutches—just as bad as I am. Oh, I can't *wait* for Max to take me away, and give me such a chance. They're too damned hidebound and conservative in our hospitals here."

Clem had listened in sullen silence to these statements. Charles, too, wanted to cure her. His whole world was concentrated upon her. What did she care? She had lost both faith and love.

Bitterly Clem wondered if this 'magician' in Geneva would, in the final analysis, prove any more successful with Lisa than Charles or Trevor-Johns—or Stoke Mandeville—what false hopes was Max encouraging in the wretched Lisa?

Clem lived in a state of tension; always wondering whether she might one day wake up to hear that Lisa had 'spilled the beans' and told Charles that she meant to go away with Max Kern.

Lisa, however, still intended to wait another month—until she had learned to walk with more confidence. She didn't really want to go away with Max until then. She was just a trifle afraid of taxing his patience, his crazy love for her too far. She explained to Clem that they were both being realistic about the situation. They would tell Charles the facts quite soon. She was fast recovering from the shock to her nerves and the strain the accident had left on her whole system.

When Clem pointed out that her going would have a ruinous effect upon Charles, Lisa expressed her regret but merely shrugged her shoulders.

"I'm sorry. I'm still very fond of Charles. But only as though he were my brother. We aren't suited—you ought to see that for yourself."

"I do—but you married him, Lisa."

"Well, now he'll just have to learn to be a brother to me and forget I was ever his wife, won't he?"

"I don't know how you can be so cruel!"

"Life has been cruel to me," was Lisa's retort, letting her hand slide down the arm which had been broken but which was now back in use.

How many times had she wished that it had been her leg that had been broken and the arm paralysed. The stronger she got, the more restive and frustrated she became whenever she was in her wheelchair. Air-cushions, therapy, struggling to stand upright, all the exercises and treatments were irksome to her. Even music seemed to torment her. She rarely played her records. She couldn't bear to listen to the old 'dance-tunes' or 'pop-songs' she had once adored. As for taking an interest in fishing, that made her laugh. She had even been brutal enough to say openly that she didn't care a damn whether she ever pulled another trout out of the river or not. That old myth about 'fishing with father' and liking it, had faded long ago. All Lisa hungered for was to be able to move around—to dance—to enjoy again the sensuous side of her nature; the amorous play in a man's arms; the feverish desire, which had once meant so much in her life.

A constant longing for all that she had lost, tormented her. She felt no more pity for Max than for Charles. She did not love him enough to reject his offer to spend his time and money on her. If he wanted to do so, let him—that was Lisa's policy.

Clem knew that it was no use for her to look too far ahead. She had to live from day to day and risk what lay in store. She did not know, and could only dread, the consequences upon herself, as well as Charles, when Lisa finally left Charles for Max Kern.

But her main anxiety was for Charles.

Supposing he thought life no longer worth living and committed suicide?

She had to admit that was one of her worst nightmares, although she could hardly believe that so well-balanced and sensible a man as Charles would consider suicide. The coward's way out. He had too much courage, and his profession. There were his patients—his osteopathy to live for.

Anxiety began to tax Clem's whole nervous system. She suffered continually from the insomnia which had started on the day of the crash.

How things had changed since then! How simple her old existence with Tony seemed to her now. She was glad for her own sake she had been given the opportunity to serve Charles. But it hurt her intolerably to know that she could not avert his final agony. Perhaps this was her punishment, she often thought. She had originally brought this present unhappiness down on her head by reading Max's letters to Lisa. There were many occasions when she wished she *didn't* know so much.

It was raining when she reached Lockbridge House that Friday morning. In a station taxi, carrying the yellow roses, Clem looked gloomily out of the window at a typically English summer day. It was wet and unseasonably cool. She hoped the weather would improve for Lisa's home-coming tomorrow. Everything would be so much easier if they could just wheel her into the garden to sit in the sunshine.

Lockbridge House was not on the River Kennet, but a mile outside Hungerford. Clem did not particularly care for it. She preferred Hammond Portal's adorable little cottage at Hurley. But Lockbridge House had its points. It was early Victorian and recently modernised with a walled garden, a beautiful lawn, and some remarkably fine trees. The house had been brought up to date by the last owner—a Swedish doctor who sold Charles the house and furniture. Lisa liked it. They had made few alterations.

It was Scandinavian, full of ultra-modern wood furniture, gay curtains and covers and fantastic wallpapers.

The main room, which had a huge picture window with door leading into the garden had been turned into Lisa's bed-sitting-room. Since her marriage, Lisa had bought quite a few more Swedish pictures and ornaments whilst over there on holiday with Charles. Most of the rooms in Lockbridge House were decorated with green, glossy climbing vines, and plants that careered crazily around walls, windows and across ceilings. The place looked to Clem rather like a hot-house. Certainly it was a change from the London flat with all its dark antiques and subdued brocades. Down here—white and yellow rugs were spread on the pale polished wood floors, and the rooms were shaded from the summer sun by white Venetian blinds.

Clem had plenty to do as soon as she got to Lockbridge. After lunch she went to work to make perfect the new room which would become Lisa's 'Convalescent Home' during the next few months.

8

CLEM had long since accepted the fact that she had to stand by and watch Charles being tormented, but she felt thoroughly fed up with Lisa, and more than usually sad for Charles, when Lisa first joined him at Lockbridge House.

Sister Laurie, pleasant-looking in her white overall and starched white cap, was there ready to help Charles carry the patient into her room and lay her on the new day-bed which had been placed near the picture window. It had turned out to be a glorious morning. The sun streamed warmly into the room. The garden was full of the noise and chatter of bird-song. The terrace was fringed on either side with standard roses gay with bright incredibly big blooms. Rich purple violas carpeted the rose beds. Beyond, one could see a small stone fountain. Diamond drops of water sprayed over the small lead figure of a naked faun playing a flute. It was charming and a perfect picture for any invalid. Everywhere there were roses, scarlet, yellow, pink and white. The beautiful old walls were criss-crossed with espalier trees, already heavy with fruit. A tall row of green firs shut out the sight of the adjoining meadow.

Charles had spent a fortune on Lisa's room. He had changed it completely in order to accommodate his beloved invalid. There were white rugs on the wood-block floors. Most of the old sitting-room furniture had been taken out. The books were still in their shelves, on either side the carved pine mantelpiece. Her comfortable day-bed with its adjustable back, was covered with the special white fur which Lisa adored. She had always liked in the past to lie against this fur, like a sensual cat, because it showed off her gorgeous sun-browned body. Pale blue satin cushions made a perfect background for her long red hair. Today the lovely legs were covered by a light blue cashmere shawl. But Lisa could still look magnificent, and did. Clem fully admitted this.

At the other side of the room behind screens there was a new bed with every gadget and appliance that could help the invalid. This, too, was covered with Lisa's favourite white fur in order to maintain the glamour. Bowls of choice flowers stood on all the tables. Clem had taken infinite care with these trying to remember Lisa's special taste. There was a gold basket of fruit beside her. Ripe peaches, apples, cherries, muscat grapes; champagne on ice in a silver bucket; every new magazine or paper that could be bought; a television at the foot of the bed with remote control. Radio and hand-bell within Lisa's reach. Her favourite painting had been hung on the walls which were papered in palest green watered silk. This outstanding picture Clem noticed with some irony, was a long-shaped oil of Cannes Harbour. The brilliant blue water was dotted with millionaires' yachts (Max Kern's amongst them). Max had bought this painting for Lisa in Cannes, and had it shipped over to her. She had lied to Charles and said she had been given it by the artist himself as a tribute to her beauty. This, Charles believed without questioning.

As Sister Laurie had said to Clem this morning while she busied herself making the bathroom perfect and concealing all the ugly apparatus which must still be used for Lisa's injured limbs:

"I've never seen such a room or nursed in such luxury. Mrs. Maddison is lucky. Of course, we know she's had a terrible injury but think of the hundreds who get fractured spines and don't come back to *this*, plus an adoring husband like Charles Maddison."

"You can say that again," Clem had laughed back.

But Lisa grumbled from the moment she was home. Charles's first action was to pour her out a glass of champagne.

"Take it away," she said, pouting. "Champagne makes me feel sick. It's too acid for me now I take no exercise. You ought to know that."

"Sorry, darling," he said, raised his own goblet to her and added:

"Welcome home and better days to come. You look heavenly."

"Do I?" she said, hunching her shoulders. "My arm has ached all night."

"I'll soon get that back to form," put in Sister Laurie.

Lisa eyed the nurse through her lashes.

Hospital nurses to her had become enemies rather than friends—warders—keeping her in prison—always saying what she must or must not do. She loathed them as a profession. Charles had said that Janet Laurie was one of the best physiotherapists to be found in town. He had tested her out himself. She had magical hands and a lot of commonsense.

But Lisa had reached the stage where she didn't want common-sense. She longed to get away from all the trappings of illness and

94

forced inactivity; *from herself*. This only Max could do. Max and his millions. She had had a call from New York from him last night. When she had told him that Trevor-Johns now held out definite hope that she would walk again if only with assistance, he had gone mad with excitement! It was all the more essential, he said, that she should get away and join him as soon as possible and so start that world search for a complete cure.

"Honey," he had said, "you're going to figure in the newspapers one day as the miracle glamour-girl who defied that air-crash. You'll be dancing."

His enthusiasm had fired her to fresh excitement and hope.

When Charles asked his wife if she approved of her room and said how easy it would be to wheel her out or help her walk into the garden and across the hall into the dining-room, so that she could take part in normal life, she continued to sulk. Not even the promise that she would soon be walking a few steps down that garden path, cheered her up.

Who would she be with all day? That bloody, starchy nurse with her professional smile and 'now, dear, we'll soon get you right'. Even Charles was more fun! But he'd be in town all day. He had told her that he hoped to drive the sixty miles up to London in the Alfa and back every day. That meant she'd only have his company in the evenings. She broke out resentfully:

"I'd much rather have been taken up to Welbeck Street where I could see all my friends."

"Darling," said Charles gently, sitting beside her, "we didn't think it would be at all possible with all those stairs; and we'd never have got you out of doors in the way we can do here. You know how you love the sun and if we have some good weather —"

"*If*," she broke in petulantly. "I'd be better in the South of France where I can count on the sunshine."

Sister Laurie discreetly vanished to talk to Luigi about the patient's lunch. Clem, sick at heart as she saw the disappointment on Charles's thin, drawn face, started to follow, but Lisa called her back.

"You needn't go, Clem."

"Wouldn't you two like to be alone?" Clem asked quietly.

Lisa gave an ugly laugh.

"We're not exactly on our honeymoon, dear. Charles won't wrap me in a savage clinch the moment you've gone. I'm too liable to break."

Clem caught a momentary glimpse of Charles's face flushing scarlet, but he passed Lisa's remark off good-naturedly.

"Better be careful, sweet—I'm liable to insist on that clinch whether you break or not, you look so tempting."

"Ha! Ha!" she laughed bitterly and Clem winced.

God, what a bitch Lisa was! How could one be sorry for her? She was so damnably self-centred—so poisonous to this man who was stretching his nerves to please her.

Defiantly Clem said:

"I think the room is gorgeous. I'm sure Lisa thinks so, too, Charles."

Lisa now looked at Clem, tongue in cheek.

"Maybe you'd like to change places with me and sink your paralysed limbs into the white rabbit and give everybody angelic smiles and lots of dewy gratitude so that they can say how patient and good you are!"

"Come, darling, that's rather naughty," said Charles.

"Oh, I'm sure I wouldn't like to sink on to the couch in Lisa's place," said Clem shortly. "I think this must all be most frustrating for her."

"Dear Clem, you're the only one who really understands me," said Lisa with a meaning glance.

Clem thought:

I really could shoot her!

She walked out of the room. She could no longer bear the sight of Charles's embarrassment and disappointment. She made another tart observation that the patient would probably feel a lot better after her lunch, and that there would be caviare, and grilled sole, and strawberries from the garden. Lisa's voice called after her:

"I'm sick to death of sole and I can't digest strawberries."

Clem went out of the room and shut the door. *God*, she thought, *if this is how she's going on, it might be better for Charles if Max came at once and took her away. But was that true? No! Anything would be better than that—Charles did so dote on her. He was so sweet—so patient—no doubt he would excuse her 'bitchiness' and put it all down to her state of health.*

When Lisa was alone with her husband she relented and ventured to thank him for all that he had done.

"You've made it all look very attractive and it must have cost you a lot of money," she said in a grudging voice.

96

Charles's face brightened. He took both her hands and kissed them.

"I'd do anything in the world to make life better for you, my love."

"It's just as well my legs were hurt and not my face," she said with a short laugh. "Can you imagine how everybody would have felt about me if I'd been totally disfigured?"

"Do you know something? I would have felt exactly the same about you except that my pity would have increased. But I'd still have adored you. I don't just love you because of your face."

She laughed again—uncomfortably. One of the things she resented, in a curious way, was the very fact that this man was so angelically good to her. She had *some* conscience. Not much, but some, and just a corner now and then nagged at her. She wished she could get away without stabbing Charles in the back. However, as she couldn't and it was a question of who was to suffer—it would have to be Charles.

She condescended to break into a smile and raise her face for a kiss.

"My nerves are in pieces, still. Sorry I'm so beastly."

Immediately he was happy again. He kissed her lips with tenderness.

He's a fool, she thought. *I don't want to be treated like Dresden china just because I'm half smashed. Max understands that. Max told me the other day that desire lies in the brain—yes, it's partly in the mind—how one thinks and feels. When Max kisses me he kisses like a lover. He almost makes me feel alive and well again.*

Her own frustration and hurt led her to lash out at Charles. He was her whipping-boy. It relieved her to make him an active partner in her present misery.

She said, languidly:

"Do let me make it plain to you, darling, that as I seem to be quite useless to you as a wife, you are at liberty to go and find someone else. I wouldn't blame you at all for taking a mistress, you know."

He was silent for a moment. His blue, light eyes looked puzzled, but his lips smiled at her.

"Thanks a lot, darling. I'll remember what you say if ever the temptation seizes me, but I can't quite see myself 'taking a mistress'."

"Darling, you're only human."

"Being human to me doesn't mean that I've got to go to bed with

D   97

somebody. I'm quite happy looking after my lovely wife and being with her, and I really don't worry just because the bed is ruled out for the moment. I can hold you in my arms—can't I?" he added with a smile and kissed her hand again.

She felt impatient and utterly unresponsive, but forced a smile in response.

"I'm sorry," he went on, "I'd rather that you were a jealous wife but I suppose I must thank you for being understanding and generous."

She thought:

I wonder how understanding and generous YOU'D *be if you knew about Max.*

For a brief moment Charles had felt a bit hurt, but he decided suddenly to treat Lisa in her present mood with a sense of humour.

"I say! If you really think I need consolation, Sister Laurie will have to look out. One never knows what mad passions lie behind those starched aprons."

"Oh, she's a cow," said Lisa unkindly, "but there's always your little secretary. *She's* not unattractive and not unconscious of it either."

The idea of Clem being disparaged in this way suddenly annoyed Charles. His good-humour vanished. He got up and moved towards the open window, cigar between his teeth.

"Sweetie, let's drop this talk. I don't really intend to try and make a mistress out of my secretary. Clem's a fine girl and has been a very good friend to us both."

"Don't you think she's attractive?" persisted Lisa.

"Yes. She's charming, and clever, and she often looks delightful, but I don't happen to want any woman except my wife."

"Oh, God!" said Lisa under her breath.

There the conversation ended abruptly because Carmella came in and announced that lunch was ready.

Charles had meant that meal—the first at home since Lisa's terrible accident—to be a gay affair. He hoped that she was on the brink of some kind of recovery if not total. He had also fondly imagined that she would be thoroughly glad to be away from hospital—get over the fact that she would still have to have medical attention and enjoy her home-coming. After these months of anxiety and the pain he had suffered for *her*, he had so longed to hear her laugh again—to see her eyes shine at him with something of the old warmth. After his intense loneliness without his adored wife, he had looked forward so much to holding her in his arms again; just *holding* her, caressing her, trying to give her some of his strength, warmth and fervour. Above all, he wanted to feel close mentally, as well as physically, to her again.

Deliberately, perhaps, he had blinded himself to the fact that for quite a while before the air-crash, Lisa had changed towards him. There had been nothing concrete that he could fasten on. When they were together, she used to be as charming as ever, yet gradually he had come to realise that she was no longer as much in love with him as she used to be. And she was so rarely with him, nearly always out—or away. He had blamed himself, of course. He was busy. He could not always escort her to parties, or take her abroad when she wanted to go. There had been that long holiday she had taken in France and Italy (which he had encouraged because she hadn't been so well). But it never entered his mind that she was staying away longer than she need have done, or that just before she left she used to try and avoid his love-making. She did it so subtly. With a cheek pressed to his murmuring: 'Not tonight, darling—I'm dreadfully tired . . .' or 'You look exhausted. Just kiss me and let's sleep, darling . . .'

But she had never actually refused him. She had never been unpleasant. It was only now when she *was* in fact being very unpleasant, that the idol Charles had built threatened to topple from its pedestal.

Naturally he excused everything on the grounds that Lisa's whole nervous system had received such a violent shock that she was out of control. He tried to convince himself that it was only natural and it would be months more before Lisa would be herself again.

But quite definitely she spoiled their lunch.

They wheeled her into the dining-room—such a beautiful cool-looking room with dark green walls which made a good background for a set of beautiful paintings—Scandinavian scenes. The flowers on the long table were lovely—roses arranged, Charles imagined, by Clem.

The menu had been carefully chosen and well cooked as usual by Luigi. But Lisa refused the caviare, only toyed with the sole and left the salad and fruit uneaten. When Sister Laurie handed her a roll, Lisa snapped:

"You know I don't eat bread. Do you want me to look the size of a house when I do get on my feet again?"

Sister Laurie put the basket of rolls down. She said nothing. Clem glanced at Charles. His eyes, she thought, were watching his wife with extraordinary sadness. He, too, had been snapped at by Lisa several times.

Now Lisa attacked Clem:

"Do you propose to go back to Town with Charles on Monday?"

"Yes, of course."

"And leave *me*?" Lisa said in a venomous tone.

Clem looked puzzled. Charles said:

"What do you mean, darling? You'll have Sister Laurie."

"Agreed. But I presume Sister Laurie doesn't type. I have a whole pile of letters to answer and I need a secretary like Clem just as much as you do, Charles."

He gave a tolerant laugh.

"Well, really darling, I wouldn't have said so!"

"Oh, very well—then Clem goes back to Welbeck Street with you," said Lisa sullenly. "I'm sure she'll prefer that to being buried alive with me down here."

Clem had never felt more awkward. She flung Charles an agonised look, hoping for a lead. But he gave in to Lisa—much to her chagrin.

"Well, if you really need Clem, of course she can stay with you, darling. But as she knows so much about my work it'll be a bit inconvenient to let her go during the week. Couldn't you get a social secretary from some typing bureau in or near Hungerford?"

"I don't for a moment suppose there is one and anyhow I *know* Clem. She takes down letters at such marvellous speed. It would help me tremendously."

Clem searched her brain for an explanation of this strange request from Lisa. She could only suppose that it had something to do with Max and *she*, Clem, was the only person who could deal with the situation. Her heart plunged at the thought of Charles struggling with a strange secretary in Welbeck Street but she might have known that as usual he would spoil Lisa and sacrifice himself. Oh, what an *idiot* he was, she thought furiously. How could any man be so much in love? So completely unselfish?

Sister Laurie maintained a discreet silence. This little matter had nothing to do with her. But the atmosphere, she thought, could be cut with a knife and she really had scant use for the beautiful Mrs. Maddison. She was very tough.

It all ended, of course, in Lisa getting her way and Charles promising to leave Clem down at Lockbridge House. Then suddenly Charles realised that nobody had really consulted Clem. He turned to her. He caught her unawares—her large brown eyes staring at him with such deep feeling that he could hardly mistake the meaning. He was unable to analyse the look, but it hit him like a lightning flash. He remembered what Lisa had said about her before lunch: "Your little secretary . . . really quite attractive . . ." etc. And his own acid comment that he *didn't intend to try and make a mistress out of his secretary.*

His face felt suddenly hot. He turned away quickly from Clem, who was now talking to Lisa about spending the forthcoming week down here.

"It's okay by me if it is by my employer. I've nothing to keep me in Town except a dinner appointment with my friend Hammond Portal—I can easily phone him and put it off."

"Good," said Lisa, and told Charles to light her a cigarette which she smoked in sulky silence.

Charles felt thoroughly put out. His own nerves were shattered. He had better take a grip of himself. It was ridiculous of him to think that Clem felt in the least sentimental about him. He had made a mistake about 'that look'. But that she was attractive, he wasn't going to deny. He always had admired the smooth darkness of her hair, the delicacy of her features and her neat, *petite* figure. She had beautiful ankles too. But dammit, he thought, he never *had* looked at his secretary in the way a man looks at an attractive woman. And he had told Lisa he didn't happen to want any woman except his wife. And he objected to having Clem pushed, so to speak, into the front line of his sexual thoughts.

He felt suddenly bad-tempered but speedily controlled himself. He began to wheel Lisa back into her own room.

"I suppose," he said in a light voice that gave no indication of his feelings, "you couldn't get all these letters done with Clem over the weekend?"

Lisa looked up at him with a pout.

"Oh—are you on at this business of not wanting me to use Clem for a few days? Oh, very well, take your sweet little secretary back to Welbeck Street. Why not this afternoon—the pair of you."

"Darling, don't be a bitch," said Charles in sudden anger.

It was the first time Lisa had ever heard him speak to her like that. For an instant she was on the verge of saying something dangerously disagreeable, but instead began to laugh.

101

"*Darling*, Charles—have I made you cross with me at last? How very funny!"

"Well, I'm glad I can at least make you laugh. I can't say we had a very amusing lunch."

"I expect I spoiled it," said Lisa bitterly, "but then you don't any of you realise how difficult it is for me to be sweet and sociable. I just want to scream all the time. You none of you understand me."

That was enough to make Charles regret his impatience and become the devoted husband again.

He had wheeled her up to the open french window where the sun could reach her. He now bent over her, caught her right hand in his and kissed the palm with tenderness.

"Lisa, my sweet, I'm a wretch to be cross with you. My God, you're right. None of us can know what you've been through. And if Clem will be a real help to you, just keep her down here as long as you want."

Lisa relaxed. She patted her husband's cheek.

"Sweetie you're so good to me. I *am* a bitch. Sorry, darling. I'll only want Clem for a few days—are you sure you can manage without her?"

Charles lied heroically.

"Sure."

He must speak to Clem, he thought—get her to ring one or two London bureaux first thing on Monday morning and try and line up a temporary stenographer. It was one hell of a nuisance that Lisa had suddenly decided to dictate all these letters and with Dorothy Pugh away too.

He left Lisa, who now seemed in a better mood, to the attentions of the nurse. He joined Clem who was out in the garden smoking her after-lunch cigarette.

"Sorry about this," he said.

"I don't mind at all," she answered, determined that he shouldn't guess how bitterly disappointed she was not to be driving to London with him on Monday as arranged.

Those fine dark eyes of hers smiled up at him with the old familiar friendliness. He told himself again that he had made a mistake in thinking just now that there had been anything unusual about her expression while they were at the lunch table.

He said:

"You really *are* the family friend—necessary to all of us, Clem."

"Thank you," she said.

"I'm sorry if you have to postpone a dinner date."

"It isn't important—if I can help Lisa, *of course* I will, and I think she has hundreds of letters to answer, you know. She had a pretty good fan mail from all the admirers who wrote her after the crash."

"This man—Hammond Portal—you mentioned his name at lunch—wasn't he a patient of mine?"

"Yes, he said you treated him for slipped disc before I came back to you."

"I do remember. A big chap—interested in fine arts."

"You have a good memory," smiled Clem.

"And he is the new boy-friend?" Charles asked with one of his sudden smiles—all too rare these days—thought Clem.

She answered with a lightness to match his.

"That's it. He's an old friend of *my* friends, the Grants. I have been seeing quite a bit of him. They call him The Emperor, because he looks like an early Roman."

"I remember that, too. Rather a handsome chap."

"He's just bought a beautiful little cottage in Hurley. He's going away next week. He has offered me the key in case I'd like a week-end by the river. He was giving it to me tomorrow but he can easily send it to me by post. I'll ring him."

Charles looked at her curiously. It struck him not for the first time that this girl was unusually withdrawn. She so rarely talked about herself or her private affairs. She had seemed—and of course it was wrong of him to imagine it—to be so much part of *his* life. He had forgotten that she must lead one of her own. He found himself wondering whether Hammond Portal was serious about her, and she about him. But surely not—she had only been a widow for a few months or so, and he felt pretty sure she was not the type to think of marrying again quickly.

He knew suddenly that he hoped that she *wouldn't*. It was damnably selfish of him but he *did* hope that. He didn't know what he would really do if Clem married again, and left him for the second time.

9

EVER since she could remember Clem had heard Aunt Anne use the term 'Black Monday'. It used to be one of her private jokes; 'Lazy weekend over—now for Black Monday and hard labour.'

The Monday on which Charles went to Town to try rather miserably to cope with his job minus his secretary, was one of the blackest Clem could ever remember.

It started well enough. She had put in a telephone call to an old friend who had been in the secretarial college with her. Miraculously the girl turned out to be free and able to bridge the gap. She was a good shorthand-typist and Clem knew she would attack the job with intelligence. But Clem didn't like seeing Charles drive off by himself. He had looked so unhappy. For nobody else save Charles would she have consented to forsake him and stay down at Lockbridge House just to please Lisa.

But once Lisa had been given her exercises and massage, Clem learned exactly why Lisa had insisted upon her staying here.

Pen and pencil in hand, calm and unruffled as usual, Clem had seated herself ready to take Lisa's dictation, while Sister Laurie finished dressing the patient. It wasn't a nice day. It was sultry, and raining. There was thunder in the air. Clem had a headache. She had to admit as she watched Lisa walk slowly and weakly with the aid of Sister Laurie and the crutches, that the girl had made wonderful progress. She was courageous. She attacked the unpleasant tasks before her with amazing determination, and she looked wonderful, Clem thought. She was wearing for the first time since her accident, a pair of slacks and sleeveless silk shirt. Her hair was brushed and shining, her face beautiful, flushed with the effort she had to make to get one foot in front of another.

But once Lisa was back in her chair and began to speak, cigarette between her fingers, Clem knew the worst.

She had realised of course that it was no mere need to dictate social letters that had made Lisa ask her husband to sacrifice his secretary.

Lisa said:

"I won't mince words. I'm going to come straight to the point, whether you like it or not. The night before I left Stoke Mandeville, Max put a call through to me from New York. Incidentally we talked for half an hour."

"How nice to be a millionaire," said Clem dryly, trying not to betray her inner agitation.

"Very nice," said Lisa with a cold smile, "and things should be much nicer for me in the future. Max and I have decided that we are only wasting time. He is chartering a special plane to fly me to Nice. He has taken a villa in Beaulieu—one of the most beautiful on the coast—with a divine garden. A specialist from Paris will be waiting for me and two trained attendants. I shall want for nothing and Max and I will be together—at last."

Clem sat very still. She betrayed her feelings only by her change of colour. She could almost feel her cheeks growing pale. Her heart thumped.

"You don't mean this, do you, Lisa?"

"I certainly do. Max and I haven't just been playing a game, you know. But until this week I haven't felt well enough to face the air journey. Now I do. Now we both know that I can stand on my feet and crawl around, we are also sure that I'm well on the way to recovery. Max intends to cover Europe first, then if we fail, fly back to America and go on looking until we *do* find a specialist who can put me absolutely right again."

Clem let her pencil fall on to the carpet. She didn't even bother to pick it up. She stared at Lisa. She was fascinated by the hard glitter of triumph in those marvellous eyes.

"Oh God!" at last Clem said in a hopeless voice.

Lisa puffed at her cigarette, and hunched her shoulders.

"I'm sure it's a shock for you, Clem; you never really thought I'd do it, did you?"

"I hoped you wouldn't, Lisa. My God, I hoped it."

"For poor Charles's sake if not for your own. Yet I'm quite sure it will benefit you if I leave him. In spite of you not wanting him to be hurt, you'll love it if he turns all his attention to *you*." Lisa gave a brief laugh . . . "In fact the thought of you consoling him will be my chief consolation. I feel dear Charles will be in the best possible hands, comforted and fortified by his efficient little Clementine!"

Clem's colour, burning red, scorched her face; her eyes blazed.

105

"I didn't think anybody could be quite so *bloody*! You *defeat* me!"

"You must be thinking of a number of horrible names for me. I don't really blame you. I don't particularly admire myself for what I am doing. No woman could want to be cruel to Charles. He's such a dear, good man. Whether you believe me or not, I don't *like* hurting him, Clem. But I've been in love with Max for a long time and I need him. He does something for me no other man has ever done."

Clem found herself shaking.

"You mean, no other man in your life can *afford* what he is going to do. It's all a question of £ s. d."

"That's not very nice—or true. I'm crazy about Max."

"And do you realise that quite apart from smashing up Charles's life, you've just insulted both of us by suggesting that I—I would console him? I'm not hypocritical enough to deny that I'm deeply fond of Charles but *he* has no eyes for anybody on earth but you, *and* you know it! I don't know how you can suggest anything else."

Lisa shrugged her shoulders.

"I was just saying that once I've gone, he's sure to turn to you. Is that true or isn't it? I'll bet on it."

"Your imagination carries you too far. To Charles I'm a good secretary and friend. That's as far as it will ever go."

"Okay, okay," drawled Lisa, "don't let's argue. We'll agree he mightn't carry you straight to the double bed. But I'd have thought you'd be glad to believe that Charles won't be left absolutely high and dry so long as you're around."

Clem stood up.

"Oh, yes he will be. He will be!" she said with passion and despair. "You're his life. Everything he does is for you. Once he finds out that you're in love with another man and about to leave him, it'll kill him. It'll be murder for him."

A sullen look crossed Lisa's face. She looked down at her cigarette.

"Obviously you only see the whole thing from his point of view. I can't expect otherwise but I *would* like to remind you that *I've* got a side. It'll be murder for me if I let Max go, and stay with Charles. What about that?"

Clem's throat felt dry. She felt ridiculously near to tears of rage and impotency. Disaster was drawing nearer and nearer Charles and she could do nothing to prevent it; absolutely nothing.

Lisa continued:

"You're so odd. I know you've been married and I presume you must have been in love with your husband. Or was it Charles all the time?"

"This conversation is not about Charles and me—it's about Charles and you!" Clem said harshly.

Lisa shrugged.

"All the same, it's obvious that you don't know what it is to be madly in love with a man. I'm mad about Max I tell you—crazy about him. I can't sleep some nights for wanting him. Yes, that must surprise you. You may think I'm just a paralysed cripple . . .!" she broke into hysterical laughter, "but I still have feelings. I want Max, and I mean to have him. He's going to fetch me and there is absolutely nothing you can say or do to make me change my mind."

Clem sat down again. She felt weak and stupid. She was still trembling. All kinds of wild thoughts flitted through her brain. Thoughts about Charles and herself. Until Lisa had suggested it, she had never once considered the possibility of Charles turning to *her*. Lisa might call her 'odd' and think she didn't know what love was, but how wrong could she be? She, Clem, had lain awake in her turn—unable to sleep because of the torture of longing. She knew only too well what it meant to be crazily and hopelessly in love. Sometimes when she was alone with Charles it hurt her physically to keep from touching his hand—from throwing herself into his arms—behaving like a lunatic. She loved him with every drop of blood in her body but she had to keep all that burning desire locked away, because it was as futile as it was wrong.

Suddenly she put her face in her hands, and try as she would, could not stop the bitter tears from falling—the first she had shed since Tony died.

"Oh, Lisa, Lisa—don't do it—don't hurt him like this," she whispered.

"My goodness, you *have* got it badly for poor Charles," came Lisa's light mocking voice, "what a pity life is so twisted. It's you he should have married. I never was right for him."

Clem lifted her face. It was wet with tears and distorted.

"But you must have been in love once. You married him in the first place for love, not money. He never was very rich."

"I don't deny that. I found him very attractive. He was always sweet to me, and I admired him. I still do. He's a famous man in his own sphere. When he came along I was a bit fed up with my life and thought it was time I settled down. So I got tied up with Charles. But I've found that it was a mistake. Domestic life didn't suit me. I've also found out that Charles doesn't suit me. His standards are too high. He's too idealistic. I'm a primitive. I need the primitive streak that is in Max. He *possesses* me—my mind as well as my body. Charles never did. I liked sleeping with him once but even that . . ."

"Oh, shut up!" broke in Clem, her nerves on edge. "Shut up. I can't stand it."

Lisa made a little whistling sound.

"You *are* showing up in a new light. I little thought our Clem could lose her self-control. You're quite human after all, dear."

"I always have been," Clem said between her teeth. "And I admit that I love Charles. I don't want him hurt. I'd be happy to go away this night and never see him again if only I thought you'd stay with him."

"Darling, don't be a heroine. All this self-sacrifice is so out-of-date," said Lisa in a bored voice.

Clem snapped back into control. She suddenly grew cold and calm again. She stared at the other girl.

"Do you realise what Charles has been through since the crash—how much he's suffered over you?"

"Yes, I realise it and I told you I'm sorry, but I'm the one who has suffered most."

"Yes, I'm sure," said Clem, "but if you care for Max as much as you say, you'll be happy in future. Charles will never recover."

"Oh, don't be too pessimistic. I don't believe in broken hearts. Charles *will* get over it."

"I hope to God you're right."

"Right or wrong, Clem, I'm leaving him."

"When?"

"Fetch me my diary," said Lisa, "and I'll tell you. It's on the table beside my bed."

Clem fetched the diary and handed it to her. With every moment that passed she was growing more composed but she felt as though she had been hit over the head. Her temples throbbed. Her whole body was hot and damp.

She had always faced this, yet had never believed the day would come when Lisa really would leave Charles. She watched the gir's slender fingers flipping through the pages of her blue leather diary.

"Is Max going to marry you?" Clem suddenly asked her.

"No," said Lisa and looked up with a cool smile, "we neither of us particularly want to be tied down. Personally I think the way to keep a man is to be his mistress. I could quote you dozens of rich attractive men who have left their wives but lived with a mistress for the rest of their lives."

"All very modern," said Clem, unable to restrain the wish to sneer.

Lisa looked at her through her long lashes.

"I suppose *you're* so holy you would never become any man's mistress—even Charles's."

Clem flushed scarlet.

"No, in fact I wouldn't. Not because I'm holy. It's just a question of principles. Anyhow, as we're being so frank, let me tell you that I *did*, in fact, live with my husband before I married him. But I regretted it. I think in a funny way it spoils things. But I believed I was going to marry Tony. I would never have dreamt of sleeping with a man I didn't intend to marry. I think marriage gives one a sort of security that a girl needs. Especially if she wants a family."

"Well, Max and I don't, and I don't suppose that I could ever have a child now, anyhow. It's something I haven't discussed with any of the specialists yet. It's never come up. If it did turn out that Max wanted a son, and I could give him one, he would probably marry me. Always of course, providing that dear Charles is willing to divorce me. But Max and I are not looking too far ahead."

Clem stared at Lisa. She didn't know whether she despised her or envied the cool way in which she could plan her life; and her utter lack of conscience or honour. Clem and Lisa were much of the same age but this morning Clem felt that she, the married woman, was years younger—just a simple, unsophisticated girl—certainly not what Lisa would have called '*with it*'.

"I'm a square," Clem told herself with sarcasm, "*just a square!* ..."

"Now to work," said Lisa.

"What work?"

Lisa shut the diary and turned it over and over nervously between her fingers.

"Max is arriving in England on July 2nd—a Tuesday. I shall go away with him on Wednesday, July 3rd. I want to discuss the plans with you."

Clem gasped.

"The plans?"

"Yes—you're the only one who knows about Max, and can help me."

"I won't!" said Clem, her breath quickening, "I won't help you to leave Charles. I've told you so several times—I won't!"

Lisa finished her cigarette and stubbed the end of it in an ashtray beside her chair.

"I think you will," she said.

"You're mistaken. I have no intention of doing so."

"Then I shall tell Charles tonight that you've confessed to me that you're crazy about him and that I'm furious and wish him to get rid of you immediately."

Clem looked at Charles's wife with horror in her eyes.

"You're out of your mind! You're just the most, unscrupulous cold-blooded person I've ever met."

"Nonsense, darling. There are heaps worse than me. I'm planning to let Charles down quite lightly. If we play it my way, it won't be too bad for him. But if I warn him about you, then follow it up by informing him that I'm off too, he'll have to look after himself, and he won't care for *that*."

"Oh, God!" said Clem. "You really are evil."

"Not really," said Lisa smiling. "Anyhow, you keep forgetting that I'm the victim of an air-crash—and have been in agonies of mind and body ever since—*and* thought I'd lost my boy-friend as well as the use of my legs for ever! I'm only just beginning to get back the old energy and will to live. I want to recover totally for Max. Can't you understand? Can't you see *anything*? Must you always think of Charles?"

"But Lisa, if you run away with Max it's bound to have a terrible effect on Charles."

"Darling, I really am disappointed in you," said Lisa in a 'trying-to-be-patient' voice. "I've always thought you practical and sensible. You're quite hysterical about Charles. He's a man. You know men don't often commit suicide because their wives leave them. You're so fond of Charles it's pathetic."

If Clem had ever hated anybody in her life it was Lisa at this moment. And if the girl hadn't been incapacitated in that wheel-chair, Clem would have slapped her face, she thought furiously.

"Shut up about my being fond of Charles, or I'll walk out of this room and I won't help you, and I don't *care* what you tell Charles!" she said in a low voice.

Then Lisa tried other tactics. She burst into tears, seized one of Clem's hands and hung on to it, her face contorted.

"Don't be so angry with me, please, Clem! You don't know how desperate I feel. I realise it's still on the cards I will never dance again, or be at all like the girl I once was. That isn't much fun for me. I don't even know whether Max will go *on* wanting me. He may be just taking me away for a while, then will regret it. It's pretty hellish."

"Then don't leave Charles. Stay where you know you're loved and wanted."

"I can't," said Lisa. "I've got to go to Max. I'm prepared to take the risk."

Clem shook her head. She tried to take her hand away from Lisa but it was fast imprisoned in those long slender fingers and Lisa continued to play her game of the unhappy much-to-be-pitied victim of an air-crash—*and* fate.

"I know you have no use for me," she sobbed. "And I know I'm being mean to Charles. But I must go. Please, help me, Clem—for his sake."

Now Clem snatched her hand away roughly. She walked to the dressing-table, found a box of face-tissues and flung them on Lisa's lap.

"There you are. For God's sake dry your eyes and stop crying. You'll only make yourself sick."

Lisa looked up at her with streaming eyes.

"Help me for Charles's sake," she repeated.

"How could it possibly be for *his* sake!"

Lisa stopped crying, and wiped her eyes.

"Because Charles will turn to you. It's no use you denying it. I want you to help me get away quickly and quietly, then be here to break it to Charles. You can try and make him believe that it's for the best; that I'd only make him more unhappy as times goes on. I'll write him a note, too. I'll explain that Max is the only one who can help me now, and I'll beg Charles to let me go without too much of a fuss. It's selfish to love somebody so much that you won't let them go even when they want to. If Charles really loves me and wants me to be happy—he'll give me a divorce."

Clem stared at her speechlessly for a moment then said:

"My God, and you talk about selfishness!"

"I don't pretend to be anything but an egotist," said Lisa sullenly.

"Well, you seem to have got it all settled. What next do you

111

intend to do?" asked Clem. She was fast beginning to realise that she had got to accept the fact that Lisa would leave Charles, and that nothing now would stop her. So she sat there, staring and listening to her.

She only intended to stay at Lockbridge House for another ten days, Lisa said. On Tuesday week, Max would arrive in England. And on the Wednesday morning he would come down to fetch her. There seemed nothing a millionaire couldn't buy. Max was detailing the man who looked after his yacht and car in Cannes to come over to London early next week and hire a Rolls-Royce into which Lisa could be carried, and which would take her smoothly to the Airport. There, Max's own special plane would be waiting to fly her to Nice. Meanwhile, the *Villa des Citronniers* in Beaulieu was to be prepared for her arrival.

Lisa continued to tell Clem, with mounting excitement, about all the wonderful things that were to be done for her and given her, and how madly thrilled Max Kern was at the idea of having her with him, with no restrictions, so that they could start the search for her complete restoration to health. Clem listened, stunned. She did, in truth, try to see things from the point of view of this girl who had so recently narrowly escaped death. Her nervous system had been shattered. Perhaps it was even possible that her mind was slightly unhinged, but no—that was *nonsense,* Clem decided. Lisa had been having a love-affair with Max *before* the crash, even in those days, and contemplated leaving Charles. And trying to be yet more factual, Clem reminded herself that she only felt badly about Charles because she loved him. Maybe if she had disliked him, she would have been only too glad to help Lisa get away. What a cynical thought! Yet she could not give Lisa her true sympathy. Why look upon it as being so dreadful, anyhow. Separation and divorce were common these days—it was an ordinary occurrence for husbands and wives to break up the home and leave each other. What was so terrible about it? Well, of course the answer was there again in the front of Clem's mind. Charles adored his wife with a more than ordinary love.

She let Lisa ramble on about her exciting future. She had already seen the Villa, she told Clem. It belonged to a French film star and was living up to its name—*Villa of the Lemon Trees.* It was full of fragrant trees and famous for its magnificent flowers. It had been built right on the rocks overlooking the blue waters of the Mediterranean, and had its own swimming pool. From the wonderful white marble terrace two circular staircases led down to the sea. The Villa was sumptuously furnished. Lisa had seen it when she and Max had lunched there, while staying in Cannes. The film star was willing to rent the Villa to Max for as long as he wanted it, including her first-rate Italian staff.

Lisa's bedroom had windows opening out on to the terrace where she could lie in the sun and look down at the sea all day if she wanted. But of course she wouldn't do that. She would be busy all day with massage and physiotherapy and other treatment, and she would be seeing specialists from Paris and Switzerland about her spine. Then, in the evenings, Max could invite his friends, and they would hold marvellous parties; life would begin for her again.

"And end for Charles!" Clem suddenly broke out in extreme bitterness.

"I'm terribly sorry about him," said Lisa with a sigh.

"But Max comes first."

"Yes. Max comes first."

"And where do *I* come into it?"

"As I said—you'll be here to help Charles get over the initial shock. You must make him see that he's got to carry on with his work and forget me. You must tell him that I've never been worth his sort of devotion, anyhow. I admit it," Lisa added frankly.

"My God," said Clem. "You've giving me one hell of a job, aren't you?"

"But it'll be better for him than if you had left too and he was having to face it all alone. Put sentiment right out of this, Clem. I don't for a moment suppose you and Charles will stagger into each other's arms—but at least he admires you and relies on you and you're good friends. You *will* be able to help him."

"I hope so," said Clem in a low voice.

She felt weak and sick suddenly, sick to the depth of her soul. She added:

"And you expect me to get through the next ten days knowing what's going to happen and just pretend that everything in the garden is lovely. How can I?"

"You will—for Charles," said Lisa in her sweetest voice.

Really, thought Clem, there was something superbly insolent about Lisa—the way she just shelved her responsibilities towards Charles, her marriage, everything, and intended to leave her, Clem, to pick up the pieces. Yet she knew as she sat there looking at Charles's wife, that she couldn't refuse to do it. She *couldn't* let

Charles face his hell alone. She might, in her own peculiar way, be of some use and support to him.

"What do you think Sister Laurie and the others will think if this Rolls-Royce arrives with Mr. Kern and you're all packed up and leaving without Charles having said one word."

Lisa reached for another cigarette.

"It doesn't matter what anybody else thinks. Besides, I shall tell Laurie that Charles, himself, is sending an American friend to drive me up to London in his Rolls, etc."

"She'll hardly believe that with all the special equipment down here —" began Clem, thinking resentfully of the trouble and expense to which Charles had been put on this incredible girl's behalf. How *could* she show such monstrous ingratitude?

"Oh, don't argue and worry me with details," exclaimed Lisa impatiently. "Whether you or anybody else likes it or not I am going away with Max."

Clem set her lips.

"Very well."

"I need only pack a small suitcase. Max doesn't want me to be bothered with anything. He says he'll get all that I need in Cannes. The best Paris couturiers have shops there."

Clem could only look at Lisa and, perhaps, envy a little the type of character that could please herself at somebody else's expense, with so little concern. It must be wonderful to have no conscience. Lisa certainly wasn't going to shed another tear over Charles. She was completely obsessed with the idea of going to live with Max Kern. He and all that he offered was becoming more desirable with every moment that passed.

"I should have been born in the reign of Queen Victoria," Clem told herself. "I don't really like modern marriage. It can bust up too easily, and with such cruelty. I'd really like to have been one of those meek and mild wives in the eighties who took her husband for better or worse, put up with him if she didn't like him, and sat at the foot of the table facing her lord and master, with a row of little jammy faces on either side."

"What are you smiling at?" Lisa's voice interrupted Clem's reflections.

"Was I smiling?" Clem asked. "I assure you I don't feel very amused."

"Perhaps you're planning to tell Charles this evening what I've just told you?"

114

Clem flushed angrily.

"I didn't know that I'd betrayed your confidences so far, Lisa. As a matter of fact, I've had this business of Max and you on my mind far too long and I haven't much liked it. I shall be glad when it's over."

"I'm sure you will," Lisa sneered.

Clem got up and walked out of the room.

10

CHARLES MADDISON— like many husbands about to be left—seemed to be the last person in the whole circle to dream that his wife had a lover. He was far too occupied in his profession and with trying to help Lisa regain her health and spirits. In fact he was rather pleased, because when he got home that Monday night, Lisa told him that she had got through her correspondence earlier than expected so Clem could go back to London with him the next day if he wanted her.

"I certainly do," was Charles's fervent reply. "Your girl-friend" —he turned to Clem who was in the room when this conversation took place—"is not a bad stenographer but of course she doesn't know where anything is nor can she deal with the patients so it's been pretty good hell today."

"I think if you don't mind I'll go up to town tonight. There's a fast train after dinner," said Clem.

She was looking at Lisa—not Charles.

Lisa was wearing one of her most ravishing negligées of oyster pink chiffon which suited her colouring. She was being particularly nice to Charles which savoured so much of hypocrisy that it made Clem feel rather sick. How she could lie there holding her husband's hand, flirting with him, calling him 'darling' in that succulent voice —knowing all the time that she meant to stab him in the back in less than ten days, Clem did not know. And poor Charles looked so pleased. No doubt he found the moments when Lisa was sweet to him like this all too rare. He was nicely deceived into thinking her good humour the result of better health, and real affection for him.

'I can't stand it!' Clem decided, 'I'm off. The less I see of Lisa the better until she goes.'

Before Clem left the house, Lisa reminded her that she would like her back to 'do some more letters' next Wednesday week. Clem flushed. This impudence was *too* much, Clem knew perfectly well why she was wanted down here on Wednesday week. Charles made only a feeble protest.

"Oh *sweet* . . . can't you use Clem during the weekend, if she'd be kind enough to stay? I do need her during working hours."

Clem walked out of the room. She seemed to do nothing else she thought, but she could no longer 'take it'. She abhorred Lisa and wondered how Charles could be so weak, so ready to indulge his exacting wife? Maybe this was why he was losing her. Lisa needed a stronger man; someone like Max Kern who seemed to hold her not only by the cords of his wealth but by his breath-taking vigour —they were both people who would snatch their own happiness over the dead bodies of others—and he possessed a determination to match hers. Clem was beginning to realise for the first time that her adored Charles was not as powerful a character as she had once thought. Yet that touch of weakness in him—all his kindness and consideration, was very endearing. It brought out all that was strong and protective in Clem. God! how right Lisa was when she said that Charles needed her—*her, Clem*. She couldn't really believe that she would be able to comfort him when Lisa left—but at least she could give him everything in her power. And she excused even the weak side that made him indulge Lisa, believing that he was possibly still a victim of the shock he had suffered on the day of her crash. Nothing mattered to him—nothing except that Lisa should be happy. Let her disorganise his working life—let her make stupid excuses for doing it—and accept them. Even as Clem left the room, she heard Lisa's voice:

"Surely you understand why I don't want Clem this weekend. I want to be alone with you. I never am."

Clem let the door slam quite viciously. She felt murderous towards Lisa. What she had just said was enough to hoodwink the wretched Charles so completely that he would be glad to let Clem come here on Tuesday. As for Lisa, *of course* she wanted Clem to see to everything when Max and the Rolls arrived on the Wednesday morning.

Clem was almost blind with helpless rage as she ran into Lisa's nurse in the hall.

"You're in the devil of a hurry," laughed Sister Laurie. Then added on a more serious note: "Hey, what's wrong? You look upset."

"Oh, I'm all right," said Clem, "I'm just going to pack."

"Are you off, then? I *shall* miss you."

"Thanks," said Clem, and rushed up the stairs anxious not to be further cross-questioned by Sister Laurie. She could hardly endure

117

this atmosphere of intrigue and treachery. It was so absolutely against her own standards. By all means commit a sin if you must that was only going to affect *you*, but to hurt somebody else so gratuitously—that was in itself a sin.

Clem returned to London. She felt in a turmoil. She wondered whether in fact she ought to tell Charles what was about to hit him, so that he could be prepared. But of course she wouldn't. It would only make things worse. She must play this damnable game the way Lisa wanted.

For Charles's sake.

This was what Lisa kept saying. This was what Clem drummed into her mind.

Back in Town she found her flat stuffy and airless. The storm that had been hanging over the country all day had not yet broken. It was ten degrees hotter in London than down at Hungerford. Clem felt stifled. She opened all the windows then tried to settle down to writing her weekly letter to Aunt Anne, but she soon gave that up. She had too much on her mind.

She wondered what the cherished aunt up in Wales would have thought if Clem could have written the truth.

> Lisa is leaving Charles. She is going away shortly with a German-born millionaire (now a naturalised American). He was in love with Lisa before the crash. I thought at first that he was going to walk out on her but now that she can walk a few steps he thinks he can find a specialist somewhere in the world to cure her completely. He's taking her away in his private plane. I don't know what this will do to Charles but I think it will just about kill him. He doesn't deserve this. Oh, God, I love him so much. Can you think what it means to me to have to stand by and wait, then watch her put the knife in, and turn it? ...

What would Aunt Anne have said to that? Clem could imagine that even that practical, intelligent woman-doctor might admit she had no solution to such a problem. It was futile to try to alter Lisa's mind. Now it was a question of '*Que sera, sera!*' The old popular song put it in a nutshell.

Hammond Portal rang up. By that time Clem had smoked six cigarettes, drunk two gins—most unusual for her ever to drink alone but tonight she felt that she needed the tonic—and was wandering around the flat in slacks and shirt, with her hair hanging untidily down her back. Clem was not at all her tranquil organised self. She had grimaced at herself in the mirror just before the phone bell rang and muttered to her reflection:

"What a sight! Imagine you being able to console *any* man . . . !"

Into the confusion of her thoughts tonight there had continually seeped the remembrance of Lisa's innuendoes about Charles 'turning to her'. He wouldn't. She didn't want him that way, anyhow. God knew, she didn't.

Hammond Portal was irritatingly cheerful. He asked how she was and talked blithely about his forthcoming holiday abroad and a new art gallery that he was going to visit in West Berlin. Then he mentioned the key of the Hurley cottage.

"Are you going to let me come and have a drink with you and give the key to you?"

She told him now that she was having an early night and begged to be forgiven. There was a crisis on in the Maddison household. She was half inclined to confide the whole thing in Ham who she knew would be understanding and sympathetic but she could not betray Lisa. It wouldn't do any good anyhow.

She talked to Ham for a few moments and apologised for disappointing him about tonight. She felt rather badly about it because it was quite obvious these days that the Emperor was more than interested in her. She could have entertained him now that she was back in town but somehow she didn't want to face Ham tonight. She had too much on her mind. It ended by Ham telling her that he would drop the key in at her flat—just put it through the letter-box. He begged her to take advantage of it.

"You'll be able to relax down there by the river, my dear."

She needed relaxation. This was for sure, she thought bitterly. But she had to remain at Lisa's beck and call—*always*, for the sake of Charles.

She wished Ham a pleasant holiday and put the receiver down.

At Welbeck Street the next morning she felt that she hardly knew how to face her employer. He was looking less strained than he had done for weeks; he was quite gay. She knew perfectly well why. The treacherous Lisa had been especially nice to him last night. Charles more or less intimated it.

"I think she's so plucky—she was marvellous last night, giving us an exhibition of the progress she's made—struggling towards me in her harness, and with Sister helping. She was so pathetic and so lovely."

"God!" Clem muttered to herself.

"She seems bent on having you down there with her next week if you care to go, Clem. I find it rather nice that she's got such confidence in you."

"Yes," said Clem without looking at him.

What would he say when he learned the truth, and learned too that she had known about Max all this time. Would he hold it against her? Should she have warned him? *Should she warn him even now?*

Clem felt torn in two yet in the final analysis believed that she must keep the facts from him. In a curious way she felt that it might be best if Lisa were gone—far away—when the bomb exploded. If he knew now he would only spend ten anguished days of fruitless pleading with her not to leave him. Alternatively he might so resent what she meant to do that he would see Max Kern and have a fight with him when he arrived. An ugly row might result which, again, could bring no satisfaction. Lisa meant to go with her millionaire whatever happened. Charles couldn't win.

Clem maintained a grim silence. Charles gave her a closer look.

"You a bit off-colour? You're not looking one hundred per cent—rather pale."

Clem kept her head lowered and pretended to write on her pad.

"I'm fine thanks. Must be my poor complexion."

"You haven't got a poor complexion. It's rather a nice one—not a blemish."

She felt her cheeks grow hot.

"All out of the pot, I assure you."

"Nonsense."

Charles laughed. Somehow his cheerfulness this morning irritated Clem beyond belief. How she longed to say: *"You fool! You fool! You're like the sailors who used to be lured on to the rocks by the siren's song. You're letting Lisa twist you round her little finger."* Yet her thoughts carried her further. It was sweet of him—pathetic and so sweet of him to be pleased because his wife had been charming to him last night. God! What a husband! Why did the wrong sort of woman seem to get *that* sort of man?

Clem raised her eyes to the level of the desk and Charles's hands. Those strong fine hands busy with papers and reports. She knew that she would have given half her life (no, all of it) just for one year, or less, to be in Lisa's shoes, possessed by *him*. To feel those hands on her hair—on her breast—holding her—*wanting* her.

The perspiration broke out on Clem's forehead. She drew the back of her hand across it. If Charles was a fool, so was she, she reflected, and a worse one. She had no right to feel this burning hopeless passion. He had every right to love Lisa.

Charles unconsciously upset his secretary by a well-meaning enquiry as to her feelings generally.

"Don't think I'm so busy that I don't notice all the countless little things you do for me and for Lisa," he said. "There are times when I think you do too much and ought to spend more time on yourself—your own personal life. Are we wearing you out? You always seem ready to come here or go there or do this at a moment's notice—and never a complaint. Isn't it rather imposing on you, Clem?"

She wished that he would keep quiet. Poor darling, how little he knew what lay behind her devotion, her stress. She resorted to joking.

"If you want to know I've been seriously thinking of approaching my union. I'm only supposed to do a limited number of hours' work."

"Oh, lord, that isn't really funny. You're dead right. Your present salary doesn't cover the amount of work that you do."

With her nerves jangling, this upset Clem thoroughly. She changed from the normally placid and unruffled secretary into a woman with a personal grievance. White-faced, big brown eyes blazing, she said:

"That's insulting. How can you possibly suggest that I do what I do for *money*? I know I am employed by you, but I'm well-paid and what extra I do is because I—because I—"

She stopped. Confused, scarlet, she turned and walked out of the consulting-room.

In her own office, she sat trembling, on the verge of tears. She pulled a powder compact out of her bag and hastily dusted her face. She was shocked by the violence of her own feelings. What on earth must Charles think of her, rushing out like that?

Charles, like most men, was merely puzzled. How could any man understand the feminine mentality? Clem's extraordinary display of feeling distressed and worried him. He told himself wryly that he certainly knew more about slipped discs than women's emotions. But he was surprised by Clem. He had always thought that behind the wall she had put up between herself and the world, she probably had deep feelings, but was just not excitable, or very emotional. She had never struck him as being 'touchy', either. He hadn't meant to insult her; far from it. He felt that he owed her a tremendous lot for the loyal service she had given him since she came back to work for him.

He was a bit afraid to say any more to her just now. He did not want to make another blunder and he certainly didn't want any kind of misunderstanding to arise between Clem and himself. She was far too necessary to him. Just how necessary, he was fast beginning to realise. The mere idea of Clem walking out on him for some silly reason, and himself having to work permanently with a girl like her friend Miss Coles, or that other 'stand-in'—Miss Garner—upset Charles. Somehow, efficient though they were, these girls seemed mere machines compared with Clem. She was so human. She had such extraordinary understanding of his needs. He rarely asked her to do anything. He just found things done. And she was as good as ever with the patients. Not one, but several lately, had complimented him on having 'Miss Wright' as they still called her, for an assistant.

Now the first patient of the day had arrived. Charles forgot about Clem and plunged into work.

It was a hot, close day. The expected storm had never broken and there was still thunder in the air. He was glad that he would be back in Hungerford tonight.

By the end of the morning, the little fracas with Clem was forgotten. She certainly made no reference to it. She gave him the usual smile when she came in to ask if there was anything more she could do before going off to lunch.

Then he said:

"Look, Clem—you know I was only pulling your leg about salary just now. After all, you pulled mine about going to your union. We're quits. I wouldn't dream of insulting you—of thinking you were after more £ s. d."

"Of course not. It was silly of me to take you seriously," said Clem in a bright, brittle voice. "Oh, well—I'm off! See you at two-thirty."

"Got a lunch date?"

"Yes," she lied, because she was sure he meant to ask her to have a snack with him and she wasn't going to do it. She was in too much of a state—brooding on the memory of that ghastly secret which she must still keep. She didn't want to be involved in any fresh discussion about Lisa, or listen to Charles gaily making plans about their future.

So, all that week, she avoided personal contact with her employer and carried out her work quietly in the background.

It was a hard week, too. Charles had several bad cases. There were the usual numbers in need of osteopathy; the inevitable grumblers who suggested that Mr. Maddison had done them more harm than good, and those who thought him marvellous. Clem took as much off Charles's back as she could, exercising the tact and charm which had made her so popular as his assistant.

Her own affairs seemed of no account—just as her flat had become a place in which she only ate her evening meal, slept, and occasionally entertained a girl-friend. It was an odd week. In a kind of hiatus she waited in despair for the end. She slept abominably and had nightmares; in which Charles and Tony became all mixed up. When she woke up she felt more restless than ever. And at times ashamed and scared of herself.

There was a night when she actually dreamed that Tony was alive—lying there at her side. She heard his lost, once-familiar voice saying: 'I love you, Clem. I don't show it, perhaps, but I do love you, darling.'

She began to cry, then Tony's face seemed to dissolve and change into the face of Charles. It was Charles who was holding her, his strange light blue eyes searching hers for what might have been the answer to all the problems and mysteries in the world. Searching desperately for truth—for light in the darkness. For faith when all faith seemed to have been destroyed. It was in Charles's arms she lay. He made passionate love to her. He whispered those same words: that she dreamed Tony had said to her.

'I love you, Clem—I don't show it—but I do love you, darling.'

She woke up, every nerve in her body quivering and the tears pouring down her cheeks. Half exulted and half ashamed she turned her face to the pillow and sobbed his name:

"Charles, *Charles*."

That was certainly a dream that nobody in the world would ever know about. It seemed terrible to her that it should have been so vivid, and meant so *much*. *And* that the one about poor Tony meant less than nothing.

The next morning she went to work feeling quite ill. She presented a bright enough face to her employer. She was thankful he was too busy to ask her any questions. But when she first looked up into those light blue eyes of his and he said: "Hello, Clem,"—

123

she felt sick—guilty—destroyed by the memory of the sensual, sorrowful dream in which he had figured.

So the days went by. Clem was thankful when the weekend came. This time she was not invited to Lockbridge House. She was glad. She didn't want to go near Lisa until she had to.

Hammond Portal had put the key of his cottage through the letter-box for her. She broke the date she had made with the Grants and drove herself down to Hurley alone. She stayed in Ham's lovely little house that night feeling she must try to sort herself out and get things into better perspective, or she would become a psycho-pathic case.

But her thoughts kept turning to him and to the immense drama of Lisa, and she wondered what sort of a weekend Charles was being given this time.

She did not imagine it would be very happy for Charles. She had spoken last night to Sister Laurie over the telephone on pretext of asking after Mrs. Maddison's health. Sister Laurie answered brightly that Mrs. Maddison was making great strides with her walking. She admitted that Mrs. Maddison had 'real courage'. But, the nurse added, things were not 'too easy' down there. Mrs. Maddison was so difficult. She kept everybody on their toes, doing her bidding. She grumbled at everything and, Sister added, she felt so sorry for Mr. Maddison who, when he came down at night, had to cope with milady's moods. She had heard them quarrelling one night. Not that Mr. Maddison raised *his* voice but Mrs. Maddison had screamed so that everyone could hear her—out of control— "For God's sake, don't fuss me. Go away. Leave me alone for Christ's sake. You drive me nuts."

"Just imagine—that lovely man," said Sister Laurie indignantly. "He looks so tired but he's so patient and sweet with her. I don't know how she can be so nasty."

Clem had made no comment. She knew far too well how and why Lisa could be so nasty, so unkind to her husband. She had the other man.

Her temporary wish to ease her conscience by being 'sweet to Charles' seemed to have been short-lived. She was being herself again. Well, thought Clem, maybe it was better. Maybe if she was nasty enough, Charles wouldn't so badly regret her leaving him. No—that wasn't true. Whatever she did, he would break his heart over her, Clem knew that. He put down all her present unkindness to nerves and forgave her.

124

Worrying about Charles drove Clem crazy. She began to wonder if after all it was a good idea installing herself in Ham's house and staying there quite alone. She had too much time in which to think, and too vivid an imagination.

She decided to go back to Town again early tomorrow and spend the day, as she often did, with her godson. Timothy was at an adorable age and would cheer her up. Lucky Timothy to be ignorant of what life could do to one. Marvellous to be still a small child, Clem thought in the wretchedness of her soul.

The day before Lisa was due to leave Lockbridge House with her lover—for Clem, as well as for Charles Maddison, was grimly unforgettable.

Things did not go to plan. As soon as Clem reached Welbeck Street—she was going to work till lunch time, then take the train down to Hungerford—Charles exploded a bomb at her feet by announcing that his medical adviser insisted on him taking a week's rest, and immediately.

"I've just seen old Bill and he won't even let me have twenty-four hours more in Town. You won't have to go by train now, Clem. I shall drive you down," he told her before the first patient arrived. "Just phone Lisa and tell her what's afoot and that she'll have to put up with her husband for a few days, although I am quite sure I shall be able to do a lot while I am at home to help make the day pass more quickly for her."

He spoke cheerfully and looked rather pleased despite the fatigue written all over his thin face. With his mind full of his work he did not see the expression of horror in his secretary's eyes.

God, Clem was thinking, *That has put the cat among the pigeons!* Lisa had things so carefully planned. Max was arriving in London this evening. He was telephoning Lisa to discuss the details before fetching her the next morning.

Charles was putting on his white coat with the high, Russian-looking collar-band. Clem always thought how well it suited him. But he *did* look tired. He was saying something about being forced to retire from the profession anyhow if he went on cancelling appointments. Clients would be getting tired of it, and this morning it would be up to Clem once again to phone the afternoon patients and apologise because he couldn't see them. She had better say he was not well and under doctor's orders.

"I feel an absolute hound about it but to be quite frank, I had a dizzy spell on the way up in the car this morning and nearly

125

blacked out. The damned blood pressure is not so good, and I'm afraid I've just got to call a halt—if only for a week. I'll take a longer holiday later on."

Clem pulled herself together.

"About time, too, and you want more than a week. You've been wearing yourself out."

"Anybody would think I was an old gentleman," said Charles grimacing.

"You've had seven months of anxiety and of rushing between Welbeck Street and your wife. Sufficient to put anybody's blood pressure up!"

"I've had enough lectures for one day. You go and start your phoning," he grimaced again at Clem.

She was thankful to get into her own room, sit down at her desk, put a hand to her forehead, and try to think what to do.

Once Charles's first patient had arrived and she knew he would be busy, she put a call through to Lockbridge House. The sooner Lisa knew the worst the better.

Lisa answered Clem and started to talk straight away:

"Oh, it's you! Well, you're not ringing to tell me that you aren't coming this afternoon, I hope. Charles and I had the mother and the father of a row over the weekend. He really makes me want to scream. I can't stand all those loving attentions, and sweet little plans for my happiness. Incidentally, I've just had a call from New York. Max is on his way—and not before time. I've about had it down here."

"Just a moment," said Clem—and told Lisa the news.

An instant's silence—then a furious Lisa snarled at Clem.

"Oh *hell*! He *would* take a holiday today. Of all the sickening maddening stupid things —" she broke off, choking.

Clem shut her eyes and prayed for patience. Would there never come a day when Lisa Maddison would think of others rather than of herself? It didn't seem to matter at all that Charles was not well.

Clem remembered once hearing a discussion between Hammond Portal and Guy Grant, about a woman they all knew and who had just left her husband. How utterly callous she had been to him, Hammond had said, although by nature she was not selfish or cruel. Clem could recall Guy's remarks:

"It's odd, when a woman decides to end her first marriage, she is often so beastly to the man she's leaving, and all her pity and feeling are for the one she's going to. It's psychological. I suppose she knows she's doing wrong and that seems to stir up a monumental resentment in her towards the wretched husband. It's only after the divorce she starts to remember how nice he really was."

At the time, this had struck Clem as being too cynical and exaggerated. Today, she began to think that Guy knew quite a lot about women and human nature. Certainly Lisa was behaving with unexpected brutality to Charles.

Lisa began a tirade. She insulted first her husband—then Clem.

"*You've* cooked this up! You're arranged for him to take a holiday before Max arrives. You've told him about me—and he's going to pretend he doesn't know, and try to win me back tonight, or some such idiocy."

Clem interrupted.

"Not true, but I refuse to discuss it. Look Lisa, you're round the bend. You should know that the last thing I want is for Charles to come face to face with Max. You haven't given me breathing space to explain that he had a near blackout in the car driving up to town this morning and that is what made him go along and see his doctor. And you might remember, Charles has been killing himself trying to do things for you."

"So you keep telling me. I'm not prepared to listen to your infatuated outpourings about my husband's nobility. Save your admiration for him after I've gone. I *am* going! This isn't going to stop me—do you hear? Nothing is. I don't belong to Charles any more. I belong to Max."

Clem looked hastily around her as though somebody might hear Lisa's crazy reckless words. She said:

"Oh, for heaven's sake, get a hold of yourself. You can't let Max go and fetch you from Lockbridge House. You can't."

"Well, just because Charles's blood pressure is slightly up I'm not going to cancel all Max's and my arrangements. And it's no good being angry. Despise me if you want to, and worship Charles. But I'm off."

The sweat broke out on Clem's forehead. She stared miserably out of the window. It was no fine summer's day. Rain had been pouring down ever since dawn and the forecast was 'More rain'; 'Temperature below normal'. She felt her courage fail at the thought of Charles driving blithely down to Lockbridge House this afternoon to receive the *coup de grâce*.

Suddenly in a choked voice, she said:

"Oh, Lisa, Lisa, I know things have been bad for you and

that you're in love with Max, but please, *please* don't do this to Charles."

"I'm sorry," said Lisa in a less aggressive voice, "but it's all settled. You know that. Just face up to it. Charles must, too."

"Do you intend to tell him tonight?"

"Yes. Then he can decide whether he wants to talk to Max tomorrow or push off. Be your age, Clem. We aren't living in the days when husbands pulled out a pistol and shot the co-respondent. We're civilised people. I'd quite like it if Charles became friends with Max and we all met in the future. I don't *dislike* Charles, you know. He can be quite wonderful at times. I just don't want to stay married to him, that's all."

The front-door bell rang. Clem set her teeth.

"Charles's next patient has come. I've got to go. There seems nothing more to say. We'll both be down by about half-past four, I expect."

"Okay. And whether you believe it or not, I'm very sorry he's not well, poor sweet. I'll be very nice to him. Don't worry, and . . ."

Clem did not hear the rest of that sentence. She put the receiver down. She found herself trembling. The anguish she felt for Charles was past belief; just as she knew that if she lived to be a hundred she would never understand the mentality of a human being as supremely egotistic as Lisa.

11

To Clem, the drive down to Hungerford was about as miserable as that other one she had taken months ago with Charles from Gatwick to Redhill Hospital—when he had been so afraid he might find Lisa dead or dying.

Today he was blissfully unconscious of what awaited him, but she felt as though there was a ton-weight on her own mind. She kept wondering at what time Lisa meant to break the news and how Charles would react to it. She couldn't begin to guess, but her apprehension became almost unbearable.

There were only moments when she felt a vestige of admiration for Lisa. She might have insisted on Max being with her to back her up. She had courage, if she was willing to face her husband alone.

Clem tried, rather stupidly, to imagine what she would have done if she had decided to leave Tony and elope with some man *she* loved. Could she have stayed to witness his hurt, his pain? No, she was sure she would have gone off in a cowardly way, leaving the inevitable note on the mantelpiece. She had always had some sympathy and feeling for Tony in spite of their disagreements and incompatibility. She would never have left him, no matter how great the temptation. No, not even for Charles, her dearly-belovèd.

Then again, Clem argued with herself, *who knows? Perhaps I might have left Tony for Charles. Who can tell how one would behave in the circumstances. Perhaps I feel this antagonism towards Lisa because I love Charles so much. I shouldn't judge her too harshly. I'm no angel!*

Charles was asking why she was so quiet.

"Got something on your mind?"

"No," she lied.

"I'm driving slowly. I think one should when one isn't feeling one hundred per cent. I damn nearly passed out over the wheel coming up, you know."

Clem tried to turn her thoughts from Lisa and Max.

"You really must look after your health, Charles. Would you

like me to drive? I'm a very safe driver, you know, although you probably won't want to trust the Alfa to me."

"Why not? You've taken me around in your own car on occasions and I've always admired your driving. Would you like to take over the Alfa? You can if you like."

She looked at him, a trifle flushed and bright-eyed.

"Oh, I'd love to!"

He pulled the car up at a layby and smiling, handed the wheel over to Clem. She felt flattered that he was willing to trust the beautiful powerful car to her. To be trusted by Charles in any way was a great comfort to her, and it would be nice to save him the fatigue of driving even this short journey down the Great West Road.

She handled the Alfa well and carefully, thankful that it had stopped raining. The sun glittered now on the broad road. Charles complimented her, and having to concentrate on the gears, and watch the heavy traffic, Clem escaped from the frightful turmoil of her thoughts. Before they had gone another ten miles, Charles was so silent that she turned and looked at him. He was sound asleep. He must be dead tired, she thought, with deep tenderness. She was glad that he could sleep—be peaceful—before the storm broke over his unhappy head.

It is terrible to realise that disaster threatens somebody you love and you can do nothing to save them. Clem learned in these few hours how very terrible it was.

Charles slept almost until they reached their destination, then woke up, amazed to find that they were passing through Hungerford and nearly at Lockbridge.

He patted Clem on the shoulder.

"Full marks. I shall be engaging you as a chauffeur soon as well as a secretary. What would I do without you?"

"Put somebody else in my place," she said in a snappy voice, just to hide the intolerable poignancy of her emotions.

There was so much to be gone through yet.

Lisa obviously did not intend to say one word to her husband straight away. Sitting in her wheel-chair in her beautiful bed-sitting-room, she looked a dream of loveliness, in white slacks, and a thin black silk jersey that flattered her exquisite breasts. Her face was carefully made-up, her hair brushed and shining. She lifted her face for Charles to kiss and sympathised with him about his health.

130

"Rotten luck, sweetie. Glad you've decided to knock off work for a bit."

As Clem and Sister Laurie were both in the room, Charles contented himself with kissing the back of his wife's hand instead of gathering her into a lover's embrace.

"I feel an awful heel leaving my patients, but Bill convinced me that I've got to play it cool for a week—(isn't that what the teenagers say?)—so I gave in. I'll just do sweet damn all until the end of the week."

"Splendid," said Lisa. "Did you bring me those cigarettes I asked for?"

"Oh, I'm sorry," he said, remorsefully, "I forgot. Can I nip out and get you any other brand?"

"Never mind," she said, "I've got others."

"I'll ring the shop and tell them to post you down your specials. A couple of hundred do you?"

Clem listened to all this, thinking bitterly that Lisa wouldn't need two hundred cigarettes down here. She'd be gone before she had smoked half a box.

Clem didn't much like watching and listening to Lisa being nice to Charles. The treachery of it all seemed so appalling. In her opinion if ever there was a female Judas, it was Lisa.

She walked out of the room followed by the hospital nurse who didn't make her feel any better by giving her a more detailed account of the row the Maddisons had during the weekend. Lisa was a devil, although so brave as a patient. Odd creature, said Sister Laurie.

Clem thought cynically that Sister Laurie might have understood more if she had known that Lisa was a brave patient because she was trying to get strong and well for her lover—not for her husband. Not once but many times that day, Clem was tempted to confide in the sensible strong Scotswoman, but could not bring herself to do so. She was still not prepared to break the promise she had given Lisa to keep the secret. Anyhow, no matter what Sister Laurie thought or advised, it would do little good now.

During tea, Charles, although he still looked very dark under the eyes, kept shutting them as though he felt it hard to keep awake. But he was in better spirits than Clem had seen him for some time. He announced that he intended to enjoy this week at home. He would do a bit of gardening. He'd sunbathe if only the damn sun would keep out. He'd ring them up at Stoke Mandeville and ask them if there was any reason why he couldn't take Lisa for a drive—not in the Alfa but in a bigger, more comfortable car, which he'd hire. If it was fine tomorrow, they might even have a picnic somewhere in the forest near Marlborough. It was pretty wonderful there.

Clem listened to all this, only raising her eyes now at Lisa who returned the look with something approximating a sneer. A devilish look—as though challenging Clem to open her mouth and tell Charles how futile it was for him to make these silly plans.

Clem tried to get away after tea but Lisa called her back. This time she was able to talk to her alone. Charles went up to his room announcing that he was going to have an hour's 'shut-eye' and be fresh for dinner.

"I can see he's not well," Lisa said, "but it's only because he's been overdoing it. There's nothing seriously wrong with him, is there, Clem?"

"Would it matter?" Clem suddenly flashed.

"Don't be nasty, dear. It isn't the slightest good trying to take your own frustrations out on me. I'm to blame for a lot of things but *not* for Charles's ill-health. I did not ask him to keep rushing to see me wherever I was. It was his idea."

"Sorry, I thought you encouraged him," said Clem. "You got so bored and felt so ill, you said you wanted him to see you every day."

Lisa's good humour vanished. Her lips tightened.

"Oh, well! I see you mean to be horrid."

"I don't understand you —" began Clem.

"Nobody wants you to, so pipe down."

Now Clem gave her a steady look feeling that she had taken just as much as she could stand from this girl.

"The sooner you tell Charles the truth the better. I'm nearly through," she broke out, her face red.

"You wouldn't like me to disturb his rest and bring him down this moment, would you?"

Clem shook her head, staring at Lisa's beautiful voluptuous figure much as she might have looked at a snake, through a glass window in the reptile house, acknowledging its strange beauty but thankful not to have to touch it. Lisa saw that look and flushed.

"You despise me, don't you? You never give me one kind thought."

"Why should I?"

132

Lisa shrugged.

"I would have thought you were the type to uphold justice. You're always damned unjust to me."

"Lisa, don't let's enter into a discussion. It doesn't really matter what I think of you or what I feel towards you. Just get on with what you intend to do and don't prolong the torture."

"Why not be glad *you're* the one I'm torturing rather than Charles. You really do bring out the worst in me, Clem. I don't want to torture you—or anyone. In fact I'd planned to get Max down here while Charles was in town mainly in order to spare him. You know that. It isn't my fault that the plans have been altered."

"And do you think it'll be a good beginning to your life with Max to have him and Charles come to grips?"

Lisa's eyes opened wide.

"Oh, don't say you're worried now about how Max and I intend to begin or go on. Surely we are beneath your contempt and your only thought is for my injured husband."

"You are without doubt, one of the most maddening and beastly —" Clem started but broke off, speechless.

Lisa gave a short laugh.

"Bitches—yes. We agreed on that long ago. Sorry, Clem. You madden me just as much as I do you. I don't understand you. Perhaps I can't appreciate really good people."

"I am *not* good," said Clem, her face scarlet, "and you know it. But Charles is. He's one of the best men I have ever known. He's kind to everybody. I just don't like having to stand by and see him murdered."

"Darling, it's becoming an awful bore listening to you accusing me of murdering Charles. You know, this morning when I was staggering round this room with crutches and calipers, and all the rest of it, I felt pretty desperate. *I* need a break as well as Charles. I've been the unlucky one. Now it's got to be his turn. That's the way things go. Do accept the fact and stop trying to make me change my mind. It won't work. If I thought I wasn't going away with Max tomorrow, I'd take an overdose."

Clem took a cigarette from a packet in her bag, lit it and smoked hard for a moment. Her thoughts were with the man sleeping in happy ignorance upstairs. She gave a deep sigh:

"Well—when *do* you intend to open his eyes?"

"If you want to know—not tonight."

Horrified, Clem said:

"You mean you're going to leave us all in a state of tension another *night*?"

Lisa's sensual red mouth pouted.

"*You're* the only one in a state, dear! I've become quite calm now that I've made my final decision and I'm not going to allow pity or honour or any of these noble sentiments you're so fond of to change me. So I think it would be kind to let Charles sleep quietly tonight—he loves to lie beside me, hold me near him and caress me, and if it gives him so much pleasure then wouldn't I be nice to give it to him for the last time?"

"Without doubt," said Clem trembling, "you aren't human. You frighten me."

"How wrong can you be! Ask Max!"

Not for the first time Clem resorted to her somewhat cowardly method of retreating. She walked out of the room. She couldn't fight Lisa any more. Not even for Charles. This beautiful, mad, bad wife of his was utterly without conscience. As for letting Charles share her bed tonight—'for the last time' as Lisa called it—that seemed to Clem positively indecent. Maybe she thought in despair, she, Clem, was a prig and a prude, or was it just that she didn't understand Lisa or life or love. Clem went to her room and lay on her bed, sobbing. Maybe there was something wrong with her that she still tried to uphold honour and the decencies. Maybe a lot of girls of her age today would say she wasn't 'with it'. But she couldn't in a thousand years become a Lisa. Lisa was capable of physical suffering but nothing touched her heart. If she lay in Charles's arms tonight it wouldn't be out of kindness or generosity—but only to satisfy her appalling vanity. She enjoyed the feeling of power which she could still exert over men in general despite the fact that she was not quite the girl she used to be. But her fascination had not suffered a change in that crash. She would never lose it, Clem thought bitterly—till the end.

Never again will I like red hair or green eyes, Clem thought childishly. And now she had to try to shut out the maddening picture of Charles tonight—the triumphant lover with his beautiful Lisa in his arms. *Caressing her,* Lisa had said. All that was passionate and jealous in Clem shook her—tormented her—as she tried to fight that picture.

Sister Laurie found the atmosphere at dinner that night distinctly odd. Mrs. Maddison seemed in a state of such excitement that one would have thought she had completely recovered. Her beautiful green eyes kept dancing, turning to Mr. Maddison who himself, looked gay and rested after his few hours' sleep. He flirted like a young boy in love with his beautiful wife. Sister could not quite understand why Mrs. Maddison was so charming to him this evening. Obviously she was in an excellent mood. Not a grumble from those pink-rouged laughing lips. On the other hand, poor little Mrs. Riton (or Miss Wright as they still called her at her job), was very gloomy; scarcely raised her eyes or uttered a word. After dinner they all gathered in Lisa's room and looked at television.

At ten o'clock, as usual, the Sister put her head in the doorway and declared that she must prepare her patient for the night. Lisa begged to be allowed to stay up a little longer.

"I feel so well and strong tonight," she pleaded.

"Have an early night and we'll go for that picnic tomorrow, darling," said Charles. "And you'll feel up to it."

Clem felt an awful urge to look at him. She did so. She was shattered by the expression in his eyes. It was one of such pure happiness. Obviously the man was in heaven because his wife seemed so much better and was being so charming to him.

Clem had to grip tightly on to the sides of her chair and keep her teeth clenched, so as not to scream, when he took Lisa's hand, kissed it lightly, and said:

"Be good and let Sister have her way. I'll come and say good-night to you, my love. It's been such fun—like our old evenings. To see you so much better does me more good than old Bill's medicine. All the same, I'm not sure about the blood pressure. I think you put that up," he added laughing.

Lisa laughed with him.

"Silly old sweet," she murmured.

Sister Laurie came back into the room. As she did so the telephone bell rang. Clem heard it and her heart twisted in an ugly way. It was dead sure to be Max Kern. Lisa had left a message at the Hilton Hotel where he was due for the night, that she wished him to telephone her as soon as he got in.

Lisa lifted the telephone receiver beside her bed and shouted over her shoulder to Clem.

"Come in and see me as soon as I'm in bed, Clem. I want you and would you please take Sister Laurie into the dining-room and give her a liqueur. She was only saying yesterday that she adores *crème de menthe.*"

This was where Clem had to act according to instructions. She

135

knew she must keep Charles occupied during that call. Fortunately he had not heard the telephone bell or if he had, he took no notice. He was out in the garden, looking at his roses. Clem inveigled Sister Laurie back to the dining-room and poured her out the *crème de menthe*. The nurse sipped it happily, taking it for granted that Mrs. Maddison wanted to be alone for her telephone call—and why not?

Clem hardly knew what she talked to Sister about. Her straining ears eventually heard the *ping* of the little bell which meant that Lisa had terminated the call. It had lasted, incidentally, for a good twenty minutes.

"Excuse me one moment," she said to Sister Laurie, "I'm just going to say goodnight to Mrs. Maddison."

"I'll be along directly," said Sister Laurie, appreciatively sipping her liqueur.

Lisa, still in her wheel-chair, gave Clem a long significant sort of look; it was a hateful look, Clem thought, it was so smug, so *satisfied*. Really, Lisa reminded her of a tigress, a wounded one at that, and all the more dangerous, with her victim under her claws—still living and bleeding, awaiting the kill.

Lisa said:

"That was Max, of course."

"I presume all your plans are buttoned up," Clem's voice was acid.

"Since you ask—yes—they are. Max quite understands that he may after all have to face my dear husband tomorrow, but he's prepared for it."

Clem winced.

"Marvellous—the way you two are preparing the faggots in order to burn Charles at the stake. You really should have lived in the days of the Inquisition. You'd have made an excellent couple of torturers."

"Darling, don't be melodramatic. You're *so* out-of-date. Surely today one can walk out of a marriage without all this, 'Pistols for two, coffee for one' attitude?"

"I don't want to discuss it," said Clem. "We've been through it all and we can't see eye to eye."

"In what manner would you have left your own husband, if you had fallen in love with somebody else?" persisted Lisa. "Just gone away somewhere, written a few explanatory notes—then faded out?"

"I said I don't want to discuss it," broke in Clem, no longer even pretending to speak to Charles's wife with respect. But Lisa did not seem to mind how rude she was. She seemed amused by Clem's attitude.

She continued:

"Max and I both agree that the sudden kill is kinder than a long-drawn-out farewell. I'm trying to make Charles happy this evening —and succeeding. I intend to make him still happier later on. I think it's nice of me. He'll have a gorgeous last memory to console him."

Clem changed from white to red.

"Oh, *shut up.*"

"Darling, I always forget you're so much in love with Charles. How horrid of me to bait you!"

"Have you finished with me? Can I go?"

"Darling, I only want you to realise that Max is in town—as madly in love with me as ever and he will arrive here about eleven tomorrow morning. I've warned poor darling Max that I've got to have those horrible calipers on my legs—and my crutches, but he says it'll be such heaven to see me walk at all, he won't care. He's blissful about the whole thing, and certain I'll soon be dancing with him again."

"Splendid," said Clem, trembling with rage—a rage that she had been feeling for a long time on Charles Maddison's behalf. "So you'll have your breakfast tomorrow, then talk to Charles and put him in the picture at last. I hope you've left time for that. Now may I say goodnight and go?"

It seemed that Lisa was suddenly tired of Clem's sarcasm.

"Oh, go to bed—or to hell—whichever you like. And by the way, would you mind putting my nurse in the picture? Let her have her night's rest but tell her in the morning that her services won't be required any further. I couldn't bear to take her with me. Those homely freckles and all that Scots decency would bore me to death, and it would *kill* Max. He's got a marvellous nurse from New York. She's flown over with him. She's trained to look after my sort of case, and looks, Max says, as attractive as she's smart. Max likes pretty girls around him. This one knows the whole story and I think she's thrilled. She's coming down in the Rolls to take me under her wing."

Clem felt a singing in her head. She began to wonder if Lisa was quite sane.

But of course I'm the one who isn't sane, Clem thought. *She's driven me round the bend with all this. Dear God if anybody had ever been paid out for reading someone else's letters, I have. It would have been better for me if I'd been as happily ignorant of it all as Charles.*

Clem joined Charles in the garden.

The night was fine and the stars clear and crystalline in the sky. The 'Super Star' standard roses looked themselves, like strange deep pink stars, Clem thought, exquisite and luminous in the dusk.

"Have you ever seen such roses!" said Charles, lighting a cigar. "Come for a short walk, Clem, while Lisa's being tucked up for the night."

"If you don't mind I think I'll go to bed," she said. "I really only came out to say goodnight, Charles."

He gave her one of his deep, friendly looks. His mind had been so preoccupied with Lisa whose brilliance and beauty and seduction had bowled him completely over this evening, he hadn't really given Clem much thought. Now he saw how ill and miserable she seemed. There were dark circles under her eyes and he found her manner strange—she seemed to be under a strain. He grew concerned.

"Why Clem—you aren't ill are you? You do look queer."

"I think I've got a migraine," she said and laughed hysterically.

He took the cigar from his mouth and shook his head at her.

"Since when have you suffered from migraines?"

"Just lately," she said laughing again, "but I'll be all right tomorrow or—I may not be—oh, I don't know—goodnight, Charles."

"Sure you won't come for that walk?"

She tried to answer. No words came. Normally she would have adored to take a walk on a warm summer night under the stars with Charles. But not with this heavy burden on her mind. And tomorrow when Max Kern came—Clem's imagination refused to carry her further. Suddenly her control snapped, she ran to Charles, caught his hand between both hers and pressed it hard against her cheeks.

"Goodnight, Charles, *dear* Charles, bless you —" her voice broke. She turned and ran indoors.

Charles stared after her, frowning. He stayed still a moment feeling a trifle shocked and uncomfortable. He could have sworn that his hand which she had carried to her cheek was wet with her tears—that Clem was crying. It couldn't be migraine. Something

138

more serious must be wrong with Clem. Poor sweet—perhaps she was in love with some fellow, he thought, and the affair wasn't going well for her. How rotten! How unfair life could be. She'd already had one unsatisfactory marriage. That fellow Tony Ritson hadn't really been good for her. He hoped that she wasn't about to make a second mistake. But surely it was a bit early for her to think of marrying again, or did it matter? Whatever it was he was distressed for her. He was very fond of little Clem.

She had been so very good to him—and to Lisa—and so absolutely loyal. He wouldn't want anything to hurt Clem. Surely the right man would turn up in time and make her really as happy as she deserved to be. She was attractive—Charles didn't deny that, although she was the opposite of his fabulous Lisa. And he had never been stirred, emotionally, by his wonderful secretary. But from a man's point of view Clem's velvety long-lashed eyes could be very appealing. Besides she had a damned good brain and a fine character. He had grown to respect her as well as be fond of her.

Charles was completely in love with his wife but man-like, he was not disinterested in the attractions of other women around him. He allowed himself for a moment to imagine what it would be like for a man to have an affair with Clem. He was sure that she'd be very sweet, and warm, and easy to love. With his peculiar sensibility, Charles had quite often been aware of that lost sad Clem who lay behind the brisk efficient secretary. He had seen the hunger—the unhappiness—in those big brown eyes—misunderstood it—but knew they were there.

He began to walk down the garden towards the fountain.

Poor Clem, he thought, Lisa and I must think of something to cheer her up. Maybe I work her too hard. Maybe I ought to insist on her taking a week off now instead of helping Lisa with her correspondence. I can write Lisa's letters myself now I won't be going up to town. I'll try and make Clem clear off and stay in that Hurley cottage Portal has lent her. She probably needs a real rest.

He made plans for Clem during his solitary walk, full of solicitude for her. When he got back to the house everybody seemed to have retired. It was very quiet.

He undressed, put on pyjamas and dressing-gown, and walked down into Lisa's room again.

She was in bed, half-asleep, he thought, holding an open book in one slack hand. The table lamp—the only light on in the room—showed up the fantastic beauty of her face and hair. Very gently he lay down on the outside of the bed, put an arm across her and touched her lips with his.

"Darling, darling—you were so wonderful to me tonight. And you seem so much more yourself in every way. Oh, my sweet, I'm so happy. I feel everything's going to be all right now."

She opened her eyes. They seemed to him as they had always done, like deep green unfathomable pools. Maybe that had always been Lisa's greatest attraction for him—the fact that he never really knew what she was thinking or feeling; never understood her. She could behave with atrocious selfishness, yet be so extraordinarily sweet as she was tonight.

She smiled up at him, put up languorous arms, and drew him down to her.

12

WHEN Clem woke up she had a headache that must become near to being genuine 'migraine' she told herself. Her whole head hurt. But she was sure it was due to nerves.

She felt she knew now what it must be like to be in battle, awaiting zero hour. Eleven o'clock would mean death for Charles. She was going to die, symbolically, with him.

She would have given her whole soul to be able to arrest this avalanche fast rolling towards Lockbridge House. For a few seconds she even conceived a wild plan of going out to a call-box, ringing Max Kern and begging him to plead with Lisa to spare Charles. But she resisted this impulse because she knew first of all that it was not her business, and secondly, if Max had taken all this trouble to fly to England and take Lisa away, he must be really in love with her. He wouldn't give her up now. A man with his looks and money must have his choice of lovely girls. But Lisa had some sort of strange animal magnetism that few men seemed to be able to resist. The French call it a *je ne sais quoi*. Max certainly must feel it. The attraction must be pretty powerful, Clem reflected, to make a play-boy like Max Kern feel this urgent desire to be with Lisa and restore health and happiness to her. It was in his favour, of course. But Clem felt small admiration for the man who was coming to take Lisa from her husband—just like that!

She found herself this morning wondering what to wear. It looked like being another warm fine day. A white mist wreathed the beautiful walled-in garden. Once the sun broke through, it would be hot. Lovely for Charles and the picnic that would never take place. Clem agonised over this thought as she dressed. She pinned up her long dark hair and combed the short fringe across her forehead. "*God, I look haggard,*" she muttered to her mirrored face. She put on an extra amount of make-up and thought it made her look worse.

She chose a straight blue linen dress (shouldn't it be black for a funeral? she asked herself with grim humour). It was still very early. She needed a cup of tea. She would take two aspirin. It might cure the headache. She had heard Carmella coming upstairs to take Sister Laurie's early tea in to her.

Clem decided that she could no longer bear the awful burden of her thoughts alone. Lisa had told her to warn the nurse. Very well — she would go and see her now. She walked down the corridor towards the Sister's room. As she passed Charles's bedroom she noticed that the door was half-open. So she could see that his curtains were not drawn and his bed had not been slept in. He was still downstairs with *her*.

"Dear God," Clem said the words aloud in a rough voice.

She found Jean Laurie looking rather like an overgrown schoolgirl in her unglamorous sensible dressing-gown, sitting on the edge of the bed, sipping her tea.

"Hullo," she welcomed the secretary cheerfully, "I must say it's a braw bricht morning. I felt I must get up and take a turn round the garden before I start my duties." Then she stopped and stared: "You're dressed! Have you had a bad night, my dear? You don't look well."

"I've come to give you some bad news," said Clem harshly. "Your duties, as you call them, will end once you've got Mrs. Maddison up, and prepared her for the day. And your services will no longer be required as from eleven o'clock ack emma."

Sister put down her tea-cup and looked at Clem with almost comical dismay.

"What on *airth* do you mean?" she asked, reverting to her native dialect.

Clem sat down on the bed beside her and told her. She made the story brief. She did not spare herself — admitting to having read those tell-tale passionate love-letters just after the air disaster. She also told her what had happened since, and what was going to happen this morning.

Jean Laurie listened without interrupting beyond an occasional shake of the head to intimate what she was feeling. This was certainly something she had not anticipated. Clem ended up in tears, hiding her face in her hands, allowing herself the relief from tension. She sobbed:

"Perhaps I should have told Mr. Maddison at once. I don't know, but I hoped I might save him from ever finding out. I didn't want him to see those letters. He was in such a state about her accident."

"I understand, you poor little soul! What a dreadful weight it must have been on your mind."

"It is nearly killing me, I can't take much more."

"You have all my sympathy, and I quite see why you read the letters. I wonder how many of us would have resisted the same temptation. And you *have* saved Mr. Maddison a great deal all these trying months. You did what you set out to do."

Clem raised a wet disfigured face.

"But I haven't. He's got to go through it today. In the final analysis I haven't saved him anything."

Now Sister Laurie looked at her curiously.

"You're very fond of Mr. Maddison, aren't you?"

"Yes," said Clem, but even to this kindly understanding woman could not give away the depths of that 'fondness'. She said:

"What do you think of it all?"

Jean Laurie drew a deep breath and picked up her tea-cup again.

"During my years of nursing I've seen a whole lot of suffering. I suppose I've grown a bit hardened. But I never like to watch the pain or see people being gratuitously hurt. I quite realise how you hate knowing Mr. Maddison is to be chopped up today. It isn't at all pleasant. You've known him and worked with him for so long. As for that glamour-girl downstairs, I could willingly wring her long beautiful neck!"

Clem nodded but said nothing. She was quietly weeping into her handkerchief, still unable to regain her self-control. Sister Laurie went on:

"I told you the other day didn't I that I thought Madam Maddison a bitch. She has physical courage but she's been beastly to her husband up to last night. I know her type. I had another case not unlike it, where a girl had a lover and the husband never knew about it until the hour she walked out. It isn't uncommon, but one has to accept the fact that this type of female is heartless and not made like we are. They're just robots with the peculiar ability to draw men to them and keep them, too. My word—Max Kern, the millionaire! I've seen photos of him in the *Queen*—pictures of his yacht. Mrs. Maddison certainly seems to 'get 'em'. But what amazes me in this case is that she should be leaving *Mr. Maddison*. He's so *attractive* and I've always said he wasn't only a good osteopath but an adorable man. Everybody in the profession dotes on him."

"Except the one who should," said Clem bitterly.

"Well, you could knock me down with a feather. It's incredible. After all he's done for her, too! Where do we go from here—do we

143

just carry on? Have I got to prepare that something-something girl for her get-away?"

"So it seems," said Clem, her eyes red-rimmed, swollen with weeping.

"Isn't Mr. Maddison to be told a thing before this other fellow turns up?"

"Well—actually Mrs. Maddison said she'd tell him after breakfast. She thinks he should be given the chance to decide whether he wants to meet Max Kern or push off before he arrives."

"Phew!" exploded Sister Laurie. Then: "I'm hanged if I'll give her her massage and put her through her exercises and dress her up all ready for her millionaire. I'd much rather knock her beautiful block off!"

"I've been feeling like that for months," Clem laughed miserably. "Then one feels sorry for her because of the damaged spine and all the efforts she makes to walk and get better even if her motives are so rottenly selfish."

"Oh, yes, I grant you she has guts."

"You'll have to dress her. What else can you do. Then there's another nurse—an American coming down with Max Kern in the Rolls to take over from you."

"And I thought I was here for months!" sighed Sister Laurie. "Well—well, this is a bit of a shock for me. But nothing compared with what that poor man is going to suffer. How do you think he'll take it?"

"I daren't think," said Clem.

Now they heard Charles's voice out in the corridor.

"Good morning everybody. Hi—you two girls in there—I can hear you chattering. It's time you were both up. Our so-called invalid is wide awake and brighter than any of us. I think she wants you, Sister, as a matter of fact."

Clem and Sister Laurie exchanged glances.

"Coming," Sister Laurie said grimly.

Clem hastily wiped her eyes, waited until she thought she heard Charles close his bedroom door, then went back to her own room to remove the traces of tears from her face. She felt a slight relief for having unburdened herself to the hospital nurse. But the worst was yet to come.

Somehow or other Clem managed to eat a piece of toast for her breakfast—no more. It was a grim meal. She and the nurse kept looking at each other as though they were confederates in a crime.

They had to listen to Charles making plans for the day. He was definitely going to hire a comfortable car and drive Lisa down to the river. She was so well this morning. She wanted Sister to get through the medical routine as quickly as possible. Charles was delighted, he said. He hadn't been in such good spirits for months. There had been a remarkable improvement in Lisa's whole condition during the last forty-eight hours.

Clem didn't dare look into the gay blue smiling eyes of the man she adored. She couldn't—or she felt she must die of shame for Lisa.

When Sister Laurie came out of Lisa's room and called to Mr. Maddison that he was wanted by Mrs. Maddison, panic seized Clem.

This was it!

She rushed into the garden. She found herself trembling from head to foot. Despite the fact that the day was warm, her whole body felt cold. If she lived to be a hundred, she thought, nothing could be worse than this hour. She knew now why men kept their lips grimly shut when they were tortured yet gave away secrets once they heard the screams of their friends. She even put her hands over her ears as though she dreaded stupidly that she might hear Charles cry out. The pain of what Lisa was going to do to him would surely be unendurable.

Clem walked to the fountain. She trailed her hands aimlessly through the cool limpid water, her mind in chaos. She saw nothing —neither the roses nor the beautiful lilies which had been a speciality of the last owners of this house and which burned in orange splendour against the old grey stone walls.

Then she heard Charles calling her:

"Clem! Are you there, Clem?"

She turned and ran back to the house.

Charles stood in the hall. Her heart took a downward plunge at the sight of his face. It was ashen-grey. Those strangely light blue eyes looked terrible as though they were full of tiny broken blood vessels.

He said:

"Clem—*you knew about this?*"

Still shivering, she choked over her answer.

"Yes. I was under oath to Lisa not to tell you."

"You had no right to take such an oath—or keep it from me."

His voice was furious. She looked up at him in panic.

"I've been scared all the time you'd think this. I suppose I should have told you, but Lisa implored me not to. I thought perhaps she'd get over it so I kept quiet. Forgive me, please. I've been almost out of my mind."

He looked ghastly, she thought. He seemed to struggle with himself then calmed down and spoke more gently to her.

"Perhaps it was as well I didn't know." He looked over his shoulder towards Lisa's shut door. "But my God," he added. "*My God!*"

Clem stared at him hopelessly. There seemed nothing she could say. He was alone now in the grim, dark world that Lisa had made for him.

"That nurse," he said in a mechanical voice. "Write a cheque for that nurse, will you? Give her a month's salary in lieu of notice. She's got to leave today, of course."

"Yes. Where's your cheque-book?"

"Up in the right-hand top drawer of my dressing-chest."

As Clem moved towards the hall, Charles added:

"And bring down my wallet. You'll find it there, too. I shall be up in a second to pack."

She felt sick.

"Where are you going?"

"I don't know. But I'm not staying here."

"You're not going to—to see *him*?"

"No—to hell with Mr. Kern. I see no point in having an unpleasant scene with him. Lisa has made up her mind she wants to go off with him—let her go. In fact I'm rather sorry for Kern. Lisa will probably do the same to him as she's done to me. She seemed very much in love with me before she married me, you know. But she says I've begun to bore her. Am I a bore? *Am I*, Clem?"

"Oh, for heaven's sake, you know you're not. You know what I think about you—what everybody thinks. Don't let anything Lisa says count. She's out of her mind. The crash affected her."

He laughed.

"Thanks for trying to let me down lightly. But she started this affair with her millionaire playboy before she ever got on that Comet!"

"Oh, Charles, you look ill. You're *not* well. You know what your doctor said. For heaven's sake —"

He interrupted her:

"To hell with my health. I just want to be by myself for a bit.

146

Certainly I'd like to get away from Hungerford, and I don't want to go back to Welbeck Street where people can always get at me."

"I understand."

"I've always relied on you, Clem," he said in a low voice, "I didn't think you'd deceive me and share such a bloody secret with Lisa but I suppose I can't blame you. It must have been difficult for you. Lisa got at you. She gets at everybody. She has no scruples. I know that now. Absolutely no sense of honour and no heart. If it wasn't for that fractured spine, and the fact that she is so frail still, I'd have beaten her up just now when she told me. Do you know that, Clem? I felt like beating her up when she told me that she was going away with that fellow. At first I couldn't believe it . . . after last night . . ." his face reddened. Clem could see him clenching and unclenching his hands. "Well, I'm wasting time. I don't want to talk about it."

"Please," said Clem. "Please don't hold it against *me*. I couldn't bear that."

"I don't hold it against you, Clem, but I want to be alone."

A sudden idea struck her.

"The cottage at Hurley—I'll give you my key. Nobody on earth will find you there. Hammond Portal said I could use it just as I liked. There's some tinned stuff in the larder and you can get a bottle of milk and whatever else you need in the village, and sleep there tonight."

"Yes," he said slowly, "I might do that. But I shan't need anything but a whisky—several very strong whiskies. As you know I'm not a hard drinker but I'd like to get drunk tonight even if it puts my blood pressure up a bit more."

The way he spoke and laughed, scared Clem. She could see that the calm self-possessed, intelligent Charles whom she knew so well was in a state bordering on hysteria. She said:

"Let me come with you. Let me drive you down there."

To her immense surprise he let her offer sink in for a second, then answered:

"Very well. Drive me there since you so kindly offer. I don't care. Let's quit this bloody house and leave Lisa to her lover. Go and pay that nurse off and tell Carmella and Luigi that we won't be back for a day or two—and they can just carry on till we—till I phone them."

In a state that alternated between utter misery and a strange primitive exultation, Clem turned and walked out of the room.

So Lisa had not been wrong in this: Charles in the extremity of his loss and suffering was going to let her help him—just help if nothing else. With all her soul she wanted to do that. She must, she thought, find some way of driving that awful look out of his eyes, and keep him from drowning his sorrows in drink. It would be dangerous for him and do a lot of harm. He was normally a man of such temperate habits. She wasn't going to allow him to be weak tonight and take to the bottle.

She found Sister Laurie packing. The Scots nurse was actually in tears.

"I think it's all too dreadful," she said, sniffing.

Clem nodded.

"I agree. It's murder—but I've been facing up to it for a long time. Now it's come. By the way, this is for you."

Rather reluctantly, Sister Laurie regarded the cheque that Mr. Maddison had just signed for her.

"I don't like taking money that I haven't earned, though I admit I would appreciate it."

"Of course. You expected this to be a long job."

The nurse looked curiously at Clem. She certainly seemed in a 'state'. She looked so flushed and feverish; not at all her normal composed little self.

"What's *he* going to do?"

"Going away. He's packing now."

"What a household!" exclaimed Sister Laurie. "In all my years of nursing nothing quite as bad as this has ever happened."

"Forgive me, I must fly. I've got so much to do," said Clem.

She went down to the kitchen and interviewed the Italian servants who seemed surprised but not distressed. Of course, they understood little of what was going on. As long as they could count on their high wages and comfortable home, the personal life of their employers was of small account.

As Clem packed her things, a small warning voice suddenly told her that she was a fool to be doing this. Charles was acting under a great strain. She was not sure she ought to take advantage of his invitation—issued obviously, under stress. But she longed to be with him and so powerful was her desire to help him, it overcame her customary caution. Besides, she really did not think Charles was fit to drive alone to Hurley, or remain there alone tonight.

As she went down the stairs, carrying her bag, she could hear Lisa shouting:

"Charles, I want you. *Charles!*"

He came down the stairs. Clem saw him look with an unforgettable expression on his face, at Lisa's door. He said to Clem:

"Go and tell her to stop calling for me. She can call for the other man. He'll be here soon, I take it. Tell her I don't want to see her again. I'll wait for you in the car, Clem."

As Clem started to open the door, he added:

"Tell her also, that I'm not leaving her any money. She obviously won't want it. She'll be paid in dollars in future."

With a little gasp, feeling the sickness of misery rise like bile in her throat, Clem walked into the beautiful room that Charles, with so much love and thought, had prepared for his invalid wife.

Lisa, fully dressed in a cream wool suit with a green chiffon pleated shirt that matched her eyes, sat in her wheel-chair. She wore the calipers, and her crutches were beside her. On her lap lay a big crocodile bag. She did not look particularly happy, Clem thought with irony. She was pale and her eyelids swollen as though she had been crying. But she spoke to Clem in the familiar voice of defiance and authority.

"Where is everybody? Where is Charles?"

"He's gone."

Lisa changed colour.

"He didn't say goodbye to me."

"I don't see why you should expect him to behave with his usual courtesy."

"Then he's a fool . . ." Lisa's voice broke just a fraction of a bit, "I told him that if he'd be sensible about this—rationalise our whole position like most people do today when they divorce—we could all be friends and enjoy it. He could come and stay with Max and myself, wherever we go. Max won't mind. He's very friendly. Why has Charles got to behave with this sort of Victorian melodrama and rush out of the house?"

For a moment Clem didn't answer. She shook her head as though she failed completely to understand anything about Lisa.

"I'll say goodbye to you if you don't mind," she said, "I've delivered Charles's message."

"What message?"

"He just doesn't want to see you again."

Lisa's long slim fingers closed and unclosed convulsively over the handle of her smart bag.

"He *is* a fool. I tried to tell him that I was still very fond of him and appreciative of all that he had done."

Clem gave a sudden hard laugh.

"You show your appreciation in the most curious way. Never mind. I'm off. I hope you'll soon find a total cure for your spine. I'm not going to wish you happiness with Max Kern. I really don't care whether you are happy or not. What you've done to Charles is unforgivable."

Lisa burst into tears.

"You're all being beastly to me just because I've got the courage to leave my husband. Hundreds of women want to leave home and don't because they're scared of making the break."

Clem felt unable to resist a harsh answer to this.

"Some women stay with their husbands whether they like them or not because they believe in fidelity, Lisa. Others, I admit, stay because they can't afford to quit. You're going away with a millionaire. You've no conscience. You'll benefit most ways. I hardly think that there can be any credit due to you. But I really *must* go. Goodbye, Lisa."

"I hate you. I hate you —" began Lisa hysterically.

Clem shut the door on her.

She found Charles outside the garage, already sitting in the Alfa-Romeo.

God! he looks grim, she thought. *He looks absolutely shattered.* As she opened the car door, he turned to her, unsmiling.

"If you've had second thoughts I can go alone, you know. I doubt if I'll have another black-out, I'm taking those tablets. Incidentally—a pity they aren't lethal."

Clem made no comment on this. She got in and slammed the door.

She thought that she could hear Lisa screaming for Sister Laurie as they moved down the drive, but it might have been her fancy. But what she did see, and she knew that Charles saw it too, was the silver bonnet of an enormous blue Rolls coming down the main road in the opposite direction from themselves—obviously heading for Lockbridge House.

Max Kern had arrived.

13

CLEM heard a church clock in the distance chime twelve o'clock as she completed her shopping, stacked her basket and then walked slowly past the Old Bell Hotel back to Hammond's cottage.

She hadn't forgotten anything, she hoped. She had made a list but come out without it—typical of her for the moment. All the worry of the last few months had definitely impaired her usually first-class memory.

Two steaks for lunch; salad, fresh fruit, cheese, bread, milk, and eggs and bacon for Charles's breakfast. There were a number of tinned things, including coffee and various soups, already in the larder, left there by Hammond. And a bottle of whisky, some gin and Italian and plenty of soda and tonic water which the generous Ham had begged her not to leave unopened.

Charles, pressing a five-pound note into Clem's hand when she went out, had said:

"Buy more whisky. I want it."

Apprehensively but with a smile that pretended this was quite in order, she had taken the money and left him.

"You shop," he had said. "I want to be quite alone for a bit."

She did not argue. She knew that such was his state of mind, it was best to do things just as he wanted. She had never seen him so stern, so bitter, so harshly dictatorial. So utterly unlike the genial, sweet-tempered man she knew. But of course—this was what the wretched Lisa had done to him. It was only what Clem had dreaded.

But she knew her Charles. She knew that once he recovered from the first shock he would be himself again, and possibly sweep everything out of his life but his work—his patients—the wish he had always had to help suffering humanity.

Just now Lisa was first and foremost on his mind. He must, she thought, both love and loathe her today.

Clem's own feelings were bad enough. She could hardly bear to look at Charles's taut colourless face. Yet she felt a surge of terrible joy at the thought that he needed her today—tonight—at least. He had not spoken one word during the drive to Hurley.

When she got back to the cottage, she found him drinking—as she had expected. Half of Hammond's new bottle of Vat 69 was empty. Charles was just pouring himself out a fresh glass when Clem walked into the beautiful book-filled room.

He sat huddled, round-shouldered, in the big Queen Anne winged armchair which was Ham's favourite. He nodded, unsmiling, at Clem.

"Hullo. Brought more whisky?"

"Yes," she said, and pulled the bottle from her basket and laid it on the table.

"Thanks."

She bit her lip and turned to go into the kitchen.

"I'll get some lunch going. How about a grilled steak?"

"Can't face food."

"Please, Charles —"

"I don't want it," he broke in roughly. He looked strange and wild-eyed, she thought. Her heart sank. He went on: "Have your own lunch and forget about me, please. I just want to get quietly, gloriously drunk."

She turned and looked at him with grave steady eyes.

"You *don't* often get drunk, do you, Charles?"

"Today I do."

"Charles, it isn't good for you."

"Don't please remind me about my blood pressure," he said with a harsh laugh. "I couldn't care less if I have a stroke."

She winced.

"And don't say that. It's too stupid. You wouldn't like a stroke. It can paralyse without killing, you know. You might just go on *feeling*."

"God forbid."

"Besides—it's unlike you to be so—so —" she stopped, awkwardly, and he laughed again and finished for her:

"So weak. Oh, you'd be surprised how weak I am. Tomorrow I can be strong. Tomorrow I'll try to show the world that I can take it on the chin. But let me be a weak, drivelling, snivelling imbecile today—will you, Clem?"

She had no answer. Her eyes filled with tears. He saw them.

"Don't cry for me, for God's sake. No emotion. I don't want it."

152

"Sorry," she said.

"Thanks, Clem, for coming along and looking after me," he added more gently. "But just don't take any notice of me. When you find me unconscious please leave me to sleep it off."

Another of those laughs that Clem found so dreadful.

"By the way, Clem, while you were out, I phoned home."

"What on earth for?" she asked, startled.

"I wanted to make sure that it was Lisa's charming millionaire in that Rolls, and that he'd taken over from me. I didn't want to leave her without a nurse or anyone."

Clem felt her throat was dry.

"How like you to be concerned about her even now."

He took a long drink of his whisky.

"Habit, my dear. And medical knowledge. She's not as fit as she may think. The wish was father to the thought, you know—her belief that she is quite ready to take a *tour-du-monde* with Mr. Kern. Believe me, she's still in need of nursing and the utmost care."

"You needn't worry. Mr. Kern was bringing a trained nurse with him and they were all going to fly straight to a private villa in Beaulieu."

Charles scowled into his glass.

"You're well informed."

"Lisa insisted on telling me the details. It became more and more unendurable, I assure you."

Charles shrugged and drank again.

"Oh, I don't care. Anyhow, Mr. Kern has done what he said he'd do, and turned up. Luigi spoke to me. Poor Luigi—he sounded a puzzled man. He said the Signora had gone off for a holiday with a gentleman and a new nurse, and that Sister Laurie had just departed by taxi for the station. *Gone for a holiday*—I thought that a nice touch!"

Another laugh. Clem shook her head and walked into the kitchen.

She wished Charles would eat something. It hurt her almost physically to think of him sitting by himself drinking one whisky after another. She tried to cook her own lunch but felt as unlike food as Charles. She put the two steaks in the 'fridge' and forced down a piece of cheese and a few biscuits. Then she drank two large cups of strong coffee.

She sat quietly in the tiny kitchen for a moment, smoking a cigarette. This whole thing was one hell of a nightmare, she thought. She pictured Lisa sitting in that Rolls—moving in stately luxury towards London; Max no doubt feasting his eyes on her incredible loveliness—astonished to see how little the air-crash had affected her looks, and moved to tenderness by the sight of her crippled condition. They would be holding hands—making their plans. The American nurse would be discreetly looking at the English countryside, thinking what a lot she would have to write home about.

They were driving direct to the Airport where Max's private plane and pilot waited for him.

Did they give one thought to the man who had been betrayed and left behind? Clem wondered. She was sure Lisa did not. She would be far too thrilled and excited at being with her lover again and—so she hoped—being given the chance to see all the finest orthopaedic surgeons on the Continent.

She had 'had' England and her English husband.

Max—the man—might make a few enquiries into the existing state of affairs—he might talk about Charles. Yes, Clem reflected bitterly. Hadn't Guy Grant said that in most divorce cases the co-respondent felt a shade more compunction about the unhappy husband than the wife who had left home.

"*God*," Clem kept saying softly to herself, "*God*—how could Lisa do it?"

She finished her cigarette, lit another, and drank more coffee. Then, unable to resist it, she walked softly into the sitting-room.

At first glance, she was almost relieved to find Charles lying back in his chair, fast asleep—even if it was a drunken sleep. His face glistened—his mouth was slack, his hair rough. All so unlike her Mr. Maddison, the well-groomed osteopath—the brisk, efficient, brilliant Charles in his Welbeck Street consulting-room.

The tears brimmed into Clem's eyes and began to drip in boundless grief down her cheeks. She tip-toed towards the sleeping man and took from his hand the empty glass he was still clutching.

Although her touch was so light, he felt it and stirred. He caught at her hand without opening his eyes, and said something under his breath which Clem could not hear. She said gently:

"Go on sleeping, dear Charles."

"I love you," he said thickly, and this time the blurred speech of the man who was well under the influence of the alcohol he had been steadily drinking, was plain enough to Clem. She blushed scarlet and tried to pull away from him.

"All right—all right—go back to sleep."

"God, how I love you! *I want you* . . . darling . . . darling . . ."

With sudden strength and purpose, Charles pulled her down until her body lay fully against his. His hands slipped from her waist to her slim hips. His lips pressed hard upon hers. It was for Clem an endless, dreadful yet incredibly magical kiss. After a moment he got up and stood there unsteadily for a second. Then with his arm around her, pulled her towards the yellow brocaded sofa which was on the other side of the fireplace.

Weakly her lips framed the words:

"No, Charles, no! . . ."

But he dragged her down and she lay against him, heart hammering, eyes shut. She began to stroke his hair, to strain closer to him.

He unzipped the blue linen dress, pulled it from her shoulder and kissed her breasts.

"Darling—darling—" he muttered.

At first her body rejected him. She drew back. Her lips stayed firmly shut. Then gradually the passion and warmth of his embrace and the terrible excitement of his kisses overcame her scruples. Nothing mattered to her except that she was wanted by him—desperately needed, here, in his arms, like this. For years she had been deeply in love with him. It was more than she could stand—this wild leaping of her blood—this frantic desire to respond to his passion. She pulled his head down to hers. Now her lips parted and they kissed wildly, with mad intensity. Clem's senses swam. Her body felt on fire with love and—despair. But just for a brief while she was his completely. He was hers. Nothing, nobody else in the world, counted.

Then suddenly Charles said in a hoarse whisper:

"*Lisa, Lisa, I love you. You were quite wonderful Lisa, my Lisa . . . kiss me again.*"

Clem lay against him—every nerve in her body quivering, her face white. The delight, the passion, the fire were gone—extinguished by his words, by that hated name.

She realised that in his stupor, his crazy delirious world, Charles had thought it was his wife whom he held in his arms.

The ashes of a bitterness as terrible as death replaced Clem's ardour. She pushed away the hands that were trying to take possession of her body again. She stood up, trembling violently.

She wanted to rush out of the room and hide. She *wanted* to die. She wanted to get away from Charles. She was furious and ashamed.

She wanted never to see him again — this man whom she loved better than life itself.

But before she could so much as brush back the hair that had come unpinned and was tumbling down her back, Charles was awake again — completely in possession of his senses now. He blinked at her. He was red with confusion and remorse.

"Oh, my God," he muttered, "Clem . . . my dear . . . it was *you*."

"Yes, it was me," she whispered.

"Clem, Clem," he repeated her name as though overcome.

"It . . . didn't matter. I . . . know . . . you didn't realise . . . it."

He stared with deep dismay at her flowing untidy hair, the unzipped dress which she was trying to pull over her shoulders, and her unhappy young face.

"Clem," he said, "forgive me. I was out of my mind."

"I'd rather you didn't apologise. It makes things worse."

"I was out of my mind," he repeated. "Too much to drink, I'm afraid."

"I was fully aware of it . . ."

He went on staring at her. His eyes were red-rimmed, his head ached.

"Why in God's name didn't you crack me over the head and bring me to my senses."

With all her jagged nerves jumping and the agony of her humiliation past bearing, she faced him squarely. The words rushed out:

"Because I love you, you fool. Oh, you fool, Charles! I've always loved you. I know it's absurd and that you loved Lisa, and now it's all a ghastly mess. All my fault, actually," she added in a lower note, "I *could* have cracked you over the head, as you said, but I didn't want to. D'you hear? You needn't be so sorry for losing your self-control. I lost mine, and willingly. Now will you stop apologising please? You've got enough on your mind. So have I, if it comes to that."

Charles rose unsteadily to his feet. He stayed there, looking down into Clem's big brown eyes. They were so brave, so honest, he thought. Like Clem herself. Very brave. Very honest. And very generous. She wouldn't even let him take the blame for the outrageous way he had behaved. As his brain grew clearer, he found himself well able to remember holding and kissing her without restraint. And he remembered, too, her complete response. He

156

realised that what she had given to him had been given with all her heart; all her loyalty and love. A love such as his beautiful, glamorous wife was incapable of giving any man.

At last he drew a long breath.

"Clem—you leave me absolutely nothing to say if I am not allowed to make an apology."

"Well, you're not," she snapped and tried without success to retrieve the fallen combs and pins from the carpet and put up her hair. He noticed suddenly how attractive she looked like this, in such confusion, and with that dark hair tumbled around her flushed face. She looked touchingly young and vulnerable.

"Clem," he said, "I shall always remember your sweetness—your comfort. Darling, you *have* comforted me—I assure you. You've saved me from God knows what depths of misery. If you hadn't come here with me and taken care of me I tremble to think what might have happened to me."

That was some consolation for her. She even found it possible to recover her sense of humour.

"Okay, we comforted each other."

He shook his head.

"Really, you've more kindness and generosity in one of your little fingers than most of us have got in our whole bodies."

"Nonsense. Look, Charles—I'm going to make you some strong coffee. For God's sake don't start on that whisky again while I'm gone."

"I won't. I don't want any more. I'm sorry I behaved so stupidly . . . drinking the damned stuff when we first got down here."

"I daresay it helped," she said dryly.

He came closer and put his hands on her shoulders.

"Clem, what a darling you are! How can I thank you enough for saying that you love me. I don't deserve it."

"Shut up, Charles."

"You can't ask me to 'shut up' saying that sort of thing. I *am* deeply grateful for your love."

She made no answer but stared miserably downwards.

He shook her gently.

"Clem, look at me."

"No. I want to make the coffee. Let me go. You look ghastly."

"Thanks—so do you," he said and laughed.

Now they both laughed. But there were tears on Clem's lashes. Charles saw them glisten and suddenly caught and held her—not with passion but with great tenderness, hiding her face against his shoulder, stroking her hair.

"Clem, Clem, thank you for loving me and for being so marvellous about everything. You've always been good to me. When Lisa told me her plans this morning the bottom dropped out of my world. But it isn't nearly such a dark lonely world as it might have been if you were not in it."

Joy and relief flooded her heart. She hugged him to her and wept. He kissed her head again and tried to comfort her.

"Don't cry for me, darling. I'll get over it. And I promise you I won't let this sort of mood conquer me again."

"That's a pity," she laughed hysterically, "I—rather liked it, didn't I?"

"Oh, Clem darling, I mean I won't *drink* any more. Not another drop. It was shameful of me. But I felt if I didn't black everything out for a few hours, I'd go round the bend."

"I understand."

"You certainly do. You're terrific. And when I said I'd never let the mood conquer me again I meant the *drinking*—*not* holding you —like this!"

Her tears went on flowing but she tried to laugh again.

"Like this—well—it's very sweet, Big Brother. But I know it means nothing else. You thought just now that I was Lisa."

"Darling Clem, I wasn't fully awake and certainly not quite sane, but if you want the truth, I don't want ever to see my wife again. If she asks for a divorce she can have one. She and her boy-friend can go to hell so far as I'm concerned. And that is *that*!"

"Oh dear!" said Clem and took refuge in the kitchen where she brewed some really black coffee for Charles. She heard him running the bath upstairs. She imagined he would appreciate a hot relaxing bath now that the immersion heater had had time to act. She took a chance and grilled a steak, hoping now he would eat it.

He did. He came down from his bath, wearing slacks and a sports shirt, his hair damp, waving in consequence. He looked very pale and strained but a good deal better. He sat in the kitchen with Clem and ate his rather late lunch. To her satisfaction he ended up with cheese and biscuits.

"I feel quite good now, thanks to you," he said, sitting back to light one of his favourite cigars.

As the rich aroma curled towards Clem, she enjoyed it and enjoyed the sight of him sitting there with her under these homely

158

conditions. His gaze met hers. A rather long intimate look passed between them—a look such as they had never before exchanged. Her pulse-beats quickened to a race. She looked quickly away. She thought: *Things can never really be the same between us now. Oh, God, I love him so much. I must go away—right away from him no matter how tempted I am to stay.*

But she couldn't go. He unconsciously forced her hand by telling her, once that meal had ended, that he could not carry on without her. He spoke frankly and with sincerity.

"I fully realise that in a case like this where two people rather lose their heads, they usually feel it best to pack things in and clear out of each other's lives. But unless you hate me now—please stay with me, Clem. I give you my solemn word I won't—I won't —" he stammered and cleared his throat. "I mean I won't lose my head again."

Clem remained silent a moment. Her heart beats slowed down. She felt unhappy again.

"I don't want to leave if you really need me, Charles —" she began, "but —"

"No 'buts'—unless you loathe the sight of me."

"Oh, Charles, don't be silly," she said irritably, "I happen to be much fonder of you than I ought to be. My only legitimate reason for quitting."

"Well, don't leave me because of that. I'm so deeply grateful for your love," he began.

She broke in:

"I *hate* gratitude. Please forget everything. I will, too, and I'll do everything I can to see you through the next few months, anyhow."

His eyes—those light blue, extraordinarily sweet eyes, held hers. She felt a thickness in her throat and hurriedly got up and began to wash the dishes. He grabbed a tea-towel and dried up. She thought: *How domestic, how touching, how normal we are being now—like an old married couple. But if the truth be told he still loves Lisa and I adore him—oh, how I adore him!*

More than ever now, after they had been so close. Oh, God, if she lived to be an old, old woman, she would remember that sad, passionate embrace; the caress of his hands; the madness of their kisses.

She said briskly:

"Thanks for helping me. What are you going to do now?"

"Write one or two personal letters if you could find me some

159

notepaper. There are one or two people I must write to about Lisa, including her mother, I suppose, although I expect Lisa is sure to phone those two in Florida."

"Can I help with the mail?"

"No—they are letters I must write myself."

As she passed him on her way into the sitting-room, he caught hold of her right hand and kissed it.

"Thank you, dear Clem, for so many things."

"Oh, go to hell!" she said in a strangled voice but immediately said, "Sorry. I'm a bit on edge. I'll go up and have a nap while you're writing, if that's okay by you."

He took his cigar from his lips and looked at the fine ash. His face was very troubled. He was thinking how immensely sad it was that little Clem should be in love with him. Surprising—and even tragic. If Lisa had never come into his life, he might have grown to love Clem, she was charming and good to him. So much more worth while than Lisa. Strangely enough, he felt no love for Lisa now. Nothing but a terrible void. A dark, bitter nothingness.

Later while Charles drank his coffee, Clem sat with him and they talked—as the good friends they were, fundamentally. Neither one referred now to the cataclysm that had swamped them an hour ago. They were completely controlled—able to look at one another without any show of embarrassment. Quietly they discussed the present predicament; the affairs of the past when Clem had first come to Charles to work for him; his marriage—and hers. They spoke frankly, without making any effort to keep their views secret from each other. He seemed quite clear-minded now—rational—the old Charles she knew so well. He spoke of his first crazy love for Lisa. It had been a deep warm love that had sprung from the roots of their early passion which she had seemed to return so happily. Looking at Clem with puzzled eyes, Charles asked:

"Why did she ever marry me? She was a world-famous model—a star in her way. She had other richer men after her. What made her marry *me*? I warned her that I couldn't give her a very glamorous existence. What *was* it, Clem?"

"Chemical reaction between you—that 'something' nobody can ever explain. You have always had it for women, Charles—you know that. And Lisa fell in love with you—the brilliant attractive osteopath who happens also to be a very attractive man."

His lips took a downward curve.

"And afterwards?"

160

"She was easily bored. Perhaps she didn't realise that she needed fresh excitement and attention all the time. She may have genuinely believed she wanted to settle down with you. You were busy—you tried, I know, never to neglect her. And you didn't. But you love your work and you had to go on with it so you were sympathetic with her. You let her go abroad with her friends. You trusted her. And well—then—she met Max Kern."

"Millionaire and playboy. German blood. Thinks his dollars can buy anything—it seems they can," said Charles with a bitterness that hurt Clem.

"It's difficult for you to understand it and accept it just now—when it's all so fresh," she said. "But one day you'll realise it is for the best. As time went on, Lisa could never have made you happy—not for much longer, anyhow. She belongs to Max Kern's crowd, not to yours."

"I wanted nothing but to help her—save her—with my love—my medical learning—everything. It wasn't enough, was it?"

"No, Charles."

He gave a brief laugh.

"Well, it's all over. She's in the sun now. She loved the sun—the glamour of France or Italy. She'll be in Kern's luxury villa, with everything dollars or francs can buy. Maybe she's happier now than she could ever have been with me. Maybe I was wrong to expect her to be satisfied with Lockbridge House and just me rushing down to amuse her when I wasn't too busy."

Clem winced.

"Don't think that way. Don't belittle anything you did for her. You couldn't have done more. You've nearly killed yourself in the effort."

"Pity I didn't finish the job."

"That," said Clem, "is perfectly beastly of you and you know it!"

He got up—moved to the back of her chair, leaned down and dropped a kiss on her hair.

"Dear, marvellous Clem. You look after me, bully me, preach to me—and you're so much nicer to me than you ought to be. *Dear* Clem!"

She was glad he could not see her face—or know how she longed to rush into his arms again—be held, kissed, made mad love to. She loved and wanted him desperately. She said:

"It's four o'clock. Like a walk along the river?"

"No, we're going home," he said.

She turned to him, startled.

"Home?"

"Yes. Back to Hungerford. Let's go up and re-pack our bags. We won't stay here tonight."

She went suddenly scarlet.

"Surely you don't mean because—because —" she stopped, floundering for words, hideously embarrassed. He cut in:

"I know what you mean. Indirectly, perhaps, yes. But primarily because I have come to my senses. I feel as though I've been through a kind of mental storm. I'm through, thanks to you. I oughtn't to have run away from Lockbridge in the first place. I ought to have stayed and faced that damned fellow she's gone off with. I don't know. But I do think I behaved badly by rushing off, and still worse by allowing you in your kindness of heart, to come here with me."

She stayed silent. She felt cold and sick at heart. He was right of course, but it hurt her . . . shockingly . . . to hear him attribute her motives in coming to Hurley with him as 'kindness of heart'. Didn't he realise yet that she had come because she loved him more than life itself? But she let him do the talking.

"One should face up to one's troubles. Clearing out with you like that was the action of a defeatist. I've always despised defeatists. And you're so very brave and sweet, Clem—I'm damned if I'm going to take any more gifts from you. Come on—drive me if you like—back to Hungerford. We'll settle things up and you can take a few days off with your friends, perhaps, and I'll get hold of a doctor friend of mine who is on holiday from Australia. You haven't met him. He's a nice fellow and on his own in town. I'll ask him to stay with me down at Lockbridge until I feel a bit fitter. I don't want this blood pressure to get me right down. I want to go back to work on Monday. Will you still work for me?" he added the question, holding out a hand, smiling with all the irresistible charm that had conquered Clem from the beginning. She found herself taking that hand and shaking it. Her eyes were blind with tears. She whispered:

"Okay."

He gave a deep sigh.

"Good. I feel better. We'll treat today as though it hasn't happened. And you're dead right. I know now that Lisa would never have been happy with me nor I with her if she'd stayed. I'll try to let her go without bitterness."

'Treat today as though it hasn't happened'—Clem could hardly bear that. She knew he didn't mean to be cruel, but . . .

162

She ran up the stairs to her bedroom. She had to exert her strength not to break down and cry. She wondered if all men, including Charles and poor dead Tony—*all of them*—were alike. Made in a completely different mould from women—able to swing so quickly, so easily, from violent emotion to dead calm. Did they all find it easy to enjoy an hour of passionate love, then package it, and replace it on the shelf, and turn to the *Financial Times*? That, she laughed hysterically to herself, was exaggeration. But it was how things appeared to her today—this strange, mad unforgettable day. Lisa had left Charles. Charles had needed *her*—but only for an hour or two. Now she must go back to being his secretary and friend—back to work—to the slipped discs, the dislocated limbs, all the routine work at Welbeck Street.

When Clem went downstairs she found Charles outside ready and waiting, putting his bag in the Alfa. He looked composed. He even had a faint smile for her. She was determined to be immensely controlled now.

"Just a moment, Charles. I must act the good little housewife and stick the milk and butter in a basket and take them with us. Saves a shilling or two —" she laughed, a dreary laugh.

"Good lord, I wouldn't have thought of that," said Charles.

She laughed to herself again.

He was a man—he would not think of so many things that a woman thinks of. She was perilously near to tears again as she went into the kitchen. Feverishly she made everything as tidy as possible, resolving to come back and give Ham's little house a good clean once Charles was safely installed with his doctor friend, and no longer in need of her vigilance.

She had one wild moment of wondering whether she ought to hand in her resignation as his secretary—now—at once. How could she go on and on, pretending that nothing had happened between them?

How could she? Yet how could she leave him? It was a frightful impasse.

14

THE fortnight that followed seemed to Clem both hateful and unreal. She went through a bad patch after that day at Hurley—the day which stood out in her mind as one of the most fantastic and revealing of her life.

Charles suggested that she should stay that first night back at Lockbridge, but she refused. This seemed to upset him.

"You're not afraid of me, are you? You don't think I'll take to the whisky bottle again?"

She flared at him:

"Don't please associate what happened to—to us—with your ruddy whisky drinking! It's insulting. Do I take it that you only made love to me because you weren't sober?"

Almost immediately she said the words, she regretted them. A look of such pain, such awful embarrassment came across Charles's face.

"Oh, my God!" he groaned. "Of course not. For heaven's sake don't misconstrue what I said. I just wondered if you were leaving me tonight because you didn't dare be left alone with me."

She said wildly:

"This is getting out of hand. Surely neither of us wants to be alone with the other. Let's be sensible."

"Darling," he said, and the endearment slipped out unconsciously. "Darling little Clem. Please believe that what happened between us may well have flared up originally from the fact that I had had too much to drink. But I was pretty sober at the end, you know. You must believe that I found you very, very sweet and generous, and what love there was left in me, I gave to you."

"Okay," she said stupidly, like a child, and rushed out of the room.

There had been no further mention of the episode between them. He had been very gentle and attentive to her, very friendly and she had felt such love for him that it threatened to drive all common-sense out of her. But somehow she managed to keep her head above water. Once they were at Lockbridge, she presented a bright face to

Luigi and Carmella, giving them orders, telling them to look after the Signor when she left. They were obviously puzzled and astonished by the sudden return of the Signor and the secretary. And Clem could imagine how they must have speculated and gossiped about the beautiful Signora's departure with the gentleman in the Rolls-Royce. But they did not seem unduly troubled. They were Italians—used to dramas, tears and scenes—to swift passionate loves and hatreds. Why worry because their English employers seemed to be cut in the same pattern. It was not true, they decided, that the English were cold and unemotional.

An exhausted Clem finally took the train to London later that night. Charles drove her to the station. She had felt miserable, yet exalted by the memory of one particular thing he had said to her. At least she had that to hold on to.

'What love there was left in me I gave to you.'

She could believe that. She was glad, even though he would never give such love to her again.

She would have to be *very* careful if she didn't want their association to break up altogether. He was so important to her as a friend.

Her flat seemed horribly empty and sad. She kept thinking about Charles. She could not resist making a telephone call to him much later to see if he was all right.

She almost sobbed with relief when he said:

"To tell you the truth, I've been for a long walk. The air was so fresh. I'm pretty tired now and I'm just off to bed early. Yes, I'm fine. Don't worry any more. Sleep well, Clem, and thank you again. Thank you, my *very* dear Clem."

She put the receiver down, threw herself on the bed and cried until she could cry no more. But at least she knew that whatever Lisa and life had done to him, he had risen above it now.

Charles rang her the next day to tell her his Australian friend, Dr. Miller, had arrived at Hungerford, and was staying with him for the rest of the week.

"He's the most interesting, entertaining fellow, Dick Miller. We took our degrees together. He's done a lot since and had a somewhat checkered married life—rather like my own. His wife left him. I don't believe doctors make good husbands," Charles ended with a short laugh.

"They make wonderful husbands if you're thinking of Mr. Maddison," she said.

"My loyal supporter—if I were a politician and you were canvassing for me, I'd be sure to get a seat in Parliament."

Clem began to feel better about him. His humour had returned. And because of this she felt less unhappy herself. She was sure that the Australian would be a good tonic for Charles.

Unable to bear London alone after all that had happened, she spent the morning at Welbeck Street, answered some letters, paid some accounts, then thought suddenly:

I wonder what Charles wants done with all the things Lisa's left behind.

She phoned him that evening by arrangement, to discuss the mail. He had a ready answer to her problem.

"Lisa called me from Beaulieu late last night. Typical of her . . ." he gave a harsh little laugh. "She woke me up at midnight. Apparently she was just giving a party. All the other millionaires and their wives had come to meet her. She really is a fantastic character, Clem. She's so egotistical and callous—one can't really judge her as an ordinary human being. She seems extremely happy—being petted and adored, and so on. She was seen by a Professor Something-or-other from Paris this morning. He is certain that he knows another Professor Something-or-other in Vienna who will help speed up Lisa's mobility. Mind you, I don't believe a word of it, but she does, so she's happy. And no doubt Mr Kern thinks he is succeeding where the English husband failed."

"Oh, damn Mr. Kern!" broke from Clem angrily.

"Don't let's mind him. Lisa ended by telling me that all the things she left behind both in Welbeck Street and down here—her clothes and shoes and bags, etc., are out of date, and would you please dispose of them. She wants nothing that I gave her, she says. She took her emeralds with her by the way."

"Those lovely emeralds you gave her for your first anniversary," exclaimed Clem, shocked.

"Oh, well, I gave them to her. Jewels don't really matter much, neither does money—let's face it."

"They certainly wouldn't to me," muttered Clem in a voice Charles didn't hear.

He instructed her to get all Lisa's personal possessions out of the way before he returned to Welbeck Street.

"But what about the Black Diamond mink coat? I know that's still at the furriers," said Clem. "She asked them to clean and store

166

it in April. It was her wedding present from you. She told me about it."

An instant's pause, then from Charles:

"I'll send you a chit so that you can get it back. It was a nice coat. She looked superb in it. The famous Michel at Chiberta chose it for her. Ask him where I can sell it. I'll use the cash to buy that new X-ray plant I've had my eye on."

"You should have had that years ago," muttered Clem.

He laughed and rang off, but Clem was unhappy for him. How *could* Lisa telephone from the South of France to tell him how happy *she* was! On the other hand, if he believed her he might write her off entirely. He was a proud man. He couldn't surely go on grieving for such a shallow, worthless person. Perhaps he'd set the machinery running for a divorce. Although of course, Lisa hadn't even asked for one. She was a queer fish.

Clem took a day off and drove down to the cottage at Hurley to 'tidy up'. She was so afraid that if something happened to bring Ham back from his trip abroad earlier than expected, he would go down there and find ashtrays full, the kitchen in disorder, with empty bottles and tins lying around. She wouldn't want that.

Once there, she looked round the sitting-room with considerable feeling. It was all so beautiful and peaceful here on this sunny summer's morning. Ham's exquisite furniture, and the books that she had arranged for him, looked lovely. But it was on the winged Queen Anne armchair that her gaze lingered; and the deep-cushioned brocaded sofa. She had to clench her hands and shut her eyes in order to keep from breaking down. There, in Charles's arms, she had experienced unimagined ecstasy; and profound despair.

"Oh, Charles—*Charles!*" she said his name aloud.

After putting things in order, she locked the house up and drove straight back to London. There she spent an exceedingly unattractive few hours in Welbeck Street, sorting Lisa's possessions.

It took her all of three hours to pack up the beautiful dresses, hats, shoes and lingerie, and the many other expensive possessions that Mrs. Charles Maddison had left behind as though they counted for nothing. She felt a faint disgust as she caught the odour of Lisa's particular perfume. She could hardly bear to handle her clothes. She would give some of them to Carmella, she decided, and send the rest to be sold.

She looked around the big luxurious bedroom with the huge wardrobes, built especially for her. God, she thought, some women were never satisfied. Charles must have spent a small fortune on extravagances for his wife.

She looked, also, at the big wide divan. She pictured Lisa's voluptuous body lying there in Charles's arms; the rich red hair spread upon the pillow; the laughing, treacherous face reaching up for his kisses.

Clem hurled a pair of shoes across the bed in childish rage, then picked them up.

"That's right, Clementine. Give yourself an extra backache. How stupid can you get? Pull yourself together."

The next morning she dealt with Lisa's furs. She thought how macabre it all was really, as though Charles's wife had died in that crash. It made her feel sick.

She found little jewellery. What had been left was of no great value to Lisa now that she was living with a man who could spend a fortune on her. Clem locked her case and took the remaining valuables downstairs to Charles's safe.

She spent that weekend with the Grants. But even there with her friends, she found trouble. Timothy had to be rushed to hospital at the double, with a sudden attack of appendicitis. During the next twenty-four hours, Clem was holding the hands of the parents who were obsessed with the fear that their lovely little boy was going to die. Of course he didn't. He survived in the hands of one of the best surgeons in Great Ormond Street and two days later was sitting up in bed laughing and demanding his favourite toys.

Once again Clem found herself envying children with their resilience, their blissful ignorance of life—the pure joy that belongs only to extreme youth.

Charles came back to London. Work started again. Clem found him looking better although he was still too thin and haggard to please her. But a lot of his natural energy had returned, and he had a good report from his doctor. If he kept on like this, Bill said, his blood pressure would soon be normal again.

They had a busy week. Charles threw himself into his osteopathy with more than his usual vigour. But at the end of each day he looked, to Clem, exhausted.

What he was suffering underneath the façade of 'couldn't care less', Clem wasn't sure, but he gradually was becoming capable of discussing his wife without much emotion. She had been gone for over a month. It was now the first week of September.

"It's strange being a bachelor again," Charles told Clem one afternoon after the last patient had gone and the Welbeck Street house was quiet.

"It must be," she said and handed him the day's letters to sign.

He looked up at her suddenly—a look which she found quite astonishingly full of tenderness.

"I remember the first day you ever came to work for me, Clem. It was in September, actually, wasn't it?"

She was pleased that he remembered.

"Yes, it was —" she said.

"You weren't fussed and all over the place like so many girls on their first day at a job," he went on. "I thought how intelligent, how cool you seemed."

"I'm neither, really," she said, laughing.

"You're very sweet," he said, not for the first time, "and thank you for all the work you've done these last few weeks. By the by, I went into Lisa's bedroom today. It all looks very empty. It made me shiver."

"I wish you'd move from here," Clem exclaimed with sudden feeling.

"Dear me, no! My job's in Welbeck Street and here I remain. The only thing I might do at the end of this year—not before—is to go back to living in my little bachelor flat on the ground-floor and let the upstairs part again. I don't really need those big reception rooms."

"You might want them —" Clem began, and then stopped, embarrassed.

He cut in, dryly, without emotion:

"You think Lisa might come back?"

That wasn't at all what she had been thinking. She had been wondering if he would meet some beautiful sympathetic woman in the future and decide to marry again. It was a sudden shock to Clem to contemplate even the faintest possibility that *Lisa* would return to Charles. She supposed she ought to want it—but it made her shudder. Lisa could never make him happy. Lisa could never be any good to him. Her nature was such that she would exhaust any man she lived with; even Max Kern mightn't want her after a while, although of course, he was not a professional man. He had plenty of time to hang round her. He might be able to cope with her exigence, her egotism. He must be much the same sort himself.

"Lisa won't come back," she heard Charles say very quietly.

"Funnily enough that's one thing I am sure of. Perhaps you'd like to see this —"

He tossed a letter across the desk. Clem knew that it had come — she had seen it and left it unopened, after sorting the rest of his mail. She had recognised Lisa's big loopy handwriting and the gaudy French stamp.

With slightly quickened heart-beats she read what Lisa had written:

> Charles dear, I don't want you to think that I never give you a thought just because I am enjoying my new life so much. I fully realise how good you were to me and what an ungrateful creature you must think me but because you always wanted me to be happy I feel you would like to know that I AM. Max is stupendous. I can't describe it but he has a kind of magic for me and I am quite bewitched and he says I have the same effect on him. He hasn't let my crippled condition make any difference. I think it's so marvellous that Fate has allowed me to be so much loved by two such wonderful men as you and Max. Meanwhile I hope you're all right and your good little Clem is looking after you properly. The professor from Vienna arrived and I've started new treatment. I've asked him to let me have the whole thing on paper in medical language so that I can send it to you, as I know you'll be professionally interested.

Clem looked up from this letter, her big brown eyes flashing.

"We-ell, I don't *know* . . . *really* !"

"Her egotism has always been stupendous," said Charles, tapping his blotter with the end of his pen. He looked at Clem with a smile midway between amusement and irony. Clem snorted.

" 'Professionally interested' — *h'm*. She has no thought for what you *feel*."

"None whatsoever," said Charles coolly. "I'm now beginning to realise that I married a very beautiful robot."

"Well, good luck to her," muttered Clem, "and let's hope all the Herr Professors do more than you and Trevor-Johns *and* Stoke Mandeville."

"I find so many patients are attracted by the mistaken idea that Herr Professors know more than British doctors," said Charles.

"There's another line in that letter I don't like," said Clem giving it back to him. "That bit about 'your good little Clem'."

170

Now he gave her an endearing smile.

"That's the only correct note Lisa struck. You *are* my good little Clem."

"I'm not," she said and walked out of the room, slamming the door, which made him blink. It also pulled him up with a jerk to the full realisation that his hard-working little secretary was by no means yet *herself*.

She was still the feminine soft responsive girl to whom he had made such mad love down at Hurley.

Did he remember that hour with guilt, with shame or with a gratitude that was deeper than passion and much more lasting? He hardly knew. But he could never forget that uncontrolled hour, nor thank her enough for loving him, and for telling him that she did. He was so fond of her; but he had meant what he had said down there: 'that there was no room left in his heart now for love'. That heart that Lisa had broken felt as empty as the grave.

It was odd, but after today he found it difficult to look at Clem without a touch of embarrassment; of *remembering*. For he had hoped she had gone back to being the old self-possessed business-like little person she used to be. He hadn't worried about her until today. He was puzzled. He wondered how she would appear when he saw her tomorrow. She seemed as cool and normal as ever, so once more he stopped worrying about Clem.

September slipped into October—there was autumn coolness in the air now. Lisa's letters continued to come at intervals. She even had the audacity to telephone her husband. Clem took the call. She told Clem that she wanted to speak to Charles. But he sent back a message that he hoped she was better but did not wish to speak to her.

Lisa was annoyed.

The all-too-well-remembered voice said, peevishly, to Clem:

"Oh, I wish Charles were not so *conventional*! I was going to ask him to come out and have a holiday with us. It's superb in this lovely villa and we're having the most *gorgeous* weather."

Praying for patience, Clem quietly pointed out that Charles was not the type of man who would take kindly to a *ménage à trois*, no matter how glorious the villa or the weather.

"Oh, that's the stupid side of Charles that I never could stand," came from Lisa. "Thank God Max isn't narrow-minded and old-fashioned."

Clem shut her mouth tightly.

171

"Clem—are you there—did you hear what I said?"

"I heard."

"As usual I suppose, you hate me and are full of concern for Charles."

"Do you mind if I ring off?" asked Clem, "I'm terribly busy and another patient has just come."

"Well, thank goodness *I'm* not there —" began Lisa rudely.

Clem, feeling equally impolite, rang off.

Charles did not ask what Lisa had had to say. The call from Beaulieu was not mentioned. No further calls were made for a time. But a nasty little note came from Florida, from Lisa's mother.

> I just want you to know that I am thankful my poor beautiful girl is now in her element with a man like Max Kern who will be able to do everything for her.
>
> Both Wally and I think you were very rude to us when we were in London and I'm glad we don't have to meet any more. I presume you will be suing Lisa for divorce so I need no longer consider myself your mother-in-law . . .

Charles seemed genuinely amused rather than annoyed by this letter.

"I like the bit about her 'poor beautiful girl'. They quarrelled like mad when Mrs. Cain was over here. *Was* I very rude to her and that dreadful young man she married?"

"I think you had one or two slight misunderstandings," Clem smiled back, "but you won't let what Mrs. Cain says worry you, *I'm* sure."

"I will not. Max can take over from me and good luck to him. I am sure Lisa's father was one of the best but her mother really is a detestable woman."

Clem sighed.

"You look tired," said Charles suddenly.

"I'm not," she lied.

"Well, I think you ought to take a holiday."

"I don't want one. I had a week off while you were at Hungerford."

"A week off—clearing up after Lisa and doing jobs for me? You've had no holiday at all."

"Yes, I have."

"When do you give up the keys of the Hurley cottage?"

She looked away from him.

"I think Ham's coming back this weekend."

"Why don't you run down there now for forty-eight hours and get some real rest, Clem?"

Almost her pain-filled heart made her cry out:

"And take you with me? And let us be together as we were . . . oh, dear, dear God, how much I would like that!"

Instead she spoke in a tart voice:

"Don't try and get rid of me, please. Like you, I'm happier working—I can't bear doing nothing."

He did not try to make her alter her mind. Secretly he did not want to make her go. He never felt as secure, yes that was the word, *secure*, about everything connected with his life and his work, when Clem was away.

Then suddenly he said:

"Hammond Portal wants to marry you, doesn't he?"

She coloured and her lashes flicked up and down nervously.

"Not exactly—I mean—I believe he told my friends, the Grants, that he does. But I don't want to encourage it. I don't want to marry him."

"But you like him—I mean he's a very cultured interesting man and rather nice-looking, if I remember right."

"Very nice-looking. We call him The Emperor. Very intelligent and full of charm. I just don't happen to want to marry him," said Clem icily.

"Well, that suits me," said Charles.

For a moment her breathing quickened and her colour came and went, then she cooled down. Of course, he didn't mean anything except that it would suit him not to lose an efficient secretary.

"Okay," she said, "I'm not considering marriage for the second time or of asking for my cards, as they call it nowadays."

"Okay! I love the way you say that."

She walked to the door, turned back and made a face at him.

"We're all so Americanised. Quite frankly, I hate the word *okay* yet I go on using it."

Charles started to take off his white coat. He said:

"You must come and have an evening out with me soon, Clem. I meant to ask you if you would like to do a theatre tonight, but I've been let in for a party by Dick Miller."

"You'll enjoy that," said Clem politely.

"Possibly. His mother and sister flew in from Sydney this morning. He's holding the party actually for the young sister. I don't know what her Christian name really is—he calls her Midget, I believe.

"What on earth for?"

"Oh, he says she's very small and has huge eyes. Nineteen and smaller than you, from his description."

"She must be fascinating," said Clem in the same frozen voice.

Charles suddenly realised that Clem wasn't pleased about something, neither had she any interest in Dick Miller's sister. Then another idea shot into his head. *She might be jealous.* That struck him first of all as being comical, then disturbing.

"See you tomorrow—goodnight, my dear," he said.

"Goodnight. Have a good time," she returned.

On her way back to her flat she reproached herself for being all kinds of an idiot. What on earth had possessed her to be so catty about this Midget, or whatever they chose to call her. Possibly it would do Charles good—a party with a sweet little nineteen-year-old from Sydney. She knew from experience that Midget would like him. Young girls always fell for the handsome, blue-eyed osteopath. Yes, it would do Charles good—it was a long time since he had been to a party. During all those long weeks and months of Lisa's illness and convalescence, he had done nothing but sit at her bedside, or work. Besides, he must have lost a lot of his self-esteem when Lisa left him. The more pretty women he met who could flatter and flirt with him, the better. He needed cherishing.

The tears came into Clem's tired eyes. She squeezed them back. As soon as she got home she rang up a friend and deliberately went out with her to a film which she didn't really want to see. But she couldn't sit down and let her imagination continue to run riot. She hated the thought of a pretty curly-haired Australian girl out with Charles. He might find her attractive. Of course, he might find other women attractive, too. She, Clem, had no exclusive rights to him—none at all.

15

THE month of October was not a very memorable one for Clem. As she wryly told herself, it was rather more full of bad than good. But that was the way life went. There was a good vein—then a bad one; good luck—bad luck, all mixed up. But she had to admit that a kind of avalanche seemed to have descended on her thoroughly flattening her, since Tony died.

Until then she had been living a very simple sort of life, really. Whenever she looked back she was astonished how simple and uneventful it had been. Not that the disturbing memory of Charles Maddison had not always been present deep down in her heart, even though she had tried to abstract her mind.

When Tony was alive at least she could feel a certain security. Now it was as though she was always afraid something was going to happen and that the something was bound to be trouble. A poor mental state which she knew she should get on top of—quickly. At the bottom of everything of course was the primary fear that she might have to go away from Charles. Only the other day when she was with the Grants, Pat had said:

"You mightn't like to hear this, honey, but you're looking years older—like thirty rather than twenty-something. There are new lines around your beautiful eyes and it's all because of Charles Maddison. I wish you'd let up—stop working for him—anything —but Guy and I don't like to see you reduced to this."

Indignantly Clem argued that her appearance had nothing to do with Charles and it was all due to the mad modern pace of living and working today, and the fact that she'd never really been herself since Tony died. Pat had said no more but looked sceptical. Clem felt a hypocrite. But that night when she looked at her tired eyes which did indeed have shadows around them, she grimaced and said:

"*Pat's dead right, my girl, you're beginning to lose your youth!*"

But leave Charles? Never. Pat just didn't know—*could never know.*

Now that Hammond Portal was back in town he pursued her

with a persistence which she knew could only mean that he was seriously in love. He was upset because she refused to join the Grants and go down with them to stay at Hurley. She kept making excuses. She couldn't bear to go into that cottage again. It held too many heart-shaking memories.

Of course the day came when The Emperor actually proposed to her. He took her out to dinner—to one of his favourite West End restaurants where he had ordered a gourmet's meal with exquisite hock which he said he was sure she needed; she looked so tired. She snapped at him:

"You and Pat—*really!* Always telling me how tired I look. Most unflattering. What it really means is I look a hag."

Hammond's large eyes smiled at her.

"My dear child—you are a child to me—you could never look a hag or anything but delicious, and I find you a most stimulating companion."

"Heavens knows why!"

Then of course it all came out—he told her that he had fallen in love with her and wanted to marry her. She had hoped this wouldn't happen. It would destroy their friendship. She had grown fond of The Emperor and couldn't deny that evenings out with him were extremely pleasant and that she found him just as stimulating—if not more so—than he must find her. Gently she told him that it was impossible for her to accept his offer, flattered and grateful though she was.

The Emperor looked shaken. Little Clem with her large brown intelligent eyes, her quick perspective mind, her lovely promising young mouth, added to the fact that she had already been married, and was an experienced woman as well as a girl, still young, had captured Hammond Portal's heart.

"Is it because I've been too previous—I mean—I know it's hardly a year since you lost your husband and —"

"No," she broke in, "it isn't that. Tony would like me to marry again but —"

"But not me," it was Hammond's turn to interrupt. He sat back in his chair and sighed deeply, fingering his hock-glass.

"You've been awfully good to me—you're a wonderful friend," she said, "I feel so awful about it, Ham."

"My dear girl, you don't have to feel that way. One can't love to order. I suppose it's this osteopath fellow you love. Pat thinks so. You are in love with him, aren't you?"

176

The colour burned her cheeks.

"Yes, but I shan't marry him, either."

"You mean it hasn't reached that point—he isn't divorced yet?"

"No. But that's not why I won't marry Charles. He doesn't happen to be in love with me."

"I'm surprised. To see you every day and not love you—*mon Dieu*—is our Mr. Maddison deaf and blind?"

"Oh, Ham," Clem laughed sadly, "you see me through rose-coloured spectacles."

"I see you as you are. Unique, delightful, and very sweet . . ."

The word 'sweet' made Clem squirm a little. It wasn't an epithet she liked and yet Charles, himself, was always using it. She didn't *feel* sweet. She felt sour, bitter and frustrated, she told herself gloomily.

The evening with The Emperor ended on a note of hope; at least he begged that his proposal should make no difference to their friendship, and that if she changed her mind, he would be waiting.

She went back to her flat wondering if she wouldn't be sensible to take the easy way out of this awful net which seemed to be closing around her, and marry Ham. A net fashioned of her own wild tangled emotions was threatening her, darkly. Why *not* marry Ham? He could give her a wonderful time and perhaps not demand too much of her. She knew that he would marry her even if she told him exactly what Charles really meant. He was a broadminded tolerant man. But when she thought about it further she knew she couldn't possibly marry Ham or any other man. If it couldn't be Charles, she would remain Mrs. Anthony Ritson for the rest of her life. She would just go on being Mr. Maddison's secretary.

But she wished she did not have to hurt The Emperor. She knew too well the anguish of a love that was not returned.

When she got to work the next morning—a blustering wet October day, when London seemed particularly unattractive and the traffic impossible—she found Charles already opening the mail. He was not wearing his white coat. He looked up at her and smiled.

"Hullo, Clem. I only had that one appointment this morning with our Greek magnate, Mr. Akaladis at the Clinic, you know. You remember two or three weeks ago he wrote and said he'd be coming over and he wanted me to give him the entire morning. He has this bad back and seemed sure I alone could cure him. He said he'd pay for a full morning's work, so we agreed. *Do* you remember, Clem?"

"Of course."

"Why did I doubt it?" He smiled again. He seemed to Clem to be in good form.

He continued:

"They've just sent a cable from Athens to say he's not arriving until tomorrow. That lets me out today but I'm afraid he won't get another full morning's work from me, either at the Clinic or anywhere else. We've too much on our plates already, haven't we?"

She agreed. All these 'we's' and 'ours' coming from him—the constant use of the plural, which included her where work was concerned, warmed Clem's heart. But she frowned at him.

"Won't you see any patients this morning?"

"No. We have no other appointments, so I'm going out."

She raised her brows. Charles said, with his tongue in his cheek:

"With a pretty girl, mark you. Mr. Maddison is about to lose his reputation if he is seen."

"What *do* you mean?"

"I'm taking The Midget to the Zoo. Don't laugh—*Mr. Maddison at the Zoo!* But Midget has never seen the London Zoo and I thought it would do me good to have a nice walk on this lovely morning."

Clem gasped:

"But it's pouring with rain."

"Oh, we can do the Snake House and see the monkeys and the Aquarium, and visit the rhinoceros, cuddling in their winter quarters if they are not still in their summer ones —" began Charles airily.

Clem broke in:

"I'm sure it will be very amusing and you'll have a wonderful morning with Miss Midget."

Now Charles rose, gathered together some papers, put them in his drawer and locked it. He was no longer smiling. His mouth had a bitter twist to it.

"Quite frankly, my dear Clem, I just want to get away from Welbeck Street and work and everything for a few hours. Taking our little Australian to the Zoo seems harmless enough."

Clem nodded. She was riddled with jealousy. Charles had taken Dr. Miller's sister out more than once lately. The Midget and her mother were still in London. The Millers were not going back to Sydney until early November. Clem bit hard at her lips and walked towards the door.

"I'll get on with the mail. Have you opened all the letters?"

178

"No—only a few, including this—take a look."

She took the letter. From Lisa, of course—she might have guessed that Charles had had a letter from *her*. He was always rather bad-tempered and disturbed after getting notes from his wife. His *ex*-wife as she would soon become. Clem only wished that the divorce was not so far ahead. Lisa's last letter had told Charles that she was walking better already and that she thought that her Max had really found the most fantastic Viennese to treat her and she was terrifically happy about her legs now. Charles made little comment to Clem about Lisa's condition, but he had been rather difficult for about twenty-four hours after hearing from Lisa. Now another one! If only Lisa would leave him alone.

I can't think why you always write to me in such an un-friendly way—just two lines, when I send you lovely long letters and try to be friends with you. Max and I both want you to come and stay with us. As for the divorce you seem to want it more than we do. I hear you've filed a petition and suppose you can't stay with us because of collusion—or so Max tells me. Well, we don't mind if we just continue to live together—in sin. I suppose you still have your strong principles. Very well, my dear Charles, if you want to be unpleasant I'll be hateful, too. I shall put in a counter-petition and sue you and cite your smug little secretary. I'm quite sure if I wanted to I could get plenty of evidence about you and her. Max says he doesn't see why I should take all the blame . . .

Clem read no further. She looked up at Charles, her eyes stricken, her face burning hot.

"Oh!" she gasped, "*Oh.*"

He said:

"I was in two minds as to whether or not I'd let you see this. I didn't want you to be upset. Then I thought you ought to know how the land lies, since you are to be named. I'm terribly sorry. Frankly I did not think Lisa could behave quite so monstrously as this. Though, of course, it's all in keeping with the rest of her conduct. But now there's no knowing what malicious action she and her millionaire may take. And if they really mean to ferret out something about us—even though there's no evidence they can possibly find, it might be unpleasant for you. I won't have you implicated. After all you've done for me—and for her—it's abominable!"

Charles spoke harshly, obviously upset; all pretence at joking and laughing at an end now.

"It *is* monstrous," said Clem. "But I don't see how you are going to stop Lisa. You know how she used to make catty little remarks about us, and the fact that you haven't fed her vanity and co-operated with her since she left you, has resulted in this —" Clem tapped Lisa's last letter with her thumbnail.

He looked at her. Her eyes were pitifully bitter. Those soft brown eyes that were usually so full of warmth and generosity. Suddenly, before he could restrain himself, Charles moved towards her and took her in his arms.

"Clem, Clem, I know just how you're feeling. But you and I can hardly forget what happened on that day at Hurley after Lisa left me. We can neither of us hold ourselves up exactly as complete angels. I just refuse to allow Lisa to do *this*. It would be grossly unfair to you."

Clem relaxed, put her arms around Charles and pressed her cheeks, wet with tears, against his shoulder.

"I always dreaded this. It doesn't really matter about me. But it would be fatal for you, with your profession, to have any scandal touch you. Oh, Charles, she mustn't—she can't *do* it to you!"

"Darling, *can't* is the operative word. I am sure they won't be able to pull this one off. They have no evidence . . ."

"But not a breath of scandal must touch *you*."

He stroked her hair. His eyes hard and resentful, looking across the bowed dark head.

"Don't always think of me. Think of yourself for a change. Whatever happened between us it was —" he stopped. He was about to say—'Reaction, rebound', and in a way that was so. But somehow the words wouldn't come out. Holding Clem's small slim body against his, full of memories of that wild sweet hour in Hurley, he could not belittle one moment of it; nor deny what he felt about this girl. It had been growing more obvious to him as the days went by that she was necessary to him, not only as a secretary, but as a woman.

She was sobbing:

"This is the end. I've *got* to leave you now. I must go right away. Hammond Portal has asked me to marry him. Perhaps I had better say 'yes'. That will mean breaking with you absolutely. Then you can write and tell Lisa."

"I shall do nothing of the kind. I won't have you marry a man you don't love just because of my marital problems."

"How do you know that I don't love The Emperor now?" she asked with an hysterical laugh.

He held her away from him and looked down into her swimming eyes.

"Do you?"

"Would you mind? Wouldn't it really solve the whole problem for you if I got married to Ham?"

"I'm shocked. It's not like you to suggest marrying just to solve this sort of problem. Surely your friend The Emperor deserves better treatment, anyhow."

Then she went limp in his arms and sobbed.

"Oh, you're right! I couldn't. I don't want to. Oh, I don't know what I want. I'm so confused."

"I'm confused too, darling Clem. But there's one thing clear in my mind. I can't bear you to go out of my life."

"You've got The Midget," she sobbed.

"You little fool, she was somebody I was going to take to the Zoo—a nice cheerful child who means nothing in my life—absolutely nothing. I was being nice to her to please old Dick Miller."

Clem's heart leaped wildly.

"What do I mean in your life?" she asked fearfully.

He kissed her tear-filled eyes, then her wet cheeks.

"Darling, a damned lot. I'm pretty mixed up, but as I've said—the one thing I know I can't bear is for you to leave me again."

She tore herself away from his arms, sat down and put her face in her hands.

"You'd better go. You've got that date—at the Zoo."

"I can't possibly go now."

"Please do. Please leave me alone. I must sort things out by myself."

She felt his hand on her shoulder.

"Clem, promise you won't leave me."

"I can't promise, and you can't make any vital decisions either. We're too tied up and tangled and it's all becoming crazier every minute."

"Clem—look at me —"

She shook her head and pushed his hand away.

"Please go and take the little Australian girl to the Zoo. Keep

181

your date. Come back afterwards and we'll talk about it, but for the moment I want to be by myself."

Reluctantly he left her. In his masculine fashion he was unable to deal easily with a situation like this. When he had first read Lisa's threatening letter he had felt nothing but a furious anger against her and her lover. Then had followed his desire to keep Clem right out of this affair—to protect her. But when Clem had announced her intention of going out of his life just now and he had held her in his arms again, he had realised that he felt more than ordinary gratitude and friendship for her. He knew that something far deeper and more disturbing had crept into their relationship, and was not to be ignored.

He drove the Alfa to Regent's Park, thinking it would be comic relief, taking Midget Miller around the Zoo and listening to her rather childish meaningless chatter. He wanted to get back to Clem, but he drove on doggedly, trying to see some light in the clouds that were gathering thick and fast about them.

Left alone, Clem pulled herself together, washed her face and put on fresh make-up. Then, feeling like death, she retired to her own desk. She felt that her brain was so addled she couldn't think any more about Charles, herself, or Lisa. It was best to get down to work.

About two hours later—at midday—the telephone bell rang. She answered it. There had been several other calls. Clem took this one, as usual, pad ready for the message.

"Mr. Maddison's secretary speaking . . ."

"Hold the line. Continental trunks want you."

Clem's heart sank. This must surely be Lisa on the phone—Lisa out to create more havoc in poor Charles's life. Clem felt like putting down the receiver but could not. A voice with a foreign accent said:

"Would Mr. Maddison take a personal call from a Mr. Kern, from Beaulieu?"

So, thought Clem, there was to be a show-down between the 'outraged husband' and 'the co-respondent' after all. She wondered if Charles would have accepted the call had he been here. She said:

"Please tell Mr. Kern that Mr. Maddison is out."

"One moment, please . . ."

She held on. The voice came back:

"Who is speaking?"

"Mr. Maddison's secretary."

"Hold the line," repeated the operator.

Now suddenly she heard a masculine voice with a strong American accent.

"This is Max Kern speaking. Is that Miss Wright — the one they call Clem?"

"Yes," she answered, somewhat surprised.

"How long before Charles Maddison gets back?"

"I don't know. He went out about half past ten. He may not be home to lunch."

"Then I'd better speak to you."

"Oughtn't you to wait —" began Clem.

"This can't wait. I'm afraid I've got news that will shock you, and knock Charles out. It's done more than that to me, I assure you. There's been a terrible disaster here."

Clem felt her blood run cold.

"Something to do with — Lisa?"

"Yes — it sure is. My poor lovely Lisa."

"What's happened, Mr. Kern?"

"She's dead."

An instant's silence. Clem's heart seemed to turn over.

"It can't be true! But when — how —?"

"She dropped down dead — this morning. It was terrible . . ." Max Kern's voice was broken. "I couldn't call you sooner. I've been too upset and involved. But I thought I ought to let Mr. Maddison know at once. After all he is still her husband. When he comes in, you must tell him."

"I can't believe it," gasped Clem, with horror.

"I'm afraid it's true. They say it was delayed shock — her system had taken too much. It was, of course, the indirect result of that air-crash. A coronary — an unexpected heart-weakness. I had every doctor in the place to work on her. They tried to revive her. I gave her the kiss of life. Oh, God, it's been too ghastly —" Max Kern's voice broke again.

Clem said:

"Mr. Kern — I'm deeply sorry — terribly shaken by your news."

"Can you imagine," came his cracked voice. "She was so young and so beautiful, and getting on so darned well with her walking. They thought they were going to put her right. She was in the swimming pool earlier on. Two of us used to hold her up and she loved it, and it was doing her legs so much good trying to move in

183

the warm salt water. She was wearing a white bikini—her body was brown and beautiful. She would never use a cap, and that gorgeous red hair floated in the water. She looked *gorgeous* I tell you! We helped her out. She started to walk slowly towards her wheel-chair. Suddenly she gave a cry. And it was all over. I carried her in to the house and laid her on the bed. She was dead. I can't believe it. *I can't —*"

Clem found no words to say. She had been feeling deeply resentful of the part Max had played in taking Lisa away from her husband. But never having met Max and realising the strong irresistible attraction Lisa had for men, Clem had never actively hated Max. He had seemed right out of her life and had come into it only when she read those fatal, indiscreet letters.

She had hated Lisa. But not now. Clem's imagination quailed at the thought of all that fabulous beauty wiped out by death. At this very moment she was lying somewhere, very still, like a statue, those marvellous eyes for ever shut. Perhaps the red cruel mouth was smiling. Lisa would never be able to say cruel things again. And the most pathetic thing of all to Clem was the fact that Lisa had not died in that air disaster nearly a year ago, but had been spared only for *this*.

The end had come with terrible swiftness to all her ambition—her hopes of making a new life with Max Kern. The end, too, for Charles, to the bitter struggle which was possibly facing him in the divorce courts.

She heard Max speaking again.

"I am sure you must be very shocked. You'll tell Mr. Maddison, won't you?"

"Yes, I'll tell him."

Max cleared his throat.

"I'm a little concerned about the burial. After all one has to be realistic, Miss Wright. She is English, and she is still Mrs. Maddison. I don't have a right to bury her here without approaching Mr. Maddison, do I?"

"No," said Clem and shuddered at the thought of Lisa's funeral and Charles standing grimly beside the grave. As Max Kern said goodbye, slowly and painfully she put the receiver back on the stand. Her mind leaped ahead to the far distant future. She wouldn't have been human if she hadn't allowed herself to be relieved that Charles was free—to hope that he would now be able to become normal again—a vigorous and happy man.

For herself, she asked of the Fates only that she should be allowed to stay near him, whatever else happened.

She spent a difficult hour trying to concentrate on the morning's work and one or two unimportant calls from would-be patients. But she could hardly do anything right. She kept making mistakes and having to tear the paper up. She could think of nothing but Lisa— Lisa dying as she came out of the beautiful blue swimming pool in that wonderful sunlit Riviera garden, with her millionaire lover at her side.

How terrifying it was—the narrow gap between life and death! How deeply one needed some sort of Christian faith, rather than think that death meant total annihilation.

At one o'clock Charles came home.

She heard his key in the lock, and braced herself for what she had to do.

He walked into her office, smoothing back his hair. It was wet and glistening. He smiled:

"Still raining. I'm soaked. I really couldn't face any more of that tour of the Zoo, although our little Australian was delighted with all she saw, and couldn't care less about the rain. Tough Midget. Fortunately she had a lunch date with her mother and some other friends, so I was spared."

Then Charles paused. He saw the expression on Clem's face.

"What's the matter with you? You look very grim."

"I feel it. I've just heard some very terrible news. Please, Charles, get yourself a stiff whisky before I tell you."

The piercing blue of his eyes darkened.

"I don't need whisky. I can stand on my own feet, thank you. What is it? Tell me."

So she told him, giving him all the details, exactly as Max had given them to her.

She saw Charles grow pale, and pinched about the mouth. He sat down heavily and pulled a cigar from his pocket. But he didn't light it, he just rolled it between his fine fingers nervously, staring with blank gaze at Clem. She was inarticulate now. She simply did not know what further to say to him. She knew that in one way he would feel this badly, yet it would be hypocritical of her to sympathise. Finally he spoke:

"Well, I must say this is a hell of a shock. The very last thing in the world to be expected."

She nodded.

"Not uncommon of course, after all she went through. I've heard of one or two cases of delayed shock ending in a coronary. But to think of all her efforts to be cured; all the work Trevor-Johns put in —all the progress she made. It's absolutely tragic that now, when she seemed to be getting better, she should die."

"That's how I feel," said Clem.

"Dear God," Charles shook his head as though he still could not credit what he had just heard. "It's ghastly—incredible really. In a few minutes—like that. Poor, poor Lisa!"

Clem said awkwardly.

"Quite apart from what you feel, it may be the best thing for her. You've always been doubtful as to whether these Continental doctors could put her right and she would have been so unhappy if at the end she had had to accept the fact she would never dance again."

Unlit cigar still in hand, Charles leaned forward and stared at the floor.

"I'm pretty shaken, Clem. I can't believe it yet."

"That's what we—Max Kern and I—both said. It's unbelievable."

"Tell me the whole story again."

Clem repeated Max's story. When she came to the part where Max had said how glorious Lisa had looked in that swimming pool, Charles lifted his head and Clem saw tears in his eyes. Tears that went to her heart. It was so like Charles to feel real sorrow for the wife who had behaved so atrociously to him.

"I know how she must have looked," he said. "She was breath-taking. And I loved her. I did love her, Clem."

"I know, Charles darling."

"I suppose I don't actually feel as grim today as I did when she first told me she meant to leave me. That was another sort of death. This in a strange way seems less bitter. My grief is for her rather than for myself. But I agree with you, she might never have been cured and her playboy might have left her, so this may all be merciful."

"I must say Max sounded terribly cut up."

"No wonder. It must have been ghastly watching her die like that. These sudden coronaries can be pretty terrible for those who are present at the time."

Silence. Again Clem felt that she had nothing to say. When Charles spoke again it was quite calmly.

"I'll need a little time to get over this, but I'm not cancelling any

186

appointments. Have your lunch, then come back, Clem, and we'll get on with the work."

That pleased her, but she said:

"Let me stay with you now. Let me cut you a sandwich, make you some coffee, here."

"If you wish."

"Charles, I've got to phone Max Kern back. I don't suppose *you*'ll want to speak to him, will you?"

"About the funeral arrangements, you mean?"

"Yes."

"If you get through, certainly I'll speak to him," said Charles quietly, "I'm not going to leave you to do my job any more. Things have changed. Lisa is dead and Max can't do me any more harm — or you," he added with a sudden significant glance at Clem.

She flushed.

"Oh, don't mind about me. Just let me know if you want any help with the arrangements."

"I shall tell Max Kern to do the necessary out there. I shall suggest she is buried in Cannes. That was always Lisa's favourite place. She hated England. I shan't bring her back here."

Clem sat quiet. In a queer way it seemed that Lisa's death was bringing back Charles's old feeling of belonging to her, and her to him. Or was it just that he was a generous man who would want to do what he could for the woman who was still his wife and who had died so tragically?

He got up and started to walk restlessly up and down the room.

"I don't think one should be petty at a time like this. I could leave Max and a lot of her so-called friends in the South of France, to follow her to the grave, but I think it would be nicer if I, as her husband, were there. If Max Kern wants to be with me — well, let him."

Clem nodded. There was a lump in her throat.

"I'll get Max to phone back and tell me the day of the funeral. I'll fly over. I hope it'll be the last day I'll have to ask you to cancel my appointments. In future it will be work — nothing but work for me."

"I understand," said Clem in a very small voice and walked towards the door.

The straight brave young back filled Charles with sudden tenderness. It seemed to him that the sight of that back had all too often meant that she was going. And this time she might go out of his life for ever. He ran after her. Putting an arm round her waist, he looked down into her eyes—those fine eyes which were the mirrors of her love and loyalty.

"Clem," he said, "I'm right to go over to the funeral, aren't I? I've got to see Lisa to her resting place. Then—it will all be over."

"Of course you're right," Clem said and shut her eyes. "Only what I would expect of you," she added.

"We must both think kindly of Lisa now. What she meant to do to us—to you—it wasn't the real Lisa, was it?"

"No—we'll remember her as she was—a fabulous being—Lisa, the Magnificent," Clem choked over the name.

Charles took her right hand and kissed it.

"I love you very much," he said. "Please be here when I come back."

THE END

The Press on

DENISE ROBINS

"One of the queens of her profession"—*Daily Telegraph*.

"The key to her success is her sincerity"—*Cumberland Evening News*.

"Unsurpassed skill for capturing delicate emotion"—*Nottingham Evening Post*.

"What she has in her writing which the younger writers who talk about 'Life' with a capital L could well emulate is a freshness, an enthusiasm, and a vitality which makes every character a living person and compels the reader to think '*I've* felt like that'"—*Time and Tide*.

"For the real love story to what better writer can we turn to than Miss Robins"—*Middlesbrough Evening Gazette*.

"Her novels are known for their fast-moving plots and for their extremely professional touch; this does not preclude warmth and feeling for life, which explains their tremendous popularity" . . . *Irish Times*.